Stripped

CAROL KINNEE & KIM MCDONALD

ISBN – 978-0-9958515-6-6

ISBN (e-book) - 978-0-9958515-7-3

Acknowledgement

We wouldn't have had time to write this book if it weren't for the support of our families and friends. Thanks for giving us time to sneak away and brainstorm. Thanks to Jean Manky for editing and proof-reading this novel. More thanks to our beta readers. You know who you are.

We dedicate this book to writing conferences and pub suppers. You never know when a *"What if?"* will spark the idea for a series.

Stripped

Chapter 1

"I've lost the love of my life." Fran blew her nose loudly and added another crumpled tissue to the growing pile on the table in front of her. Choking back a sob, she rubbed her eyes with the back of her hand. They felt hot and gritty, burned by her sorrow.

"Oh sweetie, I'm so sorry," her friend Sunny comforted, as she gave Fran's shoulder a squeeze and placed a giant glass of red wine in front of her.

Through her tear-swollen eyes, Fran watched as Sunny warily eyed the fabric-covered kitchen chairs before selecting the one with the least amount of questionable stains. Whatever. Right now, Sunny's germaphobia ranked about a zero on Fran's *Should I Worry About It* list.

Fran closed her eyes and rested her head in her hands. "It's just so hard . . . it feels like only yesterday, he was strolling around here, fine as can be and today—today—he's not. Oh Sunny, how will I ever go on?"

"It will take time, Fran, but slowly, it will get easier. Look at the positives, right? At least he passed away peacefully in his sleep, warm in his bed. He had a great life. He made it to twenty-years-old. That's all anyone can ever really ask for, isn't it?"

"I guess so." Fran sniffled and lifted the wine glass to her lips. She swallowed a sizeable gulp. "I just thought we had more time. He seemed so healthy."

"Healthy, Fran, really? Didn't he have advanced diabetes?" Sunny questioned gently as she leaned toward her. "And kidney failure? And wasn't he going blind too?"

"Yes," Fran admitted. "But we had that under control. I gave him his four insulin shots a day, plus his pills with breakfast, lunch, first dinner and second dinner. I had gotten him an appointment with a top specialist and we were going to start dialysis next week—" She checked herself at that. "I guess I never really realized how sick he was until I listed it all out . . . I think he was getting dementia too, he was peeing on all of my chairs."

Sunny's nose wrinkled. She looked distastefully down at the chair she was sitting on and scooted her butt to the very edge.

That brought a momentary smile to Fran's lips. That was his favourite chair. She started wailing again.

Sunny leaned over and took Fran's hand in hers. "Okay, sweetie. You know I love you but—"

Fran knew this wasn't going to be what she wanted to hear. Sunny always started her hard truth-telling statements off with: *You know I love you but—*

"But what?" Fran challenged pathetically.

"But it was a cat. Sorry—" Sunny held her hands up in surrender. "I know you loved him. But seriously Fran? It was a cat!"

"You don't get it Sunny! You've never had any pets. He wasn't just a cat, he was my best friend."

"Really Fran? Am I not your best friend?" Sunny challenged, eyebrows raised.

"It's different." She waved Sunny off. "I just—I need more time."

"Fran, it's been two weeks! Seriously, get a hold of yourself girl!"

"I know you think I'm some crazy cat lady, Sunny, but Puss 'n' Boots wasn't just a cat; he was *my* cat. Growing up in a family with nine brothers, I didn't have many things that were just mine, but Puss 'n' Boots was! *I* found him. *I* nursed him back to health and for the last 20 years, he's been an integral part of my life. He slept on my bed almost every night. His adorable face was the first thing I'd see when I woke up in the morning, and the last thing I'd see before I went to bed at night. And now . . . now he'll never sleep with me again."

That thought brought on another round of ugly, snotty crying. Sunny slid off her chair. Wordlessly, she moved around the table giving Fran a big hug from behind, letting her cry it out.

"Oh, sweetie, I'm sorry, I really am." Sunny consoled.

"Thanks." Fran sniffled, and concentrated on breathing in and out, trying to still the heaving sobs that she couldn't stop from taking over her body. She closed her eyes and was enjoying the comfort of a rare hug from her best friend when Sunny abruptly broke the embrace.

"Okay, that's enough mushy mushy. This is out of control. We're going out."

"Sunny, no." Fran protested weakly. Going out right now was at the top of her *That's the Last Thing I Want to Do Right Now* list.

"No, don't even try it. We're going out and that's that."

Fran weighed her options: she could dig her heels in and refuse or she could lay down and let Sunny steam roll over her. Sunny was a force of nature, hard to refuse even when Fran was at her strongest. Right now, if Fran was lucky, she was maybe at thirty percent. Sunny was going to win anyway, so she might as well give in. Steam roll it was. She took another gulp of wine.

"Sunny, please," she pleaded, in a final pathetic attempt to appeal to her friend's softer side.

"Nope. Don't give me the sad puppy dog eyes. That doesn't work on me," Sunny quipped matter-of-factly. "Stand," she continued. "Wash your puffy-ass face with ice water and then let me work my magic."

Great, the second to last thing Fran wanted, after going out, was to be Sunny's Barbie for the night.

"Sunny, no."

"Ha. You know you're not going to win this battle, Franny, so why even try?"

"Ugh, I know."

"Okay then. Drink. Wash your face. And you're putty in my hands." Sunny tossed her a wicked smile.

Fran stumbled from her chair and trudged to the bathroom. She splashed water over her face and looked up at the mirror.

Ouch, Sunny was right. She did need to get a hold of herself—two weeks of crying had left her looking as worn as her old Nonna.

She made her way back to the kitchen. Sunny looked pensive. She'd spread the entire contents of her makeup bag over Fran's table and was contemplating the infinitesimal differences between two shades of primer.

"Sit," Sunny ordered, pressing a fresh glass of wine into Fran's hand.

Fran sat obediently and took a big sip of the wine as Sunny stepped back like an artist studying the blank canvas in front of her. Coming to some mysterious decision, Sunny went to work, covering every inch of Fran's face with a blend of primer, foundation, and concealer, finishing with a light dusting of bronzer. She piled on a load of goopy eyeshadow and mascara, and then roughly brushed and pulled Fran's long dark hair into a low ponytail. Nodding, she stood back to critically examine her work before pronouncing, "Voila!"

Fran attempted a weak smile and successfully bit back the tears. At least the wine was starting to numb the pain.

"Hmmm, there's still something missing," proclaimed Sunny as she scrutinized Fran like Cinderella's Fairy Godmother confronted by a plastic slipper.

"Outfit." Fran mumbled.

"Right," Sunny said, "See you're already getting into the spirit of things!" She led the now tipsy and pliable Fran to the bedroom, rummaged through

Fran's closet and threw a light gray, deep V-neck sweater and black mini skirt onto Fran's bed.

"Change!" she commanded and left the room.

"Bossy," Fran mumbled. She pulled the sweater on, stopped and yelled, "Sunny! My boobs are hanging out! This sweater is supposed to be worn with a shirt underneath it."

"Only if you're going to church!" retorted Sunny.

Fran silently rolled her eyes and hopping on one foot, managed to pull the skirt up and on, only falling into the wall twice.

"Are you ready yet?" called Sunny.

"I guess so." Fran tugged at the sweater.

Sunny flung open the door and like a proud pageant mom, paraded Fran to the bathroom mirror. "Look at you girl! You look *amaaaazing*!"

Fran studied herself. Her face was caked in makeup and the V in her sweater felt like it reached all the way to her belly button.

"I look like a ho," she grumbled, tugging the sweater up over her chest.

"You don't look like a ho. You look like a high class call girl," comforted Sunny, pulling the sweater back down.

"Great," mumbled Fran.

"There's a big difference, Fran," chastised Sunny. "Don't be a snob. Now, let's go. I'll drive."

"Where are we going?"

"It's ladies' night at Spanky's."

"Great! Strippers." Fran rolled her eyes.

"That's the spirit!" chimed Sunny, choosing to ignore Fran's sarcasm.

On the way out of the house they passed the ratty hole-filled blanket on the floor—Puss 'n' Boots' blanket. Fran slowed, almost stopping. A lump formed in her throat.

"Come on, Fran, you'll get through this," Sunny coached, gently grabbing her elbow and leading her out.

"Thanks, Sunny." Fran sighed, gratefully leaning on her friend as they walked to the car.

"Oh, and Fran?"

"Yeah Sunny?"

"No more crying, okay? You'll ruin my makeup job."

Chapter 2

Luke backed his Jeep into a corner parking space and studied the empty lot. Good. His car was the only one there. Most of the staff at Port Fling Savings and Loans were gone for the day, leaving only the all-seeing eye of the security camera to watch the after-hours goings on. From now, until eight a.m., Port Fling's banking district was just another shortcut to the main road.

Luke opened the Jeep's driver side window and pressed his cell phone closer to his ear. His gaze dropped to the thick brown paper envelope lying on the passenger seat. He growled a curse under his breath. Okay, be cool. Don't let the anger dogs get you. He forced himself to breathe deep, to stay calm, when what he really wanted to do was crawl through the phone lines and throttle the man on the other end of the call.

"Look," he started again, "You aren't getting what I'm trying to say—"

"I'm getting it, Professor Tanner. I'm getting it loud and clear. What *you* aren't getting is that this is a done deal. We are a university. You are a university professor on the verge of getting tenure. Do not screw this up. Monday morning, a grad student *will* be standing in your lab and you will do your best to make sure that student is successful in the pursuit of a PhD."

Luke gritted his teeth and tried again. Winston Etherridge the III was a pompous windbag, a dinosaur. The guy had no idea what it was like to work in a high stress lab where lack of attention could become a real life big bang, not just a theory.

"I get that you have to place these students somewhere, but after what happened last year, I'm just suggesting that maybe we should rethink this appointment." There. Hopefully he'd put enough deference into his voice to pacify the ego of his department head.

"What happened last year happened last year, Professor Tanner. Ms. Mathers was clearly having a cerebral breakdown from the stress she was labouring under."

Luke snorted. Ms. Mathers had wrapped herself in ribbon and laid out naked on his desk. That was only after she had stalked him through the halls and showered him with cookies from Luscious Buns Bakery—special cookies, not the everyday ones—

the boobie cookies with the strategically placed cinnamon heart decorations. He rolled his eyes.

"Look Professor Tanner, that won't happen again. This student has impeccable credentials, stunning grades and a dissertation in green chemistry. You should be happy. Sustainable resources are your thing, right? All that tree-hugging and enviro mumbo jumbo is right up your alley."

Luke shook his head and looked out the window. The early September sun was hot and ripples of radiant heat rose from the pavement in a shimmering wave. Only the tiny breeze ruffling the leaves of the trees lining the lot saved him from melting. Sweat slicked his wavy black hair to his head in a tight cap. He raked his hand through it as his mouth flattened into a hard line. Good old Winston. How the guy had gotten to be department head was one of the mysteries of the universe.

Winston was speaking again. "This year do try to keep your lab under control. A chemistry lab is meant for scientific studies not the perfection of Grandpa Joe's archaic gin recipe." Winston hung up before Luke could reply.

Luke jabbed his middle finger at the end call button on his phone and glared at the empty lot. One more year, he consoled himself. One more year and he wouldn't have to deal with idiots like Professor Etherridge the III any longer. He would be able to run his lab the way he wanted and choose grad students who were serious about their work.

"Hey, Luke? What are you doing here?"

"Zack," Luke looked up and greeted the pony-tailed man crossing the parking lot. He held up the empty coffee cup resting in the console beside him and nodded towards the brick building. "I had some last-minute banking and grabbed a coffee. Funny, I was just talking about you."

Zack raised an eyebrow. "Were you? Anything good?"

Luke laughed. It was hard not to like the other man. Zack was a research biologist doing field studies. He'd been tracking orcas off northern Vancouver Island for the last two months. Living rough was what he called it. Staying real.

Luke wrinkled his nose. "You just get back?" He nodded at the pony-tail.

"This morning. What, are you sneering at the hair? Hey, I can make a man bun." Zack protested, twisting the tail into a small bun on the top of his head.

Luke raised an eyebrow. "I'd like to see how that man bun would go over with Etherridge," he muttered.

"Is that why you're looking so uptight?" Zack gestured to the phone Luke still held in his left hand.

Luke dropped the phone onto the seat and shook his head sourly. "I was trying to have a logical conversation with my department head. Is that too much to ask?"

"Since when do you let Winston Blowhard the III get to you?"

"Grad students," Luke said sourly.

Zack grinned and nodded sagely. "Oh, I get it now. Here comes another round of cookies and panties."

"It's not funny," Luke said. "It's awkward. These are brilliant minds—future scientists."

"Maybe you should take a lesson from Superman—dress like Clark Kent, or Godzilla."

"Ha, you've been out in the field too long. That or the alcohol fumes are finally getting to you."

"But I figured out the missing ingredient."

"Nope." Luke flung a hand out to ward him off. "Winston's already on to you. Find another place to set up your still."

Zack shrugged. "Alright dude, but this time I've figured it out."

"We'll talk later," Luke said, glancing at his phone. "I've got to get going."

"Sure. See you Monday." Zack waved a hand in farewell and set off across the parking lot. His long strides ate up the distance. He disappeared around a corner.

Luke shook his head. Zack insisted that he had the perfect job, the freedom to do what he wanted when he wanted. Maybe he was right. Sometimes

Luke wished he could be more like him, a free spirit. Zack didn't have any issues. He did what he wanted, drifting in and out of academia without a care. His department head wanted his profs out in the field, doing real hands-on research. Sighing, Luke yanked off his tie. Winston wanted ties—he didn't care about dress pants and shoes, but he expected his professors to wear button-up shirts with collars, and proper ties. That meant no clip-ons, and no bow ties, although Winston himself always sported a nattily tied bow tie.

Luke shut the Jeep's windows and opened the door. He climbed out and paused to stretch, rolling his neck, working out the tension that conversation with his department head always raised. Opening the back door, he grabbed his gym bag from the seat beside his leather satchel. A good sweat would go a long way towards blowing off some stress. That was his way of coping with the pressures of running a cutting-edge experimental lab.

Tossing the strap over his shoulder, he crossed the lot and jogged to an alley leading to another brick building one block over. A quick inspection of the area showed that there was no one around. He pulled his wallet out of the back pocket of his jeans and approached the back door. He slid his pass-card out and swiped it through the scanner. The door lock clicked and he pushed it open. The thumping techno blast of music hit him at the same moment he realized that he had forgotten his G-string.

Chapter 3

Sweaty ladies pressed in on Fran from every direction. The bass vibrated through her body. She could feel the techno beat of the music thumping inside her chest. The club was packed fuller than a subway train at rush hour in downtown Tokyo. Fran mumbled another *'scuse* me as she and Sunny pushed through the crowd. The soles of her four-inch heels clung to the sticky, alcohol-soaked floor, making her hike to the table as treacherous as traversing a frozen pond.

"Sit and save our table while I get some drinks," commanded Sunny as they squished into the last available table in the back corner of Spanky's.

Fran sat obediently and looked out at the colourful throng of women. Who knew there were so many horny ladies in Port Fling? The club would burst its doors if they tried to cram any more people into it. It also didn't help that most of the ladies were acting like sexually-charged teenagers, ready to explode with hormones at any second.

Fran sighed. This really was the last thing she wanted to be doing, but Sunny was right, she did need to get a hold of herself. She had a lot of big opportunities coming her way, and she had worked too hard to get to where she was to blow it all now. As Nonna would say, *Ai piu potente ceda il pui prude*nte, or *better to bow than to break*. Or did that mean *a good product doesn't need advertising*? Whatever. The point was, she had to toughen up— learn to bend with the wind and all that.

"Drink." Sunny returned, interrupting her philosophizing, double-fisting vodka cranberry sodas.

Fran complied, shuddering as she took a sip. "Jeez Sunny! Are these doubles?"

"Mine is. Yours is a triple." Sunny grinned. "We're getting you *d-runk* girlfriend."

Normally at this point, Fran would pretend-sip her drink. Sunny could get a little out of control and usually needed a sober guardian. But tonight, Fran wasn't in the mood to play mother. Tonight, Fran wanted to be the one to get just a little out of control.

"I wonder if Jason's working tonight?" muttered Sunny scanning the club for her on-again, mostly off-again, stripper boyfriend.

"No, Sunny." Fran moaned. "Don't go there again. Please."

The Sunny and Jason show usually featured more drama than *Meet the Kardashians* and always ended with someone storming away in tears—usually Jason.

"Oh, I won't. We're completely done. Jason's a total drama king. He took me out to that new club Glitter, the other night, and I was innocently talking to a guy, you know Paul—the gay cycling instructor? And Jason just totally freaked out. He's so jealous, it drives me crazy."

Jason was definitely jealous and dramatic, but Sunny played her part too. She loved to get him all riled up.

"Are you sure you weren't hanging all over Paul—the gay cycling instructor—to make Jason jealous?" challenged Fran. She normally kept mute on Jason and Sunny's drama but the alcohol was loosening her tongue and she kind of liked it.

"Why Francesca Romano, you sly minx. I don't know what you're talking about!" teased Sunny. "You know me too well."

Fran shrugged silently. They had been friends since grade eight. Friends since the pink-haired, glitter-loving Sunny had arrived in the small sleepy town of Port Fling from world-weary Los Angeles. The Romano clan had wrapped their arms around her and dragged her into the craziness that was their world. Sunny had gone from lonely, only child to having nine adopted older brothers telling her what to do.

"Maybe I was trying to make Jason jealous. I guess I could have mentioned the little fact that Paul was gay," Sunny confessed. "I'm just still mad at him for cheating on me with that bimbo Serena. But I guess I haven't exactly been a saint."

"You definitely haven't!" agreed Fran, slurping her drink. Now that it was watered down with ice it was tasting a lot smoother.

"Maybe I'll just go back-stage and find him to apologize."

"No, Sunny," pleaded Fran. "Please just leave it. You've both made mistakes but you're better off apart." She knew the chances of Sunny coming back were slim-to-none if she got sucked into the Jason drama.

"Fran, I pinky swear I will return. This is something I really need to do. I just want to make things right and end it between us once and for all," promised Sunny as she linked her pinky through Fran's.

"Okay fine," relented Fran. "But get me another drink first."

Chapter 4

Luke shouldered open the door to the change room and looked around. For the moment, he had the room to himself. Good. His mood hadn't improved, if anything it was getting darker by the second. Bloody students. If he had his way—

"Hey, Darkness, you're looking like your name tonight. What's with the cranky face?"

Luke turned to confront the speaker. The other man, Dallas, loomed over him. Luke was tall, six feet-two-inches, but Dallas was taller, about six-feet-four, and bigger. He outweighed Luke by at least eighty pounds. Luke looked up at him. Dallas could probably pick him up and snap him like a twig.

Tonight, in keeping with his cowboy schtick, Dallas was wearing a faded jean jacket with the arms torn off and battered jeans worn low on the hips. The guy had to be a body builder, Luke decided. His arms were like tree trunks, the biceps bulging beneath the torn denim.

Dallas shoved back the rim on the battered felt cowboy hat he wore and took a bite out of the pepperoni stick he held in one hand. Everywhere Dallas went the signature hat and meat stick were with him. Luke thought Dallas and his pepperoni were both a bit off.

"You missed a bit," Luke said, pointing to a drizzle of baby oil trailing down one of Dallas's bulging biceps.

"Hey, thanks man."

That was another thing about Dallas. He punctuated every sentence with the word hey.

"Hey, so why are you looking so pissed? You won't be getting no tips looking like that," Dallas said idly, rubbing the oil into the rippling muscle, studying Luke, his eyes hooded beneath the brim of the hat.

Once again, Luke wondered what Dallas did in real life, but that was part of the beauty of Spanky's. The guys who worked the club kept their personal lives private. They didn't share information. That suited Luke just fine. The last thing he needed was Winston the III finding out about his weekend gig at the club. If that happened, he could kiss tenure good bye.

"So?" Dallas asked again.

Luke shook his head, shaking off thoughts of the lab. "Nothing. Real life stuff."

Dallas stared at him a moment longer.

"Well, the ladies are primed tonight. Don't get too close to the front of the stage. You might find yourself unwrapped sooner than you want."

Dallas winked at him and strolled into the costume room. That was where most of the dancers kept the props they used in their sets. Dallas kept his horse back there. It was a saw horse with a stuffed horse's head and tail—a unicorn's head. The guy was unquestionably quirky. He said the gals could have him in their dreams. That's why he rode the unicorn.

Luke dropped his gym bag onto the floor, still cursing the loss of his G-string. It was an amateur's mistake and he wasn't an amateur. He'd used stripping to pay for college. It started out as a joke when one of the guys in his study group kept mysteriously disappearing every Saturday night. Luke pointed it out to the group and they'd followed him one night. The trail had led them to a run-down club in downtown Portland.

Luke smiled remembering the night. Jared had almost fallen off the stage when he stepped out and found half his advanced molecular chemistry class lined up at the front of the dance floor. He'd dropped his lion tamer's rope. The ladies had gone wild fighting over the souvenir.

Luke had hung around, watching the crowd throw money at the dancers. It had made him think about his own cash flow. He was in good shape. If he took a few dance classes maybe he could make a little money on the side. A little money turned out to be a lot. He quit washing dishes and worked weekends at the club. He liked the stress release dancing gave him. He liked the exercise and face it, he liked the adoration on the faces of his audience. No one knew who he was. He was a mystery, in disguise.

Back then, his costume had consisted of a lab coat and a stethoscope—he'd called himself Dr. Love, until one the older guys sat him down and told him it was okay to have some class.

That's when special forces Captain Danger Dark was born. Danger Dark worked. Best of all, the camouflage paints he wore masked his identity—an important detail for a university prof stripping in a university town.

He pulled the camo paints out of his bag and carefully stroked the greens and whites across his face, covering the tiny scar on his chin, the small hairless patch nestled in his left eyebrow—souvenirs of a rough and tumble childhood spent in a chain of foster homes across the Pacific Northwest.

He grabbed a thin black t-shirt from his gym bag, pulled it over his head, and tucked it into the uniform pants he'd had specially created for the act. The pants were designed to be torn off in one swift move. He smoothed out the shirt and snapped the fake leather belt around his waist.

Stepping back, he studied the result in the mirror. Satisfied with his disguise, he nodded and bent to lift the helmet and head set from his gym bag. He settled the helmet onto his head and dropped the head set into position. After sliding his authentic Delta Force glasses onto his nose, the costume was complete. The glasses hid his eyes—his soul—from the world, protection from reality. He could have used a pair when he was a kid. He smiled crookedly.

"Hey, Danger. You're on in five, after J-Dawg."

That was another thing he liked about the club. The dancers were addressed by their stage names. Luke headed for backstage. Dallas had called it; the club was really *bumpin'* tonight. Hoots and cat calls hammered his ears as he approached the stage. The mingled scents of cheap and expensive perfumes assaulted his nose—musk, florals, patchouli oils— they were all there. Yes, the ladies were ready to be entertained. He grinned and climbed the stairs to the stage holding area.

Chapter 5

So far Fran had seen three strippers, two penises and the bottom of five drinks (or was it six?) and still no sign of Sunny. She stretched out her legs. At least she had the entire back of the club to herself. The latest dancer, Dallas, really had the ladies pushing for the stage. Who knew that a routine with a sawhorse unicorn could get a roomful of randy ladies so hot and bothered? Speaking of hot and bothered, it felt like a million degrees in here. Right now, Fran wanted nothing more than to rip her itchy sweater off. Her modesty had gone out the window with drink three (or was it four?) and her V-neck was now sitting at full capacity putting 'the girls on display,' as Sunny would say.

Fran looked around, purposefully ignoring the act of pretend bestiality that was going on onstage— she would never look at a unicorn the same again. It was nuts in here. Panties were flying from every direction.

Where the heck was Sunny? Fran reached for her purse and blindly fished around for her phone. Her hand finally closed over the solid comforting rectangular shape. No missed calls, just a clock reading 11:46 p.m. and a background screensaver picture of Puss 'n' Boots when he was just a young guy. He had been so handsome and proud in that picture. She'd taken it right after his litter of kittens with Princess Fiona, her other cat, was born. He was such a good daddy, always playing gently with his kittens, making sure they were safe. He was irreplaceable. She had kept the litter of five kittens (now full-grown cats) and his mate but it just wouldn't be the same without him. Tears welled up at the thought of life without her favorite cat. She took a deep breath and stilled the pain by gulping down the rest of her drink.

"*Laadiess,* put your hands up in the air and get ready to get sweaty! *Heeerre's* J-Dawg!"

Fran looked up. Good, now maybe Sunny would get her butt back out here. She watched the stage as Jason's song "*Hot in Herre*" by Nelly started to play. The stage remained awkwardly empty. Disappointed club-goers began filing back to their chairs. Over the music, Fran thought she heard Jason's frantic screaming, "Sunny! Sunny! *Nooooo*! Don't leave me. It was just one time!"

The music cut off abruptly. It was followed by a loud bang that sounded like a door being slammed.

More Sunny and Jason drama. Why was she not surprised? Right on cue her phone vibrated. She looked down at the text from Sunny:

So sorry. Jason and I got in a huge fight. He wants to talk and won't leave me alone. I need to get out of here now. Can you cab it home?

No problem. End it already! She texted back.

Sunny texted: **I will. Call me tomorrow.**

Fran had seen enough penises and flying panties for the night. She grabbed her purse and started to make her way to the exit door when the lights blinked out. The sudden darkness cast a spell of silence over the crowd. The choppy whir of helicopter rotor blades started.

"Daaannngggeerrrr Daaarrrrrkkkk!" announced the DJ. A cheer arose from the expectant crowd.

One of her favourite songs *The Hills* by The Weekend started. Fran stopped and turned back to watch the dancer. The strobe-light was on for his intro, driving the ladies crazy with flashing hints of his amazing body and swivelling hips. Fran was intrigued—dark song choice, dark outfit—she'd always had a secret thing for tall bad boys in camo. Danger Dark, was no exception. How could he see with those dark glasses on? Curiosity lured her away from the exit and led her back towards the stage.

The guy could actually dance. He moved effortlessly, flowing like water, from one sequence to the next. He wasn't terrible to look at either—actually he was totally gorgeous. Fran swallowed hard as he swiveled his hips and expertly teased, lifting his shirt, revealing a perfectly chiseled six-pack.

She had a momentary vision of licking salt off of that rock-hard stomach and drinking tequila out of his belly-button—she didn't even like tequila! Danger tore off his shirt and slid to the ground, dry-humping the floor in perfect rhythm to the music. Fran joined the other ladies, screaming for more. Heat coursed through her body. She wanted to slide in there, right beneath him.

She elbowed her way past a pushy brunette. She had to get closer. She needed to inspect those rippling muscles. Yep. They were just as spectacular up close as they were from far away. Thanks to Jason, Fran had always held some disdain for male strippers. She had to admit though, Danger was pretty much a specimen of perfection.

She had never felt pure animal attraction before. The guys she dated were thinkers, big brains, tiny muscles. She was attracted to their intellects and their organized patterns of thought. This was different. She had no desire to talk to this man, to know his mind. All she wanted was to rip off his clothes and feel the weight of his gorgeous, muscular body on top of hers. His hands were huge. What would they feel like sliding down her torso, cupping all of her curves?

With her eyes still locked on the stripper, she drew her hand across her mouth wiping away a speck of drool pooled in one corner. He was staring at her through those dark glasses, looking only at her, dancing just for her. It didn't matter that she was surrounded by a crowd of panting ladies and couldn't exactly see his eyes. The air between them was charged with raw sex, so thick she could taste it.

Years of experience fending off her older brothers at the nightly Romano dinner rush came into play as she artfully pushed aside the burly blonde in front of her and slid into the prime real estate right next to the stage. Her breath hitched. Wow. He was so close she could reach up a hand and graze his gorgeous body with her fingertip. She had to clench her hands together to stop herself. Then it happened—he was looking down, right at her, the corners of his mouth turned up as he reached to pull her up on stage.

Chapter 6

The closing bars of *The Hills* were approaching. Luke smiled at the pretty brunette on the stage next to him. He never let anyone up on the stage when he was dancing but there was something about her that got to him. For a minute there, it was as if he was dancing just for her. Everything and everyone else faded into the background. He didn't hear the whistles and the screams. He was drowning in her whiskey-coloured eyes, drunk on the sexy fire he saw burning there. Her lips quivered. A pair of panties smacked her in the forehead. The brunette didn't notice.

Luke swivelled and dropped to the floor. He army crawled, rolled to his side and tilted his head in a sexy come-hither move. The crowd went wild. In one step he was on his feet. He danced around the girl and gently lifted her over the side of the stage back onto the floor. Dollar bills fluttered to the ground beside him. He gave himself to the music, making up moves as he went.

He moonwalked, mixing pelvic thrusts with gyrations, stretched and bounced his pecs. He added a hip thrust and roll swaggering to the front of the stage as the music climaxed. Reaching down between his legs he grabbed hold of the tear away on the camo pants and yanked. The music ended and the stage lights winked out. The audience went crazy.

The lights flashed on. Luke blew the crowd a kiss and left the stage. The ratty velvet stage curtain swished into place behind him. He put the pants back on, loosely tacking them into place. He wasn't going to wander around back stage bare-ass naked. The janitor handed him his shirt and a stack of cash.

"Hey, dude that was weak." Dallas was standing at the edge of the stage. He looked disapproving.

"I was working them up for you. Go take your mad unicorn and ride back into their dreams there, cowboy."

"Hey, since when do you pull that move? Going commando. You're violating the art," Dallas complained.

"Since I forgot my G-string." Luke grinned. "It worked."

Dallas shook his head. "I dunno, man."

Luke tried to hide a smile. Dallas was a big man, six feet four, 280 pounds of lean baby-oiled muscle.

The saw horse unicorn with its yellow mane and pink horn should have looked ridiculous. It didn't. Dallas moved past him, carrying the saw horse in one hand. He was pulling double duty, filling in for J-Dawg who was M.I.A. The opening beat of bon Jovi's *Dead or Alive* started. Dallas took a bite of the pepperoni stick he held in his left hand and stepped onto the stage.

Luke yanked the black t-shirt over his head and watched the cowboy play to the crowd. The ladies were really into Dallas. He could definitely dance. For a big guy, he moved lightly, silent on his feet.

Back in the dressing room, Luke pulled on a camo button up shirt, added a tactical vest, and tucked the camo pants into his boots. The boots were custom- made to resemble the footwear special forces soldiers wore. In reality, they were flat dance shoes that let him move easily without slipping.

He left his Delta Force glasses on and carrying the helmet, headed back into the club. Standing at the bar, he asked for a tall glass of water and took a sip. He had one more dance at the end of the night and then he'd go home. Tonight, he didn't feel like socializing. He was still too ticked off over the whole lab fiasco.

"Good turn out tonight." Craig, the bartender said. He was leaning up against the bar, taking advantage of a momentary lull in business. "It's crazy how charged up this place gets." He shook his head in bemusement.

Luke nodded and took another sip. The bar at the back of the club let him see into the corner furthest from the stage. The brunette he'd invited up on stage was alone at a table in the darkest corner. He looked over his glasses at her. She was sitting, actually more like propped up, against the wall. There was a row of glasses in front of her—they ranged from wine to martini to beer steins. Luke winced. If she'd personally emptied all of them, she would be hurting by morning.

Craig said something and Luke leaned forward to hear him.

"She came in with that Sunny chick. You know the one, the wine rep, the funny one. Anyway, she's been slamming them back. I've been keeping an eye on her. She liked your dance though. It was the only time she moved out of the corner."

"Dark, you're up next," a passing stage hand called to Luke.

"Thanks," Luke said grabbing his water and heading back stage.

This time Luke did a slow number, teasing the crowd, building their expectations. He slid the tactical vest off, deliberately leading them on, playing to their imaginations. The vest fell at his feet. His chest shone golden under the glow of the stage lights. He stretched, theatrically—a world-weary warrior needing rest, ready for his woman. Almost dreamily, he unclipped the helmet. It dropped to the ground. The music changed. The alteration in pace had the audience jumping.

Not the entire audience, Luke realized feeling vaguely disappointed. The brunette was nowhere in sight. He pushed her out of his mind and gave himself up to the dance, giving the ladies what they wanted. The music ended. The club exploded in whistles and cheers. Luke flashed the audience a wicked smile and offered a mock bow. Leaning over slowly, he gathered up the discarded uniform and helmet. The stage went black as the curtain dropped signalling the end of the performance.

Luke looked at the floor. The stage was littered with money—dollars, fives, tens. The janitor swept them into a pile and handed them to Luke. Luke handed him back fifty dollars.

"Thanks, Jordy. Stick this in the baby's piggy bank for her college fund."

"Thanks, Dark. It's a few years away, but that little girl is going to university. Maybe she'll be the one to discover a new bio fuel."

Luke smiled. Not if I do it first, he thought.

Chapter 7

Luke was the last act and the last dancer back to the locker room. He grabbed a quick shower and changed into his jeans and short-sleeved white shirt. The other guys were milling around, rehashing the night. One of them, Odin, had just finished twisting his white blonde hair into a pony-tail. He reached over, grabbed a beer and offered it to Luke.

"No, thanks," Luke said, shaking his head. "I'm good. I'm going to grab a bottle of water and head home."

"It's Friday night."

"Aw, you need your binky to go night, night?" Maximum Impact smirked and upended the Coors Light he was holding. "Come on. Don't be a pussy." He crushed the can and tossed it towards the garbage.

Luke laughed and bent to tie his runners. "Nope. Sorry. I don't want to spend tomorrow hung over."

He never went out with the guys. It was too risky. Being seen hanging out with a bunch of strippers from Spanky's wasn't the way to further his career. He looked up and met Odin's eyes. Odin gave him a little nod. In real life, Odin's name was Tyler Ford. He was an investment banker. Luke had stumbled on Odin's alter-ego by chance. He'd booked a meeting with a financial advisor and Tyler walked in. That was an *oh shit* moment for both of them.

He picked up his Deltas and slid them on. Another thing he never did was take the risk of leaving off his disguise, although tonight, the ladies looked older than the usual university crowd. Still, better safe than sorry.

"See you guys," Luke called exiting the room to a series of jeers and mock insults. He headed for the bar at the back of the club. Craig was wiping down the counter, loading the industrial-sized glass washer and dumping bits of fruit peal and swizzle sticks into the garbage. He handed Luke a bottle of water without being asked. Luke cracked the top and gulped half the contents. He turned and looked towards the corner table in the back.

"Yeah," Craig nodded at the corner. "She's still there."

"Where's her pal Sunny?"

Craig shrugged. "I haven't seen her. She left with J-Dawg awhile ago." He rolled his eyes. "His stripper name should be D-Bag. You would think she'd have better taste."

Luke wrinkled his nose. He didn't like J-Dawg and tried to avoid him. The guy was a player. The thing about stripping was there was never a shortage of women wanting to take you home and guys like J-Dawg were always willing to take them up on their offers. Luke waved his half-full bottle of water at Craig and approached the table where the girl was leaning up against the back of the booth.

"Hey, you okay?" he asked, stopping beside her.

"Hmmm?" She looked up at him and smiled.

Luke half-smiled back in response.

The girl muttered something that that he couldn't make out. She'd been crying. Streaks of mascara had followed the tears down her face. She had swiped them aside staining the sleeves of her sweater with sooty black. Guy troubles, he decided, straightening. This was the last thing he needed right now. He turned to leave but made the mistake of giving her another look.

"Hey," he said, silently cursing himself for not running while he could. "Are you okay? Is there something I can do to help you? Call a cab? Phone someone to pick you up?"

She started to cry in earnest, grabbing for a ratty cocktail napkin sitting on the table.

Desperate, Luke looked around the room for help, hoping to catch the attention of one of the servers. The only person nearby was Craig. He had ducked his head and was carefully wiping down the beer taps. His shoulders shook with silent laughter at Luke's predicament.

"I don't understand," the girl whimpered. "Everything was good but now my Pussy is gone. Lost forever." She hiccoughed and groped blindly for the half-full glass of wine near her elbow.

Luke eased it out of her way, but she'd already forgotten about it. She was back to blubbering and hiccoughing about the loss of her "pussy." Okay, this was weird. He wasn't hearing her clearly. He leaned in closer. She met his gaze and his heart jumped. No way. This was not happening—he couldn't look away. The impact of her whiskey-coloured eyes was like downing a shot of 151 rum.

"What will I do without my Pussy?"

The way she was looking at him, imploring him, trusting him to make things right, got to him. She was like a kitten, a cute, funny, drunk kitten.

"I'll call you a cab," Luke said, pulling his phone out of his hip pocket.

"No," she said. "I'll come home with you. I shouldn't be alone."

Luke looked around for her purse. "Where's your purse?"

She smiled weakly and shrugged. She found the glass of wine and tossed back the contents in one big gulp. That made her remember her problems. She started crying again.

One of the servers passed the table.

"Jules, do you know her?" Luke asked nodding towards the unknown girl. The girl was looking at him like a puppy now, trusting he would take care of her.

"Nope, but can you get her out of here? We all want to go home."

Obviously, Jules wasn't going to be any help. Luke looked around hoping for someone else to rescue him.

"What's your name," Luke asked, desperate to find a way out of the situation.

"Fran." The girl sniffed and rubbed another streak of black onto her sleeve.

"Don't do that. You're getting mascara all over your sleeve."

Craig took pity on him. He probably wanted to go home too. "I told you, she came with Sunny."

Luke groaned. Sunny was sort of a friend. He owed it to her to make sure poor drunk Fran got home safely. Plus, Luke wasn't the type of guy to leave some cute, helpless, wasted girl to fend for herself. Especially when she was crying about her "pussy."

"Fran, where's your purse? I can drive you home." Luke tried again.

"*Nooo*, take me with you. I'm tired. I can't go home to a house without my poor Pussy."

Luke sighed. Clearly this drunk girl would never make it home on her own. If he walked away and left her, his conscience would make him feel like a dick. Who knows who she'd end up with? And if something happened to her, he'd never forgive himself. Guess it was time to play the hero. He led Fran out to his car and buckled her into the front seat of his Jeep.

***

Fran smiled at the gorgeous man sitting next to her in the Jeep. The breeze from her open window lifted her hair off her face, cooled the sweat clinging to her forehead and cleared her head. She felt great. Why didn't she get drunk more often? Sure, she had been crying but now it was out of her system. She felt relaxed and free, ready to take on the world.

"You're so pretty," she marvelled aloud studying the perfect lines of Dark Danger's face.

"Thanks, so are you." The edge of his mouth twitched upwards in a smile as he glanced her way, then went back to looking at the road.

"No, really. You're gorgeous. You should be a model—" She reached over and squeezed his big, firm bicep, and added, "—an underwear model!"

She giggled. "Whoops, I think the alcohol has deleted my inner voice. I have no inner voice! Everything I'm thinking just pops out." Giggling again, she leaned back in the leather seat. "Sex," she blurted. "Sex. Isn't that a weird word? *Sexxxxx.*" She stretched it out, letting the word roll off her tongue. "I mean why are we all so uptight about sex, right? It's just sex! I'm sure you get a lot of sex in your line of work. Me? Not so much. Not that I'm not interested in it," she gushed and looked down at her hands.

"Hmmm," Danger replied noncommittally.

She leaned forward in her seat to look at him. "I'm sorry. Am I making you uncomfortable? I feel like I'm making you uncomfortable."

"No, I'm fine." He drove with a faint smile on his face.

"Oh, that's good, *cuz* I'm uncomfortable."

"You are? What's wrong?"

"My sweater is driving me crazy. It's so hot and itchy! It's supposed to be worn with a shirt underneath it but my friend—you know Sunny?" she continued before he could answer "—she made me wear it by itself and now all I *wanna* do is rip this *mo' fo'* off! In fact—"

Fran grabbed the hem of the offending sweater and in one swift motion pulled it off. She twirled it around the end of her finger and tossed it out the window.

"Ah, that's better! So freeing," she proclaimed, stretching her arms over her head. "No wonder you like stripping."

"What the—where did your shirt go?" Danger did a double take at Fran, his brow furrowed.

"I threw it out the window." She shrugged.

"You threw it out the window?"

"Yep."

"Why?"

"Weren't you listening? *Cuz* I told you, it was all itchy and stuff. Who needs a shirt anyway? You definitely shouldn't have one on." She giggled. "It's a crime to cover up that hot body!" She reached over and squeezed his bicep again to drive her point home.

"Should we go back and look for it?"

"For what?"

"Your shirt."

"*Naw*, I hated that shirt anyway. What I really need is some McDonald's! Can we go through the drive thru? Please, please, please?"

Danger muttered something under his breath.

"It's a proven fact, fries stop hangovers, but with dip, you *gotta* have the McChicken sauce." Fran nodded her head sagely. ". . . and cheese burgers . . . maybe two."

"Is that all?" Danger asked.

"Yup." Fran nodded solemnly and sank deeper into her seat.

Chapter 8

A bar of sunlight stabbed his right eyelid. Luke frowned and rolled his head away from the red haze. His face felt hot. He groaned and flung his arm up to block the light. Turning over, he tried to settle deeper into the thin mattress beneath him. Why was he sleeping on the floor? He opened his eyes and squinted at the back cushions of the couch an inch from his nose.

"What the—" he muttered, flipping onto his back, trying to figure out why he had opted to sleep on the couch. It was a nice couch but it had been chosen for appearance, not comfort. As it was he hardly ever sat on it, preferring the corduroy comfort of the extra wide chair in the corner.

The weathered leather beneath his head was cool. At some point during the night, his restless sleep had knocked all the pillows to the floor. He reached down and grabbed one, bunching it up and sticking it under his head. Propped in a sitting position, he watched the slow moving second hand sweep the face of the over-sized clock on the far wall. Now he remembered. Right, the girl—Fran. She was occupying the king-size bed in his room. He'd tucked her in when they'd arrived back at his place at two in the morning. She'd insisted on going through a McDonalds drive-thru on the way home, mumbling something about McChicken sauce and extra-large fries being a hangover preventer.

That was after she'd ripped off her shirt and thrown it out the window. He hadn't pictured her as a disposable clothes kind of girl. He'd been trying not to picture her as anything other than a lost waif up to that point. The black lace push-up bra she was wearing had made it hard to keep his eyes on the road. It had made him hard too. He shook his head, disgusted. As if he would ever take advantage of a woman in that state. She had decided that she could be a stripper too and wanted to show him her moves. He'd convinced her that she should lay down for a few minutes and plan her routine. She'd been snoring in seconds. Cute snoring though, not lumberjack snoring. He smiled.

Was she still there or did she wake up and sneak out during the night? From where he was lying he could see the front door. The deadbolt was still in the locked position.

So now what? He sat up swinging his legs onto the floor. Part of him hoped she was still there. She was pretty cute, like a bunny rabbit—a very sexy, black-lace bra-clad bunny rabbit. The whole pussy thing was weird though. He frowned. He was still trying to sort that out. She'd tried to cuddle up to him, calling him her bad boy, her hot dark danger. She couldn't seem to get his name right. Luke shook his head and stood. He needed a coffee, then he'd figure out what to do.

After putting on a pot of coffee, he tiptoed down the hall and looked in the door of his bedroom. Fran was out cold, still snoring softly like a milk-sated kitted. A McDonald's-sated kitten, he corrected himself. She'd gulped down the extra-large fries and two cheeseburgers as if she were afraid someone would take them away from her.

He stepped away from the door, returned to the kitchen and poured a mug of coffee. It was Saturday morning, his last work-free weekend before the semester started. He hadn't been booked to work the night before, but he had stepped in to help them out. The truth was, he was trying to distance himself from stripping. It was too risky. Meeting Tyler was a reminder that his covert moves weren't as secret as he thought they were. He wasn't a kid anymore. He had too much riding on his career and his reputation to risk someone recognizing him. It was all too easy to picture some undergrad student with a gripe exposing him to Etherridge. He rolled his eyes at the pun.

Opening the French doors to the patio, he stepped outside. The bricks were hot under his feet, not surprising considering it was eleven o'clock. The day was half-gone. Settling into a battered

Adirondack chair, he pushed a chunk of 2x4 off of a low wooden table and propped his feet on the table's edge.

His 1950s-style bungalow was a work in progress, but he'd gotten it cheap. The view though, the view was worth a million dollars. He had an unbroken view of Puget Sound. Today, it sparkled in the sunlight. The ferry was pulling away from the dock—late of course. This time though, they could blame the slow downs on the work going on at the new pier. He could hear the pile driver working, hammering the heavy support posts into the ocean floor. The island-hopping ferry, *MV Orca Queen* ran back and forth between one of the neighbouring islands on a hit or miss schedule. That was one of the funny quirks about Port Fling. Nothing ever worked the way you expected it to.

He took a sip of coffee and watched sail boats skitter across the water. It was the calm before the storm. Monday morning would arrive and he would have to face the music with his new lab rat. He sighed.

The wooden step behind him creaked. Luke swung around to face the door. Fran was clad in one of his button up shirts, hair messy, looking sexy as hell. She looked like a model poised to take a step, one foot raised, coffee in hand.

"Good morning," he offered.

"Morning," she mumbled, smiling tentatively.

Chapter 9

Bang, bang, bang, bang, bang. The noise cut through Fran's sleep, banishing her dream just as it was getting to the good part.

"Ow." She moaned and rolled over. The bed lurched. Maybe moving wasn't such a good idea. Probably best to keep her eyes tightly closed for now.

Bang. It sounded again.

"Fluffy, stop it," she pleaded. "I'll get up and feed you in a minute."

Despite Fran's promise, her misbehaving cat, intent on being fed, continued to make the offensive noise.

"Fluffy! I'm serious. Mama needs her rest," she called. Each word punctuated the ache in her head like a nail being pounded in by a hammer.

How much did she drink last night? She scrunched her eyes. She had never been this hungover, well . . . ever. And she had *definitely* never been on stage with a male stripper before. What had happened after she'd gotten off the stage? Why did she remember crying to someone about her Pussy? And how had she gotten home? So many unanswered questions. Had Sunny come back? No, that definitely didn't happen. Maybe someone who worked at the club had put her into a cab. Yes, she vaguely remembered some guy offering her a cab.

A loud crash sounded from her kitchen. Uh-oh, the cats had knocked the cookie jar off the counter again. Enough was enough.

"Okay, okay, you win," she grumbled as she started to get out of bed, moving at the speed of a 90-year-old waking after a hard night of wheel-chair racing.

She sat on the side of her bed with her eyes closed, giving her head time to right itself before opening them to process her surroundings.

Okay, here we go. Slowly, she blinked her eyes open. Sun streamed through the window dazzling her with brightness. It took a few seconds to adjust to the light.

Um, this wasn't her room—and it definitely wasn't Sunny's room. Where the heck was she? Her heart started pounding. Had she been kidnapped? Her parents had always warned her about drinking too much. Her chest fluttered. Panic caught in her throat. The start of her *Oh my god, freak-out panic* subsided slightly as her rational voice took over, reminding her that she wasn't restrained in any way. A flashback from the night before hit her like a punch in the gut as she vaguely remembered riding home in the stripper Dark Danger's car and throwing her itchy sweater out of the window.

"*Gaw,*" she let out a little cry at the memory as she looked down and saw she was not in-fact wearing a sweater. At least her bra and bottom half were completely intact. Yikes! She needed to find her shirt. She glanced around the room, noting the absence of anything hanging on the walls. There was a man's shirt flung over the large brown, leather chair in the corner. Gingerly she swayed to her feet. Her foot knocked against something on the floor. A bucket. He had put a bucket on the floor next to the bed for her. Okay, that was a pretty good sign that the guy wasn't a psychopath.

She slid her arms into the shirt, buttoning it to her neck and rolling up the sleeves. The inviting aroma of coffee piqued her senses making her boldly ignore her Nonna's voice screaming warnings (in Italian, of course) in her head. She followed the scent to the kitchen.

"Hello?" she called quietly, and then again, a little louder, "Hello?" Maybe Danger had gone back to work. Did strippers work in the daylight? Right Fran, strippers are like vampires, they hide their poles and take cover during daylight.

A large mug had been set out on the counter for her, along with a spoon, sugar bowl and a note reading, 'I'm out on the patio.' She fixed her coffee, black with a pound of sugar, and cradled the hot mug between her hands, taking a healthy sip.

Ah, that was better. Now to find her host. She walked to the double French doors straight ahead and saw her tall, dark and handsome 'special forces' dancer sitting with his back to her, enjoying a panoramic ocean view.

She knew strippers made good money but a house with a view like this had to come from a lot of years of dancing, or something else.

She opened the door and made her way down the steps. Danger turned at the noise and gave her a smile. "Good morning."

"Morning," she mumbled, running a hand through her hair, feeling self-conscious. He was even more gorgeous in the daylight than she remembered.

"How are you feeling?" he returned, with a knowing smile.

"Not so great," she admitted. "But thanks for the coffee . . . and the bucket. I didn't use it but always a good idea. The bucket, I mean, not the coffee. I can always use coffee." She held up her cup in mock cheers. She knew she was rambling but couldn't seem to stop.

"Relax. Have a seat." He gestured to the well-worn chair next to him.

"Thanks," she said, settling in to the chair. "Wow, what a beautiful view."

"Yep, it's not so bad," he agreed.

She watched the ferry come and then go, waiting for Danger to say something else, but he remained enigmatic.

Fran had never been in this situation before. Maybe it was time to make a new list—the *Top Ten Things to Say on the Morning After* list. Only right now, she couldn't come up with a single item. Oh my god. She didn't even know his name.

She looked around, searching for something to say, noting that of the four chairs on his deck, not one was the same. Her own kitchen chairs were the same mismatched jumble.

"This is quite the set of chairs you have," she observed, gesturing.

"Yes." He laughed, tilting his head to one side as he looked at the chairs. "I have a weakness for fixing stuff up."

"Is that why you took pity on me last night? I don't remember much, but I do remember that I was quite the mess," she chanced, keeping her eyes on the view.

"That you were," he agreed. "You could barely get out of my car."

She had another recollection of the night before: his coat draped over her shoulders, his warm strong arm around her bare waist helping her walk. Her heart sped up and flipped at the memory.

She cleared her throat. "Yah, sorry about that. I don't normally drink heavily. I've just got a lot going on right now."

"Fair enough," he conceded, not pressing for any further details, turning back to the view.

She studied him out of her periphery. He made her nervous. He was one of the most gorgeous confident men she'd ever met. He seemed completely comfortable with long silences, making her feel like she needed to come to him. Nope. He was definitely a player. She'd seen Sunny get involved with too many of those to risk getting tangled up with one. The sooner she got out of here, the better.

"Thank you for your help last night." She forced herself to look at him. "This is really embarrassing to admit, but I don't even know your real name."

"Luke," he replied simply.

"Well, thank you again, Luke," she repeated and then stood. "I'll get out of your hair now. I'm sure you have stuff to do."

"Not really." He shrugged. "I was just going to go out for something to eat."

Was that an invitation or a statement? She wasn't sure. "Okay, well . . . enjoy. I'll see you later."

"Wait," he called as she made for the door.

She turned, expecting him to extend an invitation to her, instead he said, "You're wearing my shirt."

"Oh right." Her face burned. "I, uh, can't really give it back to you right now, unless you happen to know where my sweater is?" She silently begged the universe to open a sinkhole beneath her right now.

"Somewhere around Pine Tree and Main Street." He gave her a wicked grin.

"Oh, uh. Okay. Could I bring your shirt back to you later?" Seriously, where was a sinkhole when you needed one?

"Nope."

Awkward. Did he expect her to go home topless?

"How about you take me out for breakfast and then we'll call it even?" he continued.

Her face brightened. "Okay, that sounds fair. Breakfast it is." Her mood darkened, remembering. "Except, one little thing: I don't know where my purse is."

"Ah, your purse." He laughed. "Funny story, you told me you lost it but once you, er, lost your shirt, it turned out you were wearing your purse underneath the shirt the whole time."

"Oh *jeez*," she buried her face in her hands.

"It's okay. It was actually really cute."

"You say cute, I say mortifying." Fran cringed. Her face was so hot, it was going to spontaneously combust.

"No, don't be embarrassed. We've all been there. You just needed to blow off some steam." Luke reassured her.

He stood and stretched his arms overhead, giving Fran a glimpse of his washboard stomach.

"Now about that breakfast. I know the perfect little place," he said.

Chapter 10

Luke lifted his face to the sun enjoying the warmth on his skin. They'd been lucky and scored a choice table on the patio at Marietta's. The breakfast/brunch crowd was out in full force today. He studied Fran through his Deltas, wondering what she thought of the restaurant. It was one of Fling's best kept secrets, located behind an old cannery in the "bad" part of town—although in Port Fling "bad" just meant that some of the buildings were run down and the streets didn't look like a scene from *Pleasantville*.

Fran was staring out at the bay, studying the line of cars being loaded onto the ferry. She looked ready to run, perched on the edge of her seat, her back ramrod straight. She was probably asking herself how she had ended up having brunch with a stripper.

He took pity on her and broke the awkward silence. "Have you ever been here?"

Fran started and swung around to look at him. "No." She shook her head and lifted her hands helplessly.

She did that a lot, Luke decided, talked with her hands. It was cute. He liked it.

"I didn't even know this place was here . . . and I'm born and raised in Port Fling. How did you find out about it?"

"Through work. Someone mentioned it, so I thought I'd check it out. Now it's my favorite place. The food is amazing, and the prices are great."

"What do you recommend?"

"What do you like?" Luke countered.

Fran started laughing. "Why do I have the sense we have two conversations going on?"

Luke smiled. "Relax Fran. It's just breakfast. Having breakfast with a stripper isn't going to tar your reputation for life."

She looked surprised by his remark. "I'm not embarrassed having breakfast with you," she defended. "I'm trying to adjust to the fact that I let myself get blackout drunk, went home with a stranger . . . Hey, that's funny." She laughed. "Stranger Danger. Who would have thought those two words could have such a whole new meaning?

Anyway, that's not me. I've never done this kind of thing."

"Stranger Danger," Luke repeated, surprised at her quick wit. The more time he spent with Fran, the more she attracted him. "So last night wasn't your usual Friday night fun?"

"No, hardly," Fran said and laughed again. "I'm usually studying."

"Studying?"

"I'm going to college."

"What are you taking?" Education, Luke decided. Fran looked like she'd be at home surrounded by a group of kids. She had an earthy goodness about her—a big difference from the women he usually hung out with.

"I'm starting a work placement, so I'm taking a break from the classroom stuff."

So, she didn't want to talk about school. Fine with him. It wasn't as if he was going to open up about what he did in real life. It would probably bore her to death, although he had the feeling he wouldn't have to dumb it down like he usually did. It seemed Fran was as smart as she was gorgeous.

"So how about you? Do you . . . dance every day?"

"You mean: am I just a stripper?" He smiled wryly.

"No—I—I'm sorry." Her face turned an adorable shade of pink.

"Hey, it's okay. It's a valid question." He waved off her apology and felt a stab of guilt for making her blush. "I'm working on easing myself out of stripping and experimenting with something else. It's been a long time coming. I'm not quite ready to completely give up my night life." There, he hadn't told her anything and he hadn't lied either.

"Fair enough."

Fran silently toyed with her cutlery and then looked up.

"What—?"

"What can I get you folks?" The waitress interrupted. She took their orders and their conversation turned to other things.

"I keep meaning to take the ferry over to the island," Fran said wistfully, watching the ship pull away from the dock.

"Why don't you?"

Fran shrugged. "Too busy, I guess. There always seems to be something that needs to be checked off my to-do list."

Luke nodded. He knew that feeling. He'd been living it since he'd gone from two weeks in a juvenile detention center to his last foster home placement. Those two weeks had scared him silly. He had sworn he was never going back to juvie and he hadn't.

When the system had spit out another placement, he'd gone with his head down. Looking back, he couldn't decide if it was Anna Foster or the facility that scared him straight. He did know that Anna and Brent had kept him on the straight and narrow, adopting him when he turned fifteen and adding him to their family permanently.

"Why don't we do it today?" he said abruptly.

"Do what?" Fran asked, confused.

"Go check out the island."

The food arrived, saving Fran from answering. Just as well Luke decided. He didn't do spontaneous. He did calculated. That's why he had a PhD in chemistry.

They took their first bites.

"Oh my god," Fran moaned biting into her fried egg sandwich. "This is amazing."

The tiny moan sounded almost sexual. Like she'd reached down and touched him, stroked him, making him hard. Holy crap. He gulped. Where had that come from? Furtively, he adjusted and repositioned himself in his chair. He looked down at his smoked salmon Benny. It was his go to breakfast when he ate at Marietta's. Had Fran noticed him wiggling in his chair? No, she was enjoying her fried egg sandwich of pepper bacon, jack cheese, tomato and lettuce. Her eyes were half-closed, her attention focused on food. She looked almost orgasmic. What would she look like— She opened her eyes.

Luke gulped a forkful of salmon. It could have been shredded cardboard for all he noticed of the taste. They continued eating in silence until he caught Fran stealing lustful gazes at his Benny.

"Do you want a bite?" he offered.

"Oh, I couldn't."

He took another mouthful. Her eyes followed the food to his mouth. She licked her lips. He noticed that her sandwich had disappeared.

"Here." He held out a bite, waving it tantalizingly in front of her nose.

Fran leaned forward and delicately took the offering. She closed her eyes, savoring the blend of Hollandaise and smoked salmon. She gave another little moan and Luke shifted in his chair again. The tip of her tongue licked a drip of sauce from her upper lip. He felt like he was 14-years-old again, hiding his sudden erection. He looked out at the water so she couldn't see how turned on he was.

"I am so having that next time," Fran said opening her eyes, and then, "What? Is there something on my face" She dabbed at her lip.

Luke swallowed his last bite of breakfast and accepted a refill on his coffee. He didn't want more coffee, but he wanted breakfast to end even less. He leaned back in the chair.

"We should do it." Fran nodded abruptly. "Let's do it."

Damn, was she reading his thoughts?

"The ferry, let's hop the ferry and explore the island. The market's on, they have entertainment. Let's go," she repeated.

Just say no, Luke. She's not the kind of woman you're looking for. Fran was beautiful, intelligent, funny—relationship material, and Luke didn't do relationships. He opened his mouth.

"I can't think of anything I'd rather do than spend the day with you," he said, surprising himself.

Fran blinked those whiskey-coloured eyes and he was pulled into their depths—over his head—intoxicated. Hell. What could it hurt, he thought, throwing money down on the table.

"I thought I was paying," Fran protested.

"You do lunch," Luke answered with a devilish grin.

Fran was silent for a second and then muttered something under her breath.

It sounded like, "I just might."

Chapter 11

"What a gorgeous day." Fran sighed, as she stretched her legs out on the blanket Luke had bought from a local weaver. The bright reds, blues, and greens had caught her eye on their jaunt through the market, luring her back to the rack. The heavy woolen threads, woven in intricate bars of colour, had called to her. Seeing her interest, Luke had wandered over and then insisted on buying it, saying it would bring some light into his house.

At first, Fran had laughed and said no. The blanket was expensive, almost one hundred dollars. Luke had insisted. He said strippers made good money. He'd buy it with his tip money. Now as she dug her toes into the wool and leaned back on her elbows, Fran had to admit, she was glad he'd bought the blanket. Colour made her happy. She'd always been like that. While the other toddlers picked up a single crayon, and covered the page with it, Fran's pages were alive with rainbows.

"Sure is," Luke agreed. "It looks like we're not the only ones grabbing the chance to check this place out," he added. He was lying on his side, raised up on one elbow, watching the crowd. "Look," he said pointing. "It's a wolf pack." He gestured towards a woman walking three wolf hounds.

"She looks like a little girl who's dressed her puppies up for the day," Fran responded. "Do you think the dogs are all girls?" Each massive dog had a matching pink plaid bandana draped around its neck.

Sun, sea and sand—Seal Island was alive with energy. Luke and Fran had parked themselves in a prime spot for people watching. It was a Saturday and the sun shining down brought with it an eclectic mix of wacky locals, hipster Seattleites, yuppy Seattleites and 'normal' folks from neighbouring suburbs, like Luke and Fran. Fran's stomach fluttered with nerves every time she looked at Luke. She felt like she was 13-years-old again, out on a date with the most popular boy at school. Let's hope this time she didn't fall on her face, exposing her Care Bear underwear to the whole world, earning her the hated nickname 'Fransie Underpantsie.'

Fran shook her head as if she could shake that horrible memory out. It was 13 years ago but she still cringed when she thought of that day. Whatever. Deal with it Fran. You're all grown up now and Luke is certainly no gangly thirteen-year-old boy. She glanced up at him from under the veil of her lashes and her stomach did another flip-flop. He was looking out at the water, so she was free to study his profile unnoticed. She raised a hand to her mouth. Oh God, she was salivating over him like Fluffy over a fresh liver pate. She couldn't help herself. He was the best kind of eye candy and she wanted to gobble him up. She gave in to temptation and greedily eyed the hot hunk of man beside her.

Luke leaned back casually on his elbows. The motion stretched his thin shirt tight across his chest, outlining the perfect lines of his defined pecs. Fran silently added that to her list of: *Body Parts of Luke's to Drool Over*. The guy definitely worked out—a lot.

"What's that noise?" Luke asked, turning abruptly to catch Fran checking him out.

"Noise? What noise?" Fran replied, trying to act innocent and not like she was a naughty kitty caught with its paw in the fishbowl.

"The drumming." Luke smiled. "Hear it now?"

Fran listened. She heard the sound of a faint thumping in the background. She had thought it was her heart going *thunk-a-thunk* for the hunk in front of her.

"Let's go check it out," Luke said levering himself to stand and leaning down to offer Fran a hand up.

Fran took the proffered hand. She was disappointed when he let go.

"You don't strike me as a drum circle type of guy," Fran teased as they made their way towards the beat.

"I'm not a drum circle kind of guy. At all." Luke smiled and slowed his pace, turning back to her, suddenly serious. His stunning navy eyes locked with hers. "But there's something beautiful about people from different walks of life coming together and making music. I know it sounds cheesy but the way I grew up it was every man or woman for themselves. When I see people, who are able to put aside their differences and work together, well I think it's just . . . neat for lack of a better word."

"Hmmm. So, you're a lone wolf type of guy?" Fran questioned, teasing with a hint of seriousness.

"I guess you could say that. I've just always found that the only person you can rely on one-hundred percent of the time, is yourself."

"Oh, you're a control freak too?" Fran blurted. She felt her face growing warm. "Sorry, I can't believe I just said that."

"No, it's okay." Luke smiled. "You call it like it is. I like that." He caught Fran's hand in his and stopped. Fran's hand tingled as his thumb ran over her knuckle. A gust of wind blew a piece of hair into her face and he used his other hand to brush it away. His fingers lingered on her face. Time stilled. The intimate touch sparked a tingle that ran down Fran's spine and arched through her.

Their eyes locked. Fran's body leaned towards Luke. He was going to kiss her! Her heart pounded, matching the thumping of the drums as those perfect lips moved closer.

"Can I cut in for a dance?" interrupted a husky voice. A tall, thin woman wearing a brightly flowered muumuu looked expectantly at Luke. Her long gray hair reached her waist and she had wrapped a circlet of flowers around her head. "Come on, sweet cheeks," she added, pulling Luke into the middle of the drum circle and gyrating against him.

What? The?

Fran's disappointment evaporated into a wave of laughter. An exasperated Luke was trying unsuccessfully to wriggle out of the persistent hippy grandma's grasp. Finally, apparently deciding 'if you can't beat them, join them' and he gave the hippy granny a run for her money, gyrating his hips against hers.

A crowd formed around the drum-circle-dancing pair, cheering them on, clapping to the beat of the drums. Granny had some moves of her own, and soon, tears of laughter were running down Fran's face as the aging hippy bent and twerked to the beat. The pair finished with Luke lifting the woman into the air as she wrapped her legs around his waist.

Fran laughed and cheered with the crowd but she felt mildly unsettled. She'd had a flashback to being pulled up onto the stage by Luke the night before. He'd used the same move on her. She knew it was silly—he was a stripper, it was his job. But that was exactly what was bothering her. It was his job. The hippy granny didn't threaten her but she felt a stab of jealousy at the thought of Luke wrapping another young hot woman's legs around his waist.

"Did you like my moves?" Luke asked as he broke away to rejoin Fran.

"Yes. I recognized some of those from last night. I thought those moves were just for me," she joked and then silently berated herself. What was it about him that made Fran forget herself? She sounded like a jealous girlfriend.

"They were just for you."

"Sure, I bet you say that to all the ladies you pull onstage."

"I never pull ladies onstage with me, Fran."

"*Ya*, right." She waved him off. "It's okay Luke, I was just joking."

"No. I'm serious Fran. I draw a line between my audience and myself. You're the first."

Fran smiled and looked down, feeling suddenly shy. She wanted to kiss him, but there were so many people around.

"Hey." Luke caught her chin with his hand and gently lifted her face to meet his. The crowd around them melted away as Fran stared into his beautiful eyes, the colour of the sea on a moonlit night. Her breath caught as Luke leaned in.

"Hey Luke!" Again, they were interrupted. Luke turned his head away to greet the speaker.

Fran wanted to scream. *Are you freaking kidding me?* Instead she bit her tongue and pasted on a smile for the ponytailed man standing beside Luke.

"Zack! Hey, what are you doing here?" Luke greeted the man with a hearty handshake.

"It's a drum circle and I'm a free-living hippy. Dude, we go hand in hand. I should ask you what you're doing here. Nice moves by the way! You've been holding out, man."

"I have my moments. Thanks." Luke ran a hand through his hair and turned to give Fran a wink.

"Is this the girlfriend you've mentioned?" Zack gestured towards Fran.

What! He has a girlfriend? Fran was alarmed. She had known it was too good to be true.

Luke turned and winked at her again. "Sure is. Fran, Zack, Zack, Fran."

"Nice to meet you." Fran smiled and shook Zack's hand.

"Nice to meet you too, Fran. Say, Luke I wanted to ask you about—"

"No shop talks today, Zack, it's a Saturday," interrupted Luke.

"Sorry dude. I just can't shut the brain off. That's why I love drumming, I lose myself in the beat. It's like travelling to another universe, you should try it sometime."

"Sure, I'll get right on that, Zack," Luke responded. "Right after I grow my hair out and get a man bun. Catch up later?"

"Later. Nice to meet you Fran." Zack waved and turned back to rejoin his drum circle.

"He seems nice. Does he work at Spanky's? I don't recognize him, but I feel like I've seen him somewhere." Fran tried to sound nonchalant as she dug for more information.

"Nah, I've known Zack awhile. We just have similar interests."

"Hmm." Fran replied. The wheels of her mind were spinning. She wanted to know more about this girlfriend but she didn't want to go all *Fatal Attraction* on him.

They walked for a while in silence before Luke spoke again.

"I don't have a girlfriend by the way," he said, answering the hanging question that was plaguing her.

"No?" Fran answered, trying to keep the elation out of her voice.

"No. I made her up to get Zack off of my back. He's always trying to set me up with one hippy girl or another. I found the best way to stave him off was to create a fake girlfriend."

Fran smiled serenely but, on the inside, she was jumping up and down. She was really starting to like this guy.

Chapter 12

The sun sank lower in the sky, bathing the sea in a final dazzling orange glow. Fran snuggled deeper into Luke's patio chair, legs folded beneath her, with her hands wrapped around a comforting mug of hot chocolate. She wore Luke's old jacket and couldn't stop herself from nuzzling her nose into the collar, enjoying the musky scent of him lingering in the fabric.

Fran couldn't believe that she and Luke had talked, walked and eaten the day away. Maybe she was still a bit tipsy from the night before, or maybe it was the release of grief over Puss 'n' Boots' death, but Fran felt more comfortable with Luke than she had ever thought possible. It was crazy. He was a stripper. Where could this really go? How could she ever introduce a stripper to her friends and family? Fran forced herself to stop analyzing the situation. She had spent her entire life focusing on the future.

For once she was going to take a page out of Sunny's book and live for the moment.

Luke joined her on the patio. He was carrying a plate in each hand.

"I thought we'd eat out here if that's okay. Take advantage of the view?" he asked.

"Absolutely," she agreed taking the plate of spaghetti he handed her. "Serving pasta to an Italian? You're brave," she teased.

"I like a challenge," he returned, "but don't judge me too harshly."

"I'll try." Her face actually hurt from smiling so much today.

She took her first bite. "It's very good."

"You really like it?" he checked, sounding like a nervous school boy.

"I do." Fran confirmed and then smiled again at the expression of pure joy on his face. He was so cute!

They ate in silence, plates on laps and paper towels for napkins. After her first bite of the oregano and basil infused tomato sauce, Fran forgot to feel self-conscious.

"This is amazing," she said, twirling the pasta around the end of her fork and taking a bite. A tiny morsel of spaghetti dangled from her lip and she slurped it in. She grabbed the napkin and dabbed away the sauce before taking another bite.

"A fare una spaghettata" she announced.

Luke looked at her, his eyebrows raised in question.

"To eat spaghetti," Fran said and laughed. "It's a family saying, it means getting together to eat. Good friends, good food, good conversation."

"Amen to that," Luke answered *cheers*-ing her with his fork.

Luke's complete sense of ease with himself and the world around him made Fran relax. For once, she was able to just be.

"Dessert?" he asked, after Fran had polished off her plate.

"Sure," she agreed, even though she was full. She didn't want this night to end.

She stood and brought her plate and cup inside. Her steps carried her past the open door to Luke's bedroom. The king-size bed drew her like a honey bee to a particularly sweet flower, a hot sexy flower. She imagined stepping through the door with him, tugging off his shirt, slowly running her hands over his chest, his rock-hard abs. Her skin tingled. *Stop it, Fran. You just met the guy.* She didn't care. She was always telling herself to be more spontaneous, to lighten up. She'd even created a: *Ways That I Can Be More Spontaneous* list. What would Sunny do in this situation? That was easy. Sunny would grab hold of Luke, turn around, and hop back into that giant bed.

"Is it too hot in here?" Luke asked.

Damn, Fran raised a hand to her red cheek.

"No, I must have gotten a bit too much sun today," she lied, gritting her teeth. Her cheeks burned. She was the world's worst liar. Her brother Sal had always made her tell their parents when "stuff happened." He knew Fran would incriminate herself and he'd be off the hook.

"Do you need any help?" she asked, taking the focus off herself.

"No, I'm good. Take a seat."

She settled onto the couch and watched as he doled out bowls of fruit in the kitchen.

"Here you go." He handed her a bowl and sat down next to her, his leg pressing against hers as they ate. Her heart shifted into overdrive.

Fran picked at her fruit, wondering how to take it to the next level. They had been so close to kissing on the island (twice!) but each time, the moment was lost. She wanted to go back and recreate it but didn't know how. She wasn't exactly a virgin but she also wasn't very experienced when it came to intimacy either. There'd been her first—Chad Rinaldi at prom—total disaster. And then Ricky—her only boyfriend in university—that had just been blah. They hadn't had any chemistry. They were study partners who turned into more and stayed together for the convenience. In the end it just fizzled out. They went their separate ways with no broken hearts or hurt feelings. Now she was alone with this gorgeous man. He made her feel things she'd never felt before and she had no idea what to do.

"Are you feeling okay?" Luke asked, pulling Fran out of her thoughts. "You're really quiet."

"Yes, I'm fine. Just tired." Fran felt her face growing warm again at the lie.

"Do you want me to take you home?" Luke questioned, concerned.

"No!" Fran said quickly. "I just—" she checked herself. *I just want to jump your bones, drag you into your bedroom and have my wicked way with you.* "No, I'm not ready to go home yet."

She placed her unfinished bowl on the coffee table and wiped her palms on her skirt. Fruit juice had pooled on Luke's lower lip as he ate. Fran watched his tongue lick it away and greedily wished she could taste those lips. She felt like time was running out. Why wasn't he trying to kiss her again? She wanted him. She needed him. No. She wasn't the type of girl to make the first move.

So be the kind of girl who makes the first move then, Fran! She heard Sunny's exasperated voice in her head, urging her on. *You wanted to live in the moment, so seize the moment. Go for it. It's just one little move. What's the worst thing that could happen?*

He could reject you and you'd feel like an idiot, her rational voice argued. *You'll—* She silently told her rational voice to shut the *f* up.

Alright then, it's now or never. She watched Luke place his finished bowl on the table and relax back into the couch. *One, two, three*—in one swift awkward move, she straddled him. A look of shock crossed his face, and his mouth dropped open as his eyebrows shot up. *Oh my God*, she'd made the wrong choice. The shocked look altered as his eyes darkened with desire. Slowly, he ran his hands up the sides of her ribcage.

Fran shivered and wrapped her arms around his neck. She stared into his midnight eyes and her breath hitched. For a delicious instant, they stayed that way, their lips almost touching, the heat from their bodies mingling, combusting. Finally, Luke closed the distance. His soft, moist lips met hers in a slow teasing kiss. Anticipation flowered into need. The kiss changed, becoming urgent, demanding. Desire snaked through Fran, building like a chemical reaction, making her tight and restless. She moaned and wiggled closer, wrapping herself around him. She felt like she'd never really been kissed until this moment and she wanted Luke's mouth everywhere at once.

"Fran," Luke breathed kissing his way down. She fumbled with the buttons at her neck, desperate to give his lips access to move lower.

"This needs to go," he said gruffly, pulling at both sides of her shirt, tearing it open and popping off the buttons.

"Your shirt!" Fran giggled, breaking the tension.

"I've always wanted to do that."

Luke's grin was wicked. It sent another wave of need through her. His eyes travelled to her breasts, nicely plumped and pushed up thanks to Victoria's Secret. He lifted his head and stared into her eyes, not laughing now.

"You're so beautiful, Fran."

"So are you." Fran sighed and rocked against him, feeling his need for her against her own. Her hand dropped to his chest, stroking over the soft cotton of the t-shirt. She wanted to see that gorgeous body of his, to feel his skin against hers. She grasped his shirt and together they pulled it off over his head.

"I've been wanting to kiss you all day." Luke's mouth moved over hers. He pulled her closer, moving under her. It was his turn to moan.

"I've been wanting you to kiss me all day," Fran whispered between kisses. She smiled almost shyly, running her fingers through the small patch of dark hair that covered his chest.

His skin was hot, burning. She pressed closer, sharing his heat. His body melded with hers as their kisses deepened again, leaving Fran frantic for more. She needed more. The heat of Luke's skin against her own was turning her to flames. This time when he kissed his way down there was no shirt to stop his progress. He nudged her breast free of the bra, gently teasing her nipple with his mouth. She reached around behind, wiggling to release the hook on the back of the bra, sighing as he buried his face in her breasts. He wasn't still for long. He kissed and licked his way to their tips. She moaned. The feel of his mouth made her writhe. He raised his head, smiled rakishly and returned to her lips, licking, nibbling, kissing her like it was their last night on earth. She felt like a champagne bottle, shaken, ready to burst before uncorking.

"Do you want to go in your room and stretch out?" she panted.

"Absolutely." He stood with her legs still wrapped around his waist, and carried her to the bed, his mouth on hers.

"Fran, are you sure this is what you want?" he checked as he gently laid her on the bed.

"I've never been more certain of anything in my life," she answered, and she meant it.

Chapter 13

The sun was barely rising when Luke parked the car in front of Fran's two-bedroom bungalow. He yawned and turned to face her, looking down at her with sleepy eyes, bedroom eyes. Fran smiled.

"This it?" he asked.

"Home sweet home," she said leaning over to give him a kiss. "Come on," she coaxed.

Luke linked his fingers through her and hand in hand, they walked from the car to the porch. "Tell me why we're here?"

Fran responded by kissing Luke, nuzzling his neck and wrapping her arms around him.

Luke responded with a kiss that left her boneless and wanting, melting, ready to combust.

"You're bad for me," she whispered in his ear. "What if someone is watching?" At this point Fran couldn't have cared less who was looking. The only thing she was interested in was the hot sexy man standing on the porch beside her.

He groaned and pulled her in tighter. "You feel so good. We didn't have to go out. We could have just stayed in bed and . . ."

Fran wiggled even closer. "And . . ." she murmured against his lips. "Are you making me a promise?"

"Oh, I am. I am making you a big promise."

Fran laughed. "A big one eh?" She raised her eyebrows and dropped her hand to feel just how big the promise was. "Hold that thought," she said, letting him go to dig her keys out of her purse.

Luke leaned one broad shoulder up against the door frame. What was it about this woman that got him so hard? He wasn't a monk. He'd been with girls more experienced, more beautiful, but when he looked into Fran's warm brown eyes and touched her soft skin, felt her curves beneath his fingertips, he couldn't think of anything else.

"So, tell me again why you couldn't just wear my shirt all weekend?" he breathed in her ear, moving forward to wrap his arms around her, trapping her between his body and the door. He couldn't stop touching her.

"Stop!" Fran giggled and shivered. "You're tickling me."

Luke liked her laugh. It stole the seriousness from her face. It made him feel as if she'd been saving that happiness just for him. He smiled.

Fran looked up at him. "What?" she asked.

"Nothing," Luke said shrugging. "I'm just loving life."

"Me too," Fran said, leaning in for another kiss. She unlocked the door. "Umm, I need to tell you something."

"Hmm," Luke said, not really listening, pulling her closer, leaning down to steal another kiss.

Fran dodged away from him. She looked nervous. "I'm serious," she said.

Luke frowned. "You have a husband and three kids behind the door? You're running an illegal gambling den?"

Fran laughed. "An illegal gambling den? Seriously?"

Luke shrugged again. "It's all I've got. What's so important?"

Fran hesitated and then blurted, "I have six cats."

It was Luke's turn to laugh. "Six cats? I thought your cat died."

"He did, but I still have his mate and their five kittens." Fran's voice had a defensive edge as if this was a sensitive issue, as if Luke's reaction could ruin the moment.

He grinned. "No gun-toting boyfriend, or trained attack dogs? You're safe to open the door. It's okay, Fran. I know you aren't a crazy cat lady. Let's grab you a change of clothes, feed your horde and go enjoy the day."

"You promise you won't think I'm nuts?" she begged.

"Because of a cat and five little kittens?" Luke leaned past her to push open the door. The faint meows he thought he'd heard earlier, became a deafening chorus. He stepped back. A row of gray and brown tabby-coloured cats sat in a stately line. The meows stopped. Six pairs of blue eyes stared at him intently before the cats stood as one and swarmed Fran.

Fran looked at him apologetically. "I have to feed them or they get a bit out of control."

Luke grinned and lifted one eyebrow. "Like their mother?"

Fran blushed. "Not my fault. There were extenuating circumstances. Besides it's hard to stay in control with you around."

"Really, Fran? Want to find out?" He leaned in to grab another kiss but the army of giant cats blocked him. "Just what kind of cats are these anyway? They're huge." He bent down to pat one. It hissed and sidled away from him.

"Maine Coon," Fran answered. "Have a seat on the couch. I'll feed them and get changed."

Luke watched Fran disappear down the hallway surrounded by her cat pack. He shook his head in bemusement—six cats? Not just any cats either—giant cats. The smallest one probably weighed twenty-five pounds.

Left alone, Luke wandered into the living room, stopping inside the doorway to get his first look at the private Fran, the Fran she hid from everyone else. He smiled again. He couldn't seem to stop doing that. There was something about her that made him feel damn good . . . and hot and bothered. Carefully he rearranged himself, grimacing at the tightness of his jeans. If he and Fran kept seeing each other, he'd have to buy looser jeans, or sweats. The smile widened.

He stepped into the room and looked around. Colour—Fran liked colour. Now he got why she had fallen in love with the blanket in the market. When Luke bought his house, he'd hired a decorator to choose paint colours and suggest furniture. His surroundings didn't matter. He needed a bed and a couch . . . and a fridge. It was probably the result of living in so many foster homes at a young age. His need to stamp his personality on his surroundings had been beaten out of him.

He could live out of a suitcase for a month and not feel the need to put his mark on the space surrounding him. Hell, he'd done just that in foster care number eight. That was the house with the plastic on the couches and the smell of bleach permeating every molecule of air. The Weirdons, that was their name. The Weird-ones and their little crop of weirdo children who enjoyed dissecting all sorts of animals. Creepy. He'd used the emergency call number to get out of that one. He shook his head. Whenever he heard of a serial killer arrested in Portland, he thought about the Weirdon family.

Fran on the other hand used every molecule of the space around her. She'd etched her personality on everything, going crazy with colour. She'd told him that she was only renting the tiny rancher. That explained the dead white walls, the tidy white trim surrounding the mullioned window panes. Banned from colouring the walls, she'd turned her attention to the room, decorating the fat-cushioned couches with blue and white pillows in abstract lines that bent the eyes. She'd thrown down a thick-piled area rug decorated with fans of gray, white and yellow.

At the centre of the room was an old-fashioned red brick fireplace. Hanging over the mantle was a painting of a fat panda riding a bicycle. Splashes of green and yellow formed a back drop for the over-sized bear.

Brightly colored post-its were tacked on the wall. He leaned closer to read what one of them said. Scrawled in what he assumed was Fran's large, loopy writing, was a list titled: *Words I need to use Less Often!* 'Like,' 'Umm' and 'Yah' had made it to the top of the list. Beside that list was another one entitled: *Words I need to Use More Often!* 'Elucidate,' 'Obfuscate' and 'Perfunctory' made the top of that list.

Luke laughed and moved further into the room. The groupings of mismatched frames lured him in to view their whimsical works of art. The bright primary colours made him smile. They were like Fran, they breathed life into the room. One wall was dedicated to framed photographs. Luke crossed the carpet to see them. Fran had said something about a big family but this was crazy. He spotted Fran immediately. The photo looked like it had been snapped recently. It was Fran and nine men. He stepped back. Brothers? They all had wavy chocolate brown hair and cat's eyes slightly tilted up at the corners.

He sat down on the couch and stared absently at the overflowing book case in the corner. Thick text books were piled neatly on one shelf, paper backs lined the others. From where he sat, he couldn't see the book covers but he was guessing they had to do with whatever she was studying at college. Education, he decided again, grinning. Fran would be a great teacher. The top of the book shelf held a Chianti bottle with a pool of white wax at one end and a pair of gilt candle holders on the other. It should have looked messy but it didn't. It was free and light—like a happy drunk Fran.

He leaned back against the cushions and thought of Fran. Fran in the shower, Fran in his bed, Fran . . . His jeans felt tight and he changed positions. They were going to have to get very dirty and repeat that shower scene. Oh, yeah. He turned his head and his eyes met those of a stern elderly woman glaring at him from a carved wooden frame on the coffee table next to the couch. He sat up, feeling like a teenage boy caught "reading" a porn magazine.

That must be the Sicilian Nonna Fran had told him about. He studied Nonna's menacing face and decided he would not want to piss that woman off. Nonna's eyes bored into his, daring him to make one wrong move, so she could hit him over the head with a shovel and bury him in her cheerful but sinister garden, where the rest of Fran's ex-boyfriends were decomposing under-ground. Yes, he definitely was in no hurry to meet Fran's Nonna.

The cushion next to his head moved. He jumped and looked over his shoulder to find the cats had finished chowing down on whatever Fran fed them and come back to hunt for some dessert. The biggest one slunk towards him, black tufted ears twitching, flattening against its head as its blue eyes narrowed. The cat's long tail shuddered and it sank back on its haunches, growling. The sound set off a chain reaction of rumbling.

Luke stood hastily and retreated to stand next to the fireplace. It was if the cats had joined forces with stern Nonna and were warning him not to hurt Fran. No longer interested in him, the cats dropped down to the couch and settled onto the cushions for some group grooming.

"Sorry I took so long," Fran said stepping back into the room. "What's the matter? Oh," She looked from Luke to the cats. "Fluffy kicked you off the couch?"

"You call the big one Fluffy?" Diesel or Axel, maybe, but Fluffy? "Are they always like this?" Luke waved in the direction of the crowded couch.

Fran followed the gesture and sighed, nodding her head. "Were you sitting there?"

"I was," Luke said. "The big guy growled at me. I didn't even know cats could growl."

"I'm sorry. They think the couch belongs to them."

Luke looked down at his fur-covered jeans. He made a half-hearted attempt to brush them off.

Fran saw his dilemma and grabbed a lint roller. "I'm so sorry," she repeated. "I didn't get to vacuum and—"

Luke grabbed her arm, stopping her. "And if you keep that up we aren't going to get out of here."

Fran looked down at the bulge straining his jeans. She blushed and dropped the roller onto the cat pile on the couch. The wave of cat grooming stopped as six pairs of eyes glared accusingly at Luke.

He leaned in for a quick kiss and grabbed Fran's hand, pulling her in close, wanting to absorb the feel of her body against his own. Fran moaned softly and burrowed in tighter. It was Luke's turn to moan. The kiss deepened. He stepped back, bringing her along with him. His knees hit the back of the couch and he moved to sit, pulling her along. A wave of cats exploded off the cushions.

Fran started laughing.

Luke looked at the herd of cats trying to recover their dignity with a moment of personal grooming. He smiled, loving the husky timbre of her laugh. Bending over, he dropped a quick kiss onto the tip of her nose.

"Let's go explore, then I'll cook you dinner at my house."

The cats were going to take some getting used to.

Chapter 14

"So, a Sicilian Sunday supper?" Luke asked. He was propped up on one elbow looking down at Fran where she lay beside him in bed. They had tried to go out. In fact, they had made it all the way to downtown Port Fling. They had wandered into a couple of shops, poked through the back corner of Bits and Pieces, the local hardware store, and had a coffee at the Bull Cafe.

Luke needed some new neckties for work and he enlisted Fran to help pick them out. He didn't care what they looked like, they were a necessary evil for the job. He always bought them from the bargain table at Manley's Dry Goods Emporium, choosing them based on conformity and price. He'd rather spend money on renos for his house. He looked up at the ties now adorning the headboard. Who knew ties could have so many possibilities.

They had then tried taking a walk on the beach, but five minutes in, they had looked at each other and by unspoken agreement, ended back here. This is where Fran belonged . . . gorgeous and naked . . . in his bed. He traced his hand along the curve of her hip and she scooted closer to him.

"Dessert," Fran corrected, reaching up to pull his head down for a kiss.

"You taste like dessert and I'm a big fan of dessert," Luke whispered against her lips.

He pulled her up and over so that she was resting on top of him. Her long hair dangled over his face in a riot of curls. Fran swept up a hand and pushed it back. She stared into his eyes.

"I can see that," she said, rocking slowly against him, teasing him.

"Fran, you're killing me."

"Oh, poor Lukie. Should I stop," she mocked gently. "Or would you prefer I do this?"

Her mouth dropped lower and Luke groaned. In one smooth move he rolled her over.

"My turn," he said, smothering her giggles, taking his time until they were both panting and begging for release.

Afterwards, Luke held her close. He'd never shared that intimacy with any woman. Most of his relationships had been getting down, quick and dirty—it's been fun. I'll call you. Of course, he never made that call. He rested his chin on Fran's damp curly head and inhaled the scent of his shampoo on her hair. That brought memories of their earlier shower and he felt himself getting hard again.

Fran stirred, sliding away from him. "Down, boy," she said, slipping out of the bed. "I cannot be late for Nonna's dessert night. She's trying out a new bake-off recipe."

Luke levered himself up to sit propped against the headboard.

"Bake off? What's that," he asked. He gave Fran his best come-hither smile but she laughed and shook her head.

"Nonna and Sunny's grandma, Waverly, have a long running feud over who is the better baker. Waverly, Sunny's grandma, owns Luscious Buns Bakery."

Luke's eyebrows shot up. "Luscious Buns home of the boobie cookies with the cinnamon heart nipples?"

Fran nodded. "Amongst other more phallic things."

"Wow," Luke said. He moved to sit on the edge of the bed. "No wonder Sunny's so interesting."

"Waverly's a sex therapist. She's all about yoga, sex, and food. If you ever meet her, don't let your guard down. Seriously, that woman can learn all your secrets before you've finished saying hello. She's always made me a bit nervous but I do love her cinnamon buns." Fran shrugged.

"So how does your Sicilian Nonna and a sex-therapist end up in a bake-off?"

"Bad blood over cannoli. Don't even go there."

"Okay I won't, but there's a few other places I'd like to go."

Fran glanced up at the ties.

"You are a bad influence. For you, I would miss eating cannelloni. But no. I have to be strong. I need to get ready," Fran said, stretching languidly, sending Luke her own come-hither type of look. She held up one finger enticing him to follow her. "Want to help me?"

Luke forgot all about Sicilian feuds over cooking. He stood slowly, his eyes alight with desire, his body already hard and aching. "I don't know Fran? What do you think?"

Fran blushed and giggled as he stepped closer, draping his arms around her, ducking his head and capturing her lips in a long tantalizing kiss.

Fran's arms wrapped around his neck and he boosted his up as her legs wrapped around his waist. He started to back toward the bed.

"No, no, no," Fran panted into the kiss. "Shower," she mumbled.

"Bed," Luke whispered.

Fran groaned and gave in. "I am going to be so late."

Luke gave her a wicked grin and kissed her again slowly, rolling over so he was looking down into her beautiful eyes. "So, make an entrance," he whispered.

Fran stared back at him. "You," she whispered between kisses. "Are a very bad influence."

Chapter 15

Fran drove to Nonna's Sunday night *dolce* and *bevande* in a cloud of happiness. Even the muscle-bound freak who cut her off and then leaned out the window to flip her the finger didn't drop her down to earth. She just smiled and waved. Okay, so her third finger was bent a little bit more than the rest of her hand, but that didn't mean anything. She was, calm, centred, Zen. She sighed and her lips tilted into a contented grin.

For a few minutes back at Luke's place, she had been tempted to forget about dessert and stay with Luke instead. Luckily, sanity had prevailed. She shuddered to think of what would happen if she called Nonna at the last minute with some lame-ass excuse. Nonna would likely jump into her Cadillac Seville and head over with her special soup. Nope. Better to go to Nonna's than try and explain why she wouldn't be there. Besides, Sunday evenings were family nights. Nonna had tapped out of big family meals in favour of desserts and drinks. She said "You never get the gossip if you up to elbows in spaghetti water." Fran had to agree. There were less dishes too.

Fran sighed and inhaled a deep breath of fresh air. It carried the scent of salt and flowers. The sun covered the world in brilliant sparkles, birdsongs sounded sweeter, and colors were more vivid. Everything around her emerged in ultra-high-definition—brighter, crisper. Fran mentally added: like a Disney princess, to her: *How Does It Feel to Meet Someone Amazing* list. That's what she felt like, a Disney princess. Any second, she might break into song. It was almost like she was in love.

She smiled. She wasn't silly enough to believe she could be in love with Luke already, but she was definitely in lust with him. They'd gone back to his place and spent the day in bed. After the third time he was begging for a reprieve. She blushed at the memory. Nonna always said *'Italian woman are best in kitchen, and in bed.'* It had always grossed her out to hear her old Nonna talking like that, but now that she'd met someone who'd ignited her hot Italian blood, she could see Nonna had a point.

She imagined Luke's strong, warm hands on her body: sliding up her legs, caressing her hips and waist, gently kneading her breasts. It made her feel hot and achy, restless. No, she felt lustful. She grinned. He was an artist and she was the masterpiece beneath his hands. Her skin tingled at the memory. She'd never understood what the big fuss about sex was before—she'd never even had 'the big O', but

Luke had changed that (three times!). And now she definitely got what all the fuss was about.

She pulled into Nonna's driveway and took a few deep breaths to calm the flush in her cheeks and still her sinful thoughts. She wished that she'd had time to go home and style her hair and put on some make up. Nah, her brothers weren't that observant. She'd say she'd been to the beach with Sunny. That would explain the red cheeks and the sparkle in her eyes. Or she'd tell them about some obscure scientific finding and they'd zone out and leave her alone. It worked every time.

Her family could read her like a book and she definitely did not want to share what she and Luke had been up to with them. She was twenty-six-years old and all grown up, but her family couldn't seem to see her as anything other than sweet little thirteen-year-old 'Fransie Underpantsie.' Even a whiff of a boyfriend would send Fran's nine brothers into ultra-macho-man mode, especially Sal. He had been terrible when he met her ex, Ricky. The memory still made Fran cringe. Sal had made poor Ricky call him 'Sir', and worse, Ricky had complied. He had spent the afternoon jumping up and fetching beer and chips for Fran's brothers. Ricky hadn't even seen the Super Bowl half-time show. Luke now, Fran shook her head. Somehow, she couldn't see Luke waiting on her brothers.

The Romano clan was out in full force and Fran was the last to arrive. She took a deep breath, preparing herself for the chaos before she pushed open the front door.

"Aunty Fran's here!" Her nieces and nephews buried her in a flurry of hugs and sloppy kisses.

"Hey guys!" Fran bent down for some proper hugs, but the pack turned as one and headed back towards the kitchen in hopes of begging treats from Nonna.

"Franny's here!" Her brothers hooted, jumping up and surrounding Fran in a giant group bear-hug.

"Hey guys! Okay. Enough, enough." Fran was laughing as Roberto and Sal lifted her into the air and twirled her around. At her words, they dropped her down to earth and trailed back to their seats, their eyes back on the TV, their hands back on their beers.

"Where's the wives and girlfriends?" Fran asked, pushing in next to Roberto on Nonna's worn flowery couch.

"Girls weekend." Mario took a swig of his beer.

"Right." Fran had forgotten about that. She'd been invited but used the 'had to work on a Saturday excuse' to get out of it. She loved her brother's women but they were worse than a group of dirty old men when they all got together. Once the merlot was flowing, all barriers were down. They shared details about her brothers she'd rather not know. She shuddered at the memory of their trip to Vancouver, when Lisa started describing Joe's foot fetish in graphic detail. Never again. Yuck.

"So, what's up with you, Fransie? You look like you actually spent some time outside for once. Your skin is a shade of off-white instead of stark. You're practically glowing." Roberto observed, reaching across the couch and pulling on her ponytail.

"Thanks, really mature, Rob," Fran swatted his hand away. "I just thought I'd take advantage of our final days of sun before the torrential downpours hit."

"That's all? Just getting some sun?" Roberto raised his eyebrows.

"Yep, just sun." Fran leaned back into the couch and folded her arms across her chest defensively. Darn. What did he know?

"It looks like more than sun to me. What do you think Mario?"

Fran glared daggers at Roberto. He was like a cat eying up a particularly fat mouse when he set his mind to something—she knew when she was being set up.

"What do I think about what?" Mario questioned, eyes still on the game on TV.

"About Fran. Doesn't she look like she's glowing?"

"Huh?" Mario took his eyes off the game for a minute and shrugged. "Yah, maybe she's a little tanned."

"I think it's more than a tan." Roberto mused. "I think our Franny's met someone."

"What?" The remark caught her brothers' attention. Their eyes left the TV and centred on Fran.

"What? No. Why would you even say that?" Fran sputtered, feeling her cheeks heat up. She had to deflect them, otherwise they'd crack her for sure. Nine against one was not a fair fight!

"I would say that, dear sister, because I saw you." Roberto was smug.

Alarm bells were ringing in Fran's head. This could be bad. "You saw me? Where? When? How do you know it was even me?"

"Calm down, Franny. It was definitely you. I saw you on Seal Island yesterday. You were with some tall, dark muscular dude." Roberto smirked. "All cozied up on a blankie."

At least he hadn't seen her leaving Spanky's with Luke—that would have been really bad. She was going to kill Roberto. He knew better than to throw her under the bus. She had covered for him more than once. They had an unspoken agreement. Traitor.

"Oh, oh, Franny's got a boyfriend!"

All nine of her brothers were now focused on Fran, intent on getting the details. Fran was not going there, no way, no how. The last time she'd made the mistake of trusting her brothers with the name of a crush, they'd set up a stake-out across the street from his house and followed him to school. She'd been mortified.

"Whatever. He's just a friend, guys." She waved them off and left the couch. The Spanish Inquisition was her cue to get out of there and help Nonna in the kitchen.

"Friend? What's this guy's name? Why haven't we met him before? And when are we going to meet him?" Sal challenged, chest puffed out.

"You don't need to meet all of my friends, Sal." Fran called as she walked out of the room.

"Francesca!" Nonna exclaimed as Fran walked into the kitchen. Nonna was wearing a black long dress with a simple red, flour covered apron atop.

"Hi, Nonna." Fran leaned in for a kiss. "You're looking very *GodFather*-ish today. What's with the Sicilian black and the kerchief?"

Nonna hmphed and planted her hands on her hips. "I create an Italian masterpiece."

"Does this have anything to do with the bake off?"

Nonna nodded sagely. There was a spark of deviltry in her dark brown eyes. "I show that Waverly what a real cook can do. My baking does not have to look like a penis." Nonna shook her head disapprovingly. "A penis should stay in the bedroom."

Fran cut in quickly, before Nonna really got going. "Can I help you with anything?" she asked, trying to look past Nonna's shoulder at her creation.

"Taste this." Nonna commanded, holding up a wooden spoon covered in a brown dough.

Fran happily complied. "Delicious."

"You like it? I try new invention for Christmas bake-off."

"What is it?"

"Brownies with my special ingredient. See if Waverly can still brag that her brownies best at bake-off this year."

"Nonna, you beat Waverly in the bake-off last year with your cannoli, isn't that enough?"

"No." Nonna stubbornly shook her head. "Not enough. Whenever we talk baking Waverly always has to remind me that she has best brownies. Local paper voted her brownies best in town last year. We see who wins bake-off this year and gets brownie vote too!"

"I thought Waverly was your friend Nonna?"

"Yes, but that doesn't mean I roll on back and let her win. Never give up and make self small for anyone, Francesca, even if they your sister, your mother, your best friend in whole world. You make self small and you will disappear." Nonna shook her wooden spoon passionately as she spoke.

Fran nodded and stayed mute. She knew there was no point arguing with her grandmother when she'd set her mind to something and she did have a point, even if her logic was a little off.

Nonna went back to stirring the batter, then stopped abruptly. "You look different. You got some sun."

Great, not her too.

"Yep, I got outside this weekend. Last chance at freedom." Fran joked awkwardly.

"Hmmm. No, is more than sun. There's a boy. I can tell." Nonna pronounced, licking some chocolate off of her finger.

Crap!

"Boy? No, I just have a tan."

"Francesca, you no lie to your Nonna." Nonna scolded, staring Fran down.

Fran felt herself shrinking under Nonna's scrutiny.

"Okay, okay." She folded like a chair. "I met someone, but that's all I'm going to tell you. It's too new to talk about."

And he works as a stripper.

"Is he young, virile man, Francesca? Does he pleasure you? That Ricky was bland as Waverly's lemon cake."

"*Ewww,* Nonna, gross! No. I'm not talking about this with you." A wave of heat burned Fran's cheeks.

"Oh, Francesca. I'm not nun. Your Nonna was town beauty in her day. Many boys to choose from and I never like to make up my mind without, what is it you say? Checking things out first." Nonna smirked. "I could teach you few tricks. Best way to keep a man is in kitchen, and in bed. I've taught you my kitchen secrets, now you old enough to learn my bedroom secrets too."

Oh. Dear. God. Fran needed a distraction, any distraction. Where was one of her pesky brothers when she needed them?

"Sorry we're late." Fran's mom bustled into the kitchen bringing a welcome flurry of activity.

"Mom!" Fran exclaimed, practically jumping her mom with a hug. She'd never been happier for a diversion.

"Hi honey, hi Nonna. Wow, that was a nice greeting. What were you two talking about so seriously?" Elena Romano lifted a wineglass from the cupboard and filled it with Chianti. She took a sip and closed her eyes. "Delicious," she proclaimed. "Mama?" She asked looking at her mother.

"Nothing. Just silly stuff." Fran's cheeks burned.

"We talk later," Nonna threatened behind Fran's mom's back.

Great. Just what every girl wanted, sex tips from her seventy-two-year-old grandmother.

Chapter 16

Luke opened the door to the restaurant and was instantly engulfed in the aromas of bacon, pancakes and eggs. Fast fry, high fat food formulated to pack on the pounds and harden the arteries. He shook his head and smiled. Anna, his adoptive Mom insisted that on the first day of every new school year there would be a family breakfast. It was an Anna-type decree. It went along with the: *Thou shalt not climb out the window at night to sneak off with your friends and drink a case of beer* command. His smile widened at the memory. That had been a decree he'd never broken again. The thought of cheap beer and cigarettes, coupled with pizza and Doritos, still made him heave.

His adoptive dad, Brent, went along with Anna's tradition, except he insisted that the breakfast had to be at a good old American-style restaurant. He said he was entitled to one meal a year that wasn't contaminated with spinach and quinoa.

Luke stepped back and let an elderly lady with a walker move past. She smiled at him and he grinned back. He was feeling great, on top of the world. The weekend with Fran lingered over him giving him warm, fuzzy feelings. He rolled his eyes at the thought. Come to think of it, thinking of Fran was giving him other thoughts that lingered. Who would have believed a woman could get so far under his skin in so short a time?

"Luke," Anna called from a booth over by the window. She popped up, ready to give him a hug.

Luke passed through the line and approached the table. Brent grinned at him and gestured across the table at another man.

"Look what the cat dragged in," he said.

"Beck, when did you get back?" Luke exclaimed, returning his adopted brother's hug. "Why the hell didn't you call me?"

Beckett Foster blew a chunk of long blonde hair out of his eyes and shrugged.

"Sorry big bro, I got in this morning. Haven't closed my eyes since midnight Mumbai time yesterday. I couldn't miss breakfast though. Sleep is underrated." He laughed.

Brent glanced at his watch. "Beck is home for a week before he heads to China. You guys will have lots of time to catch up. Unfortunately, I don't have a lot of time. I have a briefing at eight. Let's order. I'm starved."

Anna shook her head in disgust. "You'd think I didn't feed you."

Luke settled into his seat in the booth and let the conversation wash over him. It felt good to hang out with his family. If it weren't for Anna's decrees about regimented family meetings, months might slide by before they met again.

What's with your smiley face there, Bro? You're looking pretty contented for a guy that's about to meet his new lab horror story. Got your glass cleaner ready? I hear this year's red lipsticks pack a powerful punch," Beck took a sip of coffee and leaned back. His eyes were ringed with bags larger than the tea bag Anna was swishing through her hot water. He was an electronics expert specializing in trouble-shooting. It wasn't often he got back home to Seattle.

"It's nothing," Luke defended. "It's good to see you guys."

"Lukie's got a girl," Beck chanted.

"What are you a ten-year-old?"

Anna's eyebrows raised. "Boys, boys, boys," she said. She looked happy. She didn't even comment when Brent's platter of fried eggs, hash browns, bacon, sausage and pancakes arrived.

"So?" Beckett prodded as he finished off his yogurt and granola.

"Bugger off," Luke returned, refusing to be tempted into saying anything about Fran. It was too new, not something ready for full family disclosure.

He changed the subject, relieved when Beckett's travel life took centre stage.

The server returned, clearing the plates, refilling the coffees.

"So, did you get rid of your lab rat?" Brent asked sitting back. He had one arm resting on the back of the booth and was playing with a lock of Anna's long curly hair.

Luke snorted. "Not yet. I think I'm stuck with her. That will be a pain in my ass. I tried to fix the problem, but Winston Ass-ridge is holding firm that this candidate was hand-picked for her excellent credentials."

"So, make her life a living hell. You're good at that. Look what you did to mine," Beckett observed, smirking.

Luke frowned at his adopted brother. The glint in his blue eyes meant he was about to bring up a non-flattering memory from Luke's past. Beckett had been ten when Luke joined the family. Luke was a loner. He hadn't known what to do with the snot-nosed brat who followed him around demanding he play basketball or pitch him a few balls. Beck had been a royal pain in Luke's ass. He'd shadowed him everywhere, ratted him out, and probably taught Luke more about being part of a family than anyone else at the table.

Luke grinned. "What? Like the time I caught you and Sarah Parker playing house in the shed?"

Beckett glared at him.

"Sarah Parker?" Anna repeated. "Detective Parker's little Sarah?" Her eyebrows rose.

Luke shook his head sadly, throwing Beckett further under the bus. "They had alcohol too. Of course, I confiscated that."

"And took it out to Evans Point to a party."

"Sarah's a rock star now," Brent cut in. "She's got an album out."

"Really? So, technically I made-out with a rock star?" Beckett looked interested.

Everyone laughed. Talk turned to Sarah and her new career, letting Luke off the hook.

After breakfast they said their good byes standing in the parking lot.

"Be nice to your student," Anna said sternly, standing on her tiptoes to give him a hug. "You were once a pain in the ass to someone."

"I don't want to hear about any missing lab rats," Brent said giving Luke a one-armed hug.

Luke laughed. "No, I'm going to do what Beck said, make her life a living hell so that she gives up and moves on. I have a game plan. She'll probably switch to astrophysics or some other lame ass science."

"Good one, Bro," Beckett said, fist bumping Luke.

The expression, *what are you a rocket scientist*, meant something altogether different when your mother really was one.

"Gotta go," Luke said, climbing into his Jeep.

"I'll try and catch you before I leave," Beckett called. "You can give me the dirt on the new girlfriend. Better make me the best man."

Luke waved him off and started the engine, laughing. His lips relaxed into a smile as he thought of Fran. He couldn't wait until tonight when they planned to meet again. Oh yeah.

Chapter 17

Fran woke before her alarm blared, energized and happy. She wanted to dance and break into song, something light, like *I could have danced all night,* the theme song from *My Fair Lady,* or was that from *Cinderella*? Whatever. The point was, she felt happy, like a bubbly, sparkling princess. Okay, a dirty princess. Her cheeks heated remembering the scene from Luke's laundry room yesterday. That scene wouldn't have made it into a Disney movie. Who knew washing a few towels could get so filthy. She stretched languidly, smiling at the memory, wishing it was Luke curled up beside her, instead of the six cats.

She should be exhausted. She hadn't slept much all weekend, she was too busy doing other things with Luke. Luke, she sighed and stretched, feeling tiny muscle aches down deep in places she didn't know she had.

Despite the lack of sleep, she felt great. New wonderful job, new wonderful man. The sun was shining; life was good. She rolled out of bed and showered, enjoying the feeling of the hot water rolling over her body and the memories it triggered. She dressed in her black pants and her lucky green button up blouse, the one that made her hazel eyes pop. She had conducted a careful study of her closet contents and decided on the combination weeks ago. She pulled her hair up into a ponytail and applied just a touch of red lip gloss and mascara. She didn't need any blush today—thanks to her weekend of *sexercise* with Luke she sported a natural, healthy flush.

The cats had abandoned the bed in favour of the living room. They were now lined up, waiting for her to serve their breakfast, making their opinion of her absence over the weekend very clear in a cacophony of meowing. Six Maine Coon cats made a lot of noise. She fed her fur babies, doling out lots of extra head scratches, and then giving the picture of Puss 'n' Boots a little kiss and pat, was on her way out the door.

For once, the old Honda started without any drama, or for that matter, a smoke show. She backed out of the driveway and glanced at the clock on the dash. Good. She was out of the house with plenty of time to stop at the bakery for one of Waverly's famous cinnamon buns—if the bakery was open that is. Port Fling was a sleepy town, full of locally-owned businesses operating on *'ish'* time. The hand-written hours on most of the local store windows actually ended with an '*ish*' after the time, proving her point. But she didn't mind that. It added to the town's quaint, yet kooky charm.

The windows at Luscious Buns Bakery were lit up with a comforting soft yellow light. Fran's mouth watered at the thought of Waverly's warm and gooey cinnamon delights. She had worked up quite the appetite. She blushed at the memory of how brazen she had been.

"Good morning, Waverly, it's Fran," she called opening the bakery door.

"Good morning Francesca," called Waverly from the kitchen. "I'll be right with you."

"Sure," responded Fran, as she shopped the delicious but perverted looking confections in Waverly's display case.

"I hear you went out on the town with my granddaughter the other night." Waverly came out of the back wiping her hands on an apron that featured sketches of figures engaged in differing Kama Sutra positions.

Waverly was not only Sunny's grandma, but much to Sunny's chagrin, the town gossip as well. You would think that someone who'd made a living listening to the dirty little secrets of Hollywood's finest would keep her mouth shut. Not Waverly, she delighted in knowing what was going on in the town. Maybe it was just habit. She looked at people as if they were puzzles waiting to be solved. Or maybe, after all those years of keeping secrets, she just wanted to get things out in the open.

"Wow, Waverly! That's quite the apron!" observed Fran, hoping to steer Waverly away from the topic of Sunny.

"Was she going at it with that loser Jason again?"

Or not.

Fran gave Waverly a tight, wordless smile. Sunny would kill her if she divulged any information to her nosy grandmother.

"And how about you?" Waverly waggled her finger at Fran, singling her out.

"What about me?" Fran played dumb. "I'm just here for your delicious cinnamon buns."

"You know what I'm talking about Francesca. You look great. In fact, you look so great I'd chance to say you've got the M.O. glow."

"M.O. glow?" Fran questioned. Did she really want to know?

"Multiple-orgasm glow."

Why did she even ask?

"I don't know what you're talking about." Fran widened her eyes for effect. She and Luke were still very new and she wasn't ready to share them with anyone yet, especially not the town baker/sex therapist/gossip. Worse, despite their intense competition, Waverly and Nonna talked on a regular basis—though what a sophisticated L.A. doctor of psychiatry and psychology and an Italian grandmother from a two-donkey town in Sicily had in common, she had no clue. What Fran did know was, there was no way she was giving Waverly anything to pass on to Nonna.

"Okay. Hold it close." Waverly said as she used her tongs to place a huge icing-covered bun into a bag. "I can appreciate that. But whatever you're doing, keep doing it. You look wonderful!" She passed Fran the bag and brandished her tongs in the air to drive her point home.

"Thanks, Waverly."

"Now Francesca, before you leave I have something very important to ask you. Have you tried the turning position?" Waverly asked, pointing to a very complicated looking drawing on the side of her apron. "The man spins around while he's still—"

"Okay, Waverly, sorry I can't stick around but I need to be on my way. I'll see you later," interrupted Fran, as she threw her money on the counter and ran out the door faster than an Olympian on steroids.

Fran chuckled as she slid back into her car. It was surprising how 'normal' her best-friend Sunny had turned out, considering that Waverly had pretty much raised her. That conversation was definitely a little intense for 7 a.m. but then again, that was Waverly.

As she drove, her mind wandered back to Luke. She sighed. He was so cute. He had insisted on Fran helping him pick out a couple of new ties and a new dress shirt yesterday. He'd wanted the basic blue tie, nothing fancy. She'd convinced him to choose one in iridescent purple, and another with silver geometric designs on a black background.

Fran smiled remembering. He'd looked so hot in the purple tie that they'd almost joined the *sex in a dressing room club* but Fran chickened out when the nosy saleswoman came sniffing around. Yup, she'd never look at ties in the same way again. Although, why a guy who stripped for a living needed ties, she had no clue. Maybe it had something to do with the new job he was *'easing himself into.'* She wondered what it was but he'd been evasive and tight-lipped about it. She'd let it go, not wanting to pry.

Fran made it to the university with time to spare. She was early. The parking lot wasn't full, so for once, she had her choice of places to park. She parked under a sprawling cedar tree and sat in her car as she ate her cinnamon bun, staring out at the building that was going to be her home for the next year. The dome-shaped structure with its cold cement exterior didn't look like much from the outside but inside it was akin to Disneyland for a chemistry nerd.

Wow, this was it. She had been working towards a position in Dr. Tanner's lab for the past eight years and now she had actually made it. He was a rock-star in the world of green chemistry. His paper on the potential boost mechanisms and feedback responses of crystal formation in Nano-fuel cells had changed her life. *Don't gush, Fran. You will not act like a stalker fan. You will not ask him for his autograph.* Oh my god, she was here!

Fran jumped out of her car at 7:35 a.m. She had calculated it would take her eight minutes to walk from the parking lot to the building, another two to get to the lab. That placed her there a full fifteen minutes early, enough time to look eager but not too enthusiastic.

She forced herself to walk slowly. Be Zen, she told herself. The lab isn't going anywhere. You have all year to get there. A big grin spread across her face. She'd done it! Tanner's lab! The research pinnacle of the world! Okay, maybe not the world but her world. She had to check her strides again. She was so excited she was practically running. She always moved fast. It was a legacy of having nine older brothers all of whom were over six feet. To keep up with them, she'd learned to hustle.

The chemistry wing loomed in front of her. The glass and concrete building, one of the oldest on campus, sat at the edge of the sprawling university grounds. Tanner's lab was on the second floor. She slowly climbed the stairs. The metal railing felt hot under her moist palm. She pulled open the heavy glass door, glanced at the building floor plan and headed towards the lab. This was it. Standing in the corridor outside the lab, she took a few deep breaths. Her heart was pounding. Okay, Fran, go for it, just like ripping off a Band-Aid.

Slowly, she pushed the door open and stepped across the threshold. A tiny gasp escaped her as she got her first look at the massive sterile-looking room beyond the door—white walls and stainless steel. But that wasn't what wowed Fran, it was the equipment. The centrifuge 5000 stood in a place of honour at the center of the room. She had thought that the 5000 was an urban legend but there it was. This lab truly was a magical kingdom—Disneyland and heaven all rolled into one.

Fran couldn't stop herself. The centrifuge pulled her in, drawing her like a magnet until she stood next to it, reverently examining the massive depth of its field and the long clean lines of its vertical tube rotor.

"Wow," she muttered, reaching a hand to caress its shining metal skin.

"If you value your life, you'll take your hand away from the spinnerator," warned a voice behind her.

"Sorry." Fran obediently clasped her hands together and turned to face the person who addressed her.

"It's okay. I get it. The centrifuge 5000." The woman beside her grinned and held out her hand. "I'm Monica."

"Fran."

"Fran as in Francesca Romano our new grad student?" checked Monica. Her dark, bushy eyebrows raised.

"That's me. Here and ready to work," confirmed Fran with a smile.

"Okay Fran, we've got to fix you up, and quick. Tanner will be here any minute." Monica's eyes darted around the room.

"What? Fix me up—?"

"To start with, your ponytail is way too high. That will drive Tanner nuts. And your lipstick?"

"It's just lip gloss," Fran interrupted as she yanked the elastic out of her hair and quickly smoothed it into a low bun at the nape of her neck. *What the hell was going on?*

"It's too red, trust me. Tanner had a bad experience with red lipstick last year. Lose it." Monica pulled a Kleenex out of her lab coat.

Fran took the proffered Kleenex and vigorously scrubbed her lips, silently cursing her Revlon for its staying power.

"Quick, come with me. Let's get you safely tucked away in a corner," Monica said, dragging Fran along by her arm.

"Wait. What's the deal with Tanner? Is he a jerk?" asked Fran, resisting her.

Monica stopped and slowly turned back to face Fran. "Jerk, no. Asshole, yes. Tanner is brilliant but he's very serious about his work and very particular about his students. The past two female grad students who, well, looked like . . . you." Monica gestured at Fran. "They weren't serious enough for Tanner, so he pretty much drove them to insanity, and then they quit."

"Great," said Fran. Her stomach churned. "So, he's a sexist pig."

"In one word, yes," confirmed Monica. "But you'll be fine if you dress in a potato sack like I do, don't wear any makeup and stop plucking your eyebrows for extra effect." Monica gestured down at her baggy scrub pants and loose off-white lab coat. She wiggled the caterpillars above her eyes to drive her point home.

"Professor Tanner thinks just because a woman looks like a woman she can't be smart and successful?" Fran asked, incredulous. "Who does this guy think he is?"

As if in answer to her question, a voice that must be Professor Tanner's, barked a rough order to a lab tech behind her. Fran put steel in her spine. No way is he breaking me, she thought. I've worked my ass off and sacrificed my twenties to get here. If he thinks he's going to bully me out of here he can kiss my—

"Luke?" called Fran catching sight of Luke. He was standing in the aisle staring at her. How had he figured out she was here? He was wearing the purple tie. She smiled.

"Fran?" Luke stopped. His mouth dropped. "Fran? What are you doing here?" He looked around the room furtively, grabbed her hand and pulled her aside.

"I'm a grad student with Dr. Tanner. What are you doing here? Are you lost? Is this where your new job is?" Fran asked, confused. What was a stripper doing in one of the most prestigious labs in the country?

"No way. This isn't going to work," Luke muttered, shaking his head and backing away as if Fran had the plague.

"What isn't going to work? Luke? Luke, where are you going?" she called to his rapidly retreating back.

"Where's Dr. Tanner off to?" Monica asked as the door slammed behind Luke.

Chapter 18

The heavy lab door slammed shut behind Luke, closing him off from the nightmare standing in his lab. This morning when he'd headed into work, he'd gone with a plan to rid himself of his unwanted student. He'd never expected it would mean ridding himself of Fran. Fran . . . she'd lied to him. She said that she was going to college, not university, that she was taking a break from the classroom. What the hell Fran? She'd lied. What else had she lied about? Shit. He stopped in the middle of the hall creating a dam in the flow of students.

"Hey, don't just stop."

"Jerk, get out of the way."

Luke ignored the nasty glances and snarky remarks. He started back in the direction he'd come from, dodging a pack of first year university students. After a couple of years of teaching, they were easy to spot. Their faces all wore the same first-day-of-life-after-high-school stunned look as they milled around the building plan posted on the wall, their maps clutched in their hands as they tried to puzzle their ways through the maze of buildings.

Luke *knew* where he was going. He was going to find Etherridge. This time Winston was going to listen to him because Luke was going to tell him that either Fran went, or Luke was looking for a new lab, and if Luke left so did the wealthy financial backers.

The thought of leaving got Luke even more riled up. The idea of starting over again somewhere new made him sick. He hated change. He'd had so much of it as a kid that he'd made a pact with himself to put down roots and stay in Port Fling. Moving somewhere and starting over—

"Professor Tanner?" a hesitant voice interrupted his thoughts.

"What?" he answered impatiently, turning around to greet the speaker.

The linebacker-sized man standing in front of Luke stepped back. He brushed a thick black dreadlock out of his eye and frowned. He looked like he wanted to run away.

"Uh, sorry sir. I just wanted to thank you for the reference."

"Oh, right. Sure Darian. No problem," Luke said, forcing himself to smile at his ex-student. Darian reminded Luke of himself. He'd grown up in a run of bad foster homes until he'd found one that stuck. Luckily, Darian had also found football and started university on a scholarship. In the midst of all that Luke had mentored Darian and discovered that he also had a brilliant mind. "I'm glad I could help."

"Are you looking for Professor Etherridge?"

"Yeah, how did you know?"

Darian grinned. "You're standing outside the door to his office."

Luke looked up and realized it was true. He'd gone there on auto-pilot.

"He's not there. He's outside by the track having coffee. The cheerleaders are practicing."

"Right, cheerleaders. Thanks, man."

Luke turned and walked away. Darian watched Luke leave.

"What's with Tanner," a petite girl asked as she joined him.

"I dunno. Whatever. He seems pissed about something." Darian shrugged and turned his attention to the girl.

Etherridge wasn't down by the track. The cheerleaders were though. Old Winston must have had a heart attack over the violation of his appropriate attire mandate because he was nowhere to be seen. Luke walked away from the track, hoping he'd run into Etherridge on his way back to the main offices. Where would an uptight little weasel go for a break from the first day madness?

Knowing Etherridge, he was back in his office at the faculty building, ordering amendments to the first semester memorandums he'd sent out. Luke' footsteps sped up. He would catch him there where he couldn't run away or hang up on him. He changed directions, opting to take a short cut through the construction zone for the new physics lab.

He looked up at the framework of steel girders towering over his head. Construction workers were perched high on the beams above. You wouldn't catch him up there. Even harnessed and tethered, working on those giant beams wasn't worth the risk, or the extra pay that came with it.

Luke kept moving, ignoring the signs demanding hardhats and steel-toed boots. He turned the corner and collided with a wall wearing the required hardhat and steel-toed boots. The sudden stop knocked Luke back a few feet.

"Watch it, man. What the hell are you doing in here? This area is off limits to regular civilians."

"Sorry," Luke muttered straightening. He had missed seeing the guy in the shadows, studying blueprints and eyeballing the building forms being set up.

The worker leaned down and picked up his blueprints, shaking the dirt off them. He scowled. "If you're going to cut through a construction zone, at least pay attention. You wouldn't want to run into something and damage that soft head of yours." He turned back to the prints.

Luke scowled. Who the hell did the guy think he was? He was on Luke's turf, hallowed university ground. Like the Hulk, Luke could feel his Rockstar scientist alter-ego stirring. It didn't help that the guy's dark curly hair and brown eyes somehow reminded him of Fran.

"Maybe you shouldn't stand in the middle of the walkway, dumb ass," Luke answered.

"What did you say?" The other man dropped the roll of blue prints and stepped out of the shadows. He was big and probably outweighed Luke by thirty pounds, his muscles honed from working construction. "You going to say something, Poindexter, say it out loud."

"I said," Luke answered, gritting his teeth. "Get off the walkway if you aren't moving, meat head." He straightened, bracing himself for what was likely to follow. A good old smack down would go a long way towards blowing off his negative energy.

"Professor Tanner, is there a problem here?"

Luke turned to see Professor Etherridge bustling towards him. He looked alarmed, as if he expected to see Luke and the construction worker drop their gloves and face off in front of him.

"Winston, we have to talk," Luke said, deliberately turning his back on the construction worker. He could feel the other man's eyes boring into his back. Part of him wanted to turn around and finish things with the guy. Luke had never dealt with challenge well. His adopted mom, Anna said his trust and aversion to authority were linked to his crap childhood. Luke's theory was that adversity makes you stronger, you just had to stand your ground and make your point.

"We done here, Professor Poindexter?" the other man taunted, "Cuz I got lots of time to finish things."

Luke spun around.

"Really? You think so? You want to show me what you've got?" Old habits die hard. Luke had faced too many challenges to back down first.

The other man moved one step closer.

Luke tensed. His hands clenched into fists at his side, and he moved into a defensive stance, ready for a fight. The other man chuckled and reached past Luke to pick up the blueprints.

"Gentlemen, there is no time for this nonsense. I must ask you both to walk away."

"Yeah, Doctor Tanner, run along now. Go back to your little classroom where you belong," the other man mocked.

Luke flushed. He wanted to kick the other man's ass but Etherridge grabbed his arm and steered him away. For a scrawny guy, the professor had a lot of strength in his grasp.

Luke didn't say anything until he and Professor Etherridge stood in line to grab a coffee. They found a table in the back of the cafeteria and sat down. Winston looked frazzled and short-tempered. His perfectly flattened comb-over was ruffled, making him look like a crazed rooster.

"Now what," he began testily, "Is so important that you must hunt me down all over the campus? And," he added, his voice rising. "What possible reason is there for you to get into a confrontation with one of the workers on the construction site? Truly, sometimes Professor Tanner, I question your professionalism," he huffed.

"We need to talk about the student you placed in my lab," Luke began.

Winston bristled. He raised his chin staring at Luke down his long pointy nose. "We have already discussed this. The subject is closed." He glanced down at the intricate sports watch on his left wrist and pressed a button. "But, I will give you three minutes to reopen the subject."

Luke was used to Etherridge's method of time management.

"Your placement choice, Francesca Romano, has had a recent death in her family. She's very fragile. I am concerned that she isn't emotionally ready to face a gruelling internship at this time."

Luke sat back and waited. The terms *fragile* and *emotionally ready* acted like bombs. Time to play his ace card. "I also see some worrying similarities between Ms. Romano and the student placed in my lab last year." Luke chose his words carefully, crafting them to have the most impact on Winston's fear of public scenes. He finished by saying, "I refuse to have my lab turned into a joke yet again. She goes, or I walk."

"Good heavens," Etherridge said faintly, straightening in his chair. "You make a valid point. Very well then," he said. His watch pinged, but he ignored it. "We cannot have another term of upheaval, we need to keep our investors happy. I will correct this situation immediately." He stood, nodded his head in Luke's direction and headed for the door.

Luke watched him bull his way through the lineup near the cashier. This was good, wasn't it? He wanted to get rid of Fran. He couldn't work with someone who lied to him. He slumped down in his seat. Yeah, if this was good, why did he feel like crap?

Chapter 19

Fran slumped in her chair, feeling like a school girl waiting to be penalized for cheating on a test. The air in the department head's office was warm and thick, the walls closing in around her, squishing her flatter by the second. The same thoughts kept circling around and around in her head: Luke was Dr. Tanner? Dr. Tanner was Luke? What was a world-renowned chemist doing stripping at a local club? It didn't make any sense. Any second, someone was going to jump out and yell 'You've been *punk'd*!'

Luke had never given her any indication he was anything other than a stripper contemplating finding a new area of work, not a word to her about chemistry. Then again, she hadn't been totally forthcoming with him about her level of education either. No, she had assumed he was an uneducated stripper. She had dumbed herself down, not wanting to make him feel intimidated. Hah! What an idiot she was. Dr. Lucas Tanner intimidated by her!

Fran looked up as Dr. Winston Etherridge III entered the room. He studied her as if she were a particularly dangerous specimen before pulling out his chair and brusquely sitting down. He wasted no time with niceties.

"I won't mince words, Ms. Romano. We take our Chemistry program very seriously and although Dr. Tanner is a pain, he is the superstar of that program. Having a superstar in our program means more funding from interested parties. So, when my main draw for funding is threatening to leave, I take notice."

Fran jumped to her feet.

"Dr. Etherridge, I—"

"No. Listen." Dr. Etherridge waved her off, holding up his hand to silence her.

"Now, I don't know exactly what you did or said to make my superstar upset but he's requested that we place you elsewhere. We are actively looking for an alternative placement for you. In the meantime, you will work in Dr. Tanner's lab but you will only speak when spoken to and you will keep out of his way. Do you understand what I'm saying Ms. Romano?" He spoke slowly, delivering the last line, as if she was a simple 'country girl' and not a top-ranking grad student.

"Yes, sir," Fran mumbled, looking at the floor as she dug her nails into her palms. Her face burned with rage. She stood still, feeling powerless. What she really wanted to do was scream and cry and stomp her feet but when the department head gave you a dressing down, the only thing you could do was shut your mouth and agree.

"Alright then. Go home for the day and come back tomorrow with a new attitude. You can go now." He dismissed Fran with a nod and a wave of his elegantly manicured hand. He went back to the paperwork on his desk treating her as though she were now invisible, as though she no longer existed. Fran walked out of the office, her back ramrod straight, holding herself together as she bit back tears. Don't cry here, she told herself. Not here. Wait until you get home.

The drive home was a blur. The lump in Fran's throat grew larger with every block that brought her closer to home. The sight of her driveway pricked the balloon holding her emotions together. She stumbled out of her car and ran up the driveway, blinded by tears of rage. How could Luke do this to her? He was ruining her life, her livelihood. Obviously, she meant nothing to him, just another notch on the belt. She was sure the "superstar" Dr. Lucas Tanner could have any woman he wanted. She wanted to scream, cry and vomit all at once.

Fran slammed the front door behind her, picturing Luke and Dr. Etherridge's faces. The loud, vibrating *bang* reverberated through the little house. It was as satisfying as pounding the dough of one of Nonna's batches of Italian bread. The cats scattered as she stormed through the living room. She couldn't believe the lecture Dr. Etherridge had doled out, treating her like she was some worthless blubbering idiot. He hadn't even given her a chance to explain. She knew chemistry was a boys' club. It was a reality she'd lived with throughout her career, but this was too much.

She grabbed her cell-phone and pressed '1' to speed dial Nonna. She was the only one who would understand what a blow it was for Fran to be removed from Dr. Tanner's lab. Nonna was Fran's unlikely supporter when she was a timid 17-year-old begging her parents to let her go to university to pursue chemistry. Fran's parents had wanted Fran to work as a secretary in the family business, and then marry a nice Italian boy and make fat gurgling babies like a proper Italian girl should. But Nonna had wanted more for Fran. She had gone head-to-head with Fran's parents, and won.

"Ciao," Nonna answered, picking up on the fourth ring.

"Nonna? It's Francesca," Fran said brokenly. Her shoulders shook under the weight of her sobs and fat tears slid down her cheeks.

"Francesca? What's wrong? Everyone okay?" Nonna's alarm radiated through the phone.

"Everyone's fine. It's just—just my placement."

"No! What wrong with your placement?"

"They're moving me out of Dr. Tanner's lab." Fran blew her nose.

"What!" Nonna sounded like she was going to jump through of the phone. "Why they do this? Are they stupid? You smartest girl by far."

"I kind of unknowingly got . . . involved with Dr. Tanner and now he's throwing me under the bus," cried Fran.

"*Che cazzo e*?!" Nonna swore in Italian. "He was boy who make you glow yesterday and then he throw you in bus? I kill him! No, I have better. Have your cousin Dario to kill him. We fly him out from Sicily, he do the job, go home and no one know. All good."

"No, Nonna," Fran protested with a mixed laugh and sob. "We can't kill him, even if he does deserve it," she added as an afterthought.

"Okay, we rough him up a bit. He back off. All good."

Fran could almost hear Nonna's shrug through the phone.

"Nonna, no!" protested Fran. "No killing, no roughing up. No nothing."

"Then what we do?"

"I don't know." Fran sighed.

"You not give up Francesca. We work too hard to get you here. There must be something you can do."

"I know, Nonna. Believe me, I won't give up. I'll be the best student he's ever had and if that doesn't work, well, I know things about him that could . . . persuade him to reconsider. I'll take care of this," Fran reassured Nonna, feeling stronger by the second.

"Ah, that's your Sicilian blood talking. Sicilians know how to be very persuasive, as you say."

Fran moved from denial to anger in a heartbeat, and now all that anger was focused on Dr. Lucas Tanner. She was not going to go down in a pathetic puddle of tears like some scared little girl. She swiped her arm across her face drying the tears. Time to woman up Francesca, because it was now game on.

Chapter 20

Luke slammed the front door hard enough to make the walls rattle. He dropped his computer bag by the closet and kicked off his shoes. Stomping into the kitchen, he grabbed a beer from the fridge. No. He stuck it back on the door and turned away. Beer wasn't going to cut it. What he was feeling right now wasn't a sit down and unwind kind of mood. It was a kick ass, beat someone down state.

What the hell, Fran? Had she planned this whole thing? How could she have figured out who he was? He'd been careful. No one knew, no one except Tyler and Shannia. He shook his head; Tyler wouldn't risk his own career and Shannia wouldn't be caught dead in Spanky's.

This is why he hated having students under him in the lab. Under him. He closed his eyes and pushed back the memory of Fran under him . . . on top of him . . . Fran—. No. He shook his head, forcing her image aside. What an idiot he was. Turning away from the fridge, he stared blindly out the window towards the ocean.

He'd told Winston that he'd met Fran and she'd said she didn't know if she was emotionally stable enough to deal with the stress of working in the lab. He'd said Fran had a recent death in the family and needed some time. Then he'd reminded him of the Tiffany Mathers fiasco and hammered the final nail in the coffin when he'd threatened to leave. That was all it took to send Winston searching out another spot for Fran.

Winston probably remembered the trail of panties and the cost of cleaning Scarlet Bliss lipstick off the mirrors in the university bathrooms. Not to mention the fact that if Luke left, so did ninety percent of the young wealthy backers who were fans of his work. Money always motivated Luke's department head.

Luke had to admit feeling a little guilt over throwing Fran under the bus, but in his own defense, Fran hadn't been honest with him. She said she was taking some courses at a local school. She hadn't said she was a PhD student starting in his lab. Nope. Fran had set him up. Sunny must have told her who he was. He shook his head and grabbed the beer out of the fridge. He cracked the cap and took a long swallow, feeling his guilt slide down with the beer.

Wait, Sunny didn't know who he was. He and Sunny had talked wine and germs. Sunny was a bit weird when it came to bacteria.

He put the beer down on the counter. No, he decided. Somehow Fran had set him up. There was no way that this was a coincidence. Fran deserved to be placed in Mike Piper's theoretical chemistry lab. She'd be great there. She knew how to create a convincing lie.

He picked up the beer and put it back down. This wasn't working. He needed to vent. He was going for a run. Only that would let him work off some of his rage . . . and disappointment. How the hell could she have done this? He turned and headed for his bedroom, carefully keeping his eyes off the bed. The weekend was fresh in his mind. He didn't want to think about Fran lying in his arms, her head on his shoulder. The scent of her perfume lingered on his pillow. That's it, he was washing the sheets. No, he was burning them.

He stripped naked and stalked into the walk-in closet to grab workout clothes. The only way he was going to sooth his hostility was by doing a 10-k run. A marathon would be better but the heat would kill him and he wouldn't get to see Fran's face when she found out he was onto her sneaky plan. He yanked on his shorts, pulled on a white cotton t-shirt and dug a pair of socks out of the drawer. Grabbing his runners, he laced them up and did a couple of stretches. He shoved his phone into an arm band, plugging in his headset, started a playlist guaranteed to set a killer pace. Slamming the door behind him, he locked it and started down the hill.

Running helped him focus and problem-solve. With running, he had to concentrate on breathing, on moving forward. His long steps ate up the road. Gradually, he settled into a rhythm. That worked for a while but by mile two of the 10 k run he was back to thinking about Fran. She was going to be mad. Yup. No doubt about it. Did he care? Nope, not at all. She should have been honest and up front. They could have avoided this.

He crossed the road on an amber light. A car honked. He flipped the driver the bird and turned right to take the coastal trail through the trees. The trail wound down to the waterfront and linked up with the causeway leading to the breakwater near the ferry terminal. He sped up, running away from the memory of Fran wrapped around him, Fran kissing him, Fran—. He ran harder.

What if Fran told Winston about Spanky's? Luke stumbled, staggered and settled back to a jerky run. She wouldn't do that. Would she? But what if she accidently mentioned it? No, he'd covered that. He'd made Winston think Fran was unstable. He believed that she and Luke wouldn't be able to work together—a kind of hate at first-sight thing. At this point whatever Fran said about him would be seen by Winston as sour grapes. That's the kind of guy Winston was. He could be counted on to play the sexist card and disregard any fact that didn't suit him.

Luke was starting to slow down. The killer pace he'd set at the start of the run was catching up with him. Plus, it was tough running under the load of guilt that he was starting to feel. The trail widened and joined with the breakwater. The ferry was unloading. He had to stop and let the long line of cars pass. His heart pounded. Sweat dripped down his face, stinging his eyes and dripping off his nose. He paced in a circle, sucking in deep breaths, trying to work through the stitch gnawing in his left side. The cars dwindled. He crossed the road and started the home stretch of his run.

His pace gradually slowed. He was feeling relaxed and loose, starting to see the situation with a clearer eye. He wanted to see Fran again. He liked Fran. They had chemistry. Not just the burning light-my-fire sex chemistry, but a relaxed, share the silence, be together harmony that felt right.

The hill leading up to his house stretched in front of him. He slowed to a walk and stripped off the white t-shirt, mopping his face before hanging it around his neck. Maybe he could see her again. They wouldn't be working together. There would be no conflict of interest. Shit. Look at you. Making excuses. This wasn't him. He didn't do relationships. He and Fran were done. He would make sure that he never saw her again.

His legs were really burning. The pace he had set was ruthless. A long shower and a gallon of water were calling his name. He walked past an older model Honda Civic parked on the side of the street.

Judging by its rusted tail pipe and dented fender, the car had seen better days. He reached his driveway.

"*Professor* Tanner?"

Luke stopped. Slowly, he turned to confront the speaker. He was screwed. It was Fran and there was no way that he would be able to walk or run away from her.

Chapter 21

Fran's phone conversation with Nonna had given her new life. No crying and moping around for her. She was wired, hopped up on enough adrenaline and caffeine that she could probably lift a bus, like Super Woman. A very angry Super Woman.

"Just call me Super Fran," she muttered, tossing another bag of garbage into the can outside the back door. She brushed her hands off on the front of her jeans.

She had cleaned the house from base boards to ceiling fans, organized her closet by colour and gone for a run. A run! Fran didn't do running, but today she'd dusted off her iPod, tied on her shoes and, practically growling, blasted Metallica as her legs pounded the pavement at a back-breaking speed. She'd showered, re-done her hair and makeup, drawn on a layer of extra red lipstick and donned a low-cut

V-neck shirt. If Professor Tanner had issues with a woman who looked like a woman—well, that was his problem. He hadn't minded seeing her all dolled up the other night. The other night . . . Fran sighed and gave herself one second to remember running her hands down his smooth hard abs, reaching into his pants to grab his smooth hard—

"Stop it Fran!" she yelled, sending her fur babies scattering.

"Sorry guys," she apologized to the cats. "Mommy's just dealing with a total asshole right now."

"Meow," responded Fluffy, enjoying the vigorous head rub Fran gave him.

"You guys are lucky you're cats. Your only concerns are when your next meal is and who gets the prime spot on the couch." She sighed, watching Princess Fiona weave in and out between her legs.

A wave of exhaustion swamped her. She threw herself down onto the couch and stared up at the slowly revolving ceiling fan. Her adrenaline was waning and with it her confidence. She needed a boost. There was only one person who could *Rocky* her back into the task ahead. She dialed Sunny.

"*Helllooooo* Franny!" Sunny drawled, answering on the first ring.

"Hey Sun."

"Uh oh, what's wrong? Trouble in stripper's paradise already?"

"Ugh, yes."

"Okay. . . Are you going to elaborate?"

Fran weighed her options. She wanted to tell Sunny what happened but like her Grandmother Waverly, Sunny loved a good bit of juicy gossip. Fran didn't want to be that girl, the one who went spewing hateful rumours all over town about her stripper/chemist ex-boyfriend of three days.

"He lied to me about his day job," Fran improvised.

"What? Did he tell you he was some hot-shot lawyer or something, and you found out he was really a struggling actor or waiter?"

"Yah, something like that." Fran eluded the question.

"Come on, Fran, give the guy a break. He's a stripper. You don't date a stripper for their brains and you certainly don't date them for their long-term prospects. You date them cuz they're hot."

"I know," Fran agreed, digging her nails into her palm. Damn! She just wanted to hate on Luke with Sunny but that was difficult when she couldn't tell Sunny the real story. "It's just the fact he lied that's bothering me." *And the fact he's really Professor Luke-Freaking-Tanner and he's ruining my career!* she thought but didn't say.

"Look honey, it's simple. Enjoy his hot body and the hot sex that comes with it, realizing that it's not going to last, or cut the guy loose and move on.

Seriously, if it's stressing you out it's not worth it. I should know."

"You're right." Fran nodded. *I need to cut him loose and tell him to stop messing with my life.*

"Okay sweets. I've gotta run but good-luck and try not to have break-up sex. It's hot but it always leads to more."

"Thanks, Sun."

"Love you. See you later." Sunny made a kissing sound and hung-up.

Fran threw her phone onto the pillow beside her and draped her arm across her eyes. Sunny was right. Enough stalling. She needed to get this over with. She dragged her butt off the couch, took one last look in the mirror and grabbed her keys.

"Okay, this is it guys. Mommy's going to give that jerk a piece of her mind and let him know you don't mess with a Sicilian. Wish me luck."

The cats stared back blankly. She shook her head, laughing at herself as she locked up. She was seriously losing it.

She rehearsed her speech on the drive to Luke's—no, not Luke—Dr. Tanner's house. Keep it professional, stick to the script. Keep your emotions out of it. She drove up to the house and parked on the side of the road. In the rear-view mirror, she saw Luke approaching. He was shirtless, covered with a fresh sheen of sweat.

"Oh crap," she muttered. How was she supposed to keep her emotions out of it when he was standing there, his dark hair ruffled, his hard body all muscular and sweaty, looking just like he looked after— *"Focus. You can do this Francesca."* She heard Nonna's voice in her head. *"You're Sicilian."*

"I'm a Sicilian," she whispered as she got out of the car. She glared fiercely, and repeating the phrase in her head, walked up to Luke. Had he shrunk under her evil glare? She almost felt sorry for him, almost but not quite.

"Hello, Professor. Tanner." She gave him an icy nod.

"Hey, Fran?" He didn't meet her eyes.

"I just wanted to tell you what's going to happen from here."

"Fran—" he interrupted.

"Let me finish," Fran demanded, her anger flaring. "You will go to Dr. Etherridge and you will tell him that you made a mistake. You let your ego get the better of you because you were intimidated by my credentials, but you've seen the error of your ways and you realize that I'm an asset to your lab."

"Intimidated? By you? Come on Fran, really?" His hands rested on his waist, accentuating his broad shoulders.

Fran took a deep breath. "Are you serious Lu— Dr. Tanner? Don't mess with me. I know things that could ruin you," she threatened, moving closer.

"Really, Fran?" Luke repeated. "Are you going to tell everyone that I'm a stripper? Who would believe that one of the top chemists in the U.S. moonlights as a stripper? Do you think I haven't been careful to make sure that no one finds out?"

He was right. Who would believe her? She didn't have any concrete proof of his after-school activities and it did sound preposterous. But it was true! She hated him. She wanted to punch him in his beautiful smug face or kiss him. The fact that she wanted to kiss him made her blood boil even more.

"Do you realize that you're screwing with my entire life?" she yelled. Her body shook with a hot blaze of anger. She took another deep breath and checked herself. Okay, that was a bad choice of words, but it gave her some inspiration. "You screwed me. You told me if I didn't sleep with you, I'd lose my position in your lab and then I did it and you still decided to get rid of me." Her voice sounded eerily calm and alien. What was she doing?

"What? What are you talking about Fran?" Luke didn't look as infuriatingly calm anymore, he looked alarmed.

"That's right. That's exactly what I'll tell Dr. Etherridge if you don't take back what you said."

She knew she sounded totally nuts right now. She was in way over her head, but dammit, she'd come this far. She was not going to lose this placement.

"Jesus, Fran."

Luke was looking at her like he didn't know who she was at that moment. *She* didn't know who she was at that moment.

She stepped closer to him, standing on her tiptoes to look into his eyes. "I'm serious, Luke. Call him now, or I run with a harassment story."

There was a fine line between love and hate, and right at that minute, Luke looked as if he didn't know if he wanted to kiss her or push her to the ground. They were at a stand-off breathing heavily, their faces inches from each other.

Fran felt her anger changing, fusing with her desire. She had to get out of there before she did something stupid that completely ruined her chances of staying in his lab.

She stepped back, breaking eye contact and walked to her car. His gaze burned into her back.

"I'll see you tomorrow, Dr. Tanner," she threatened and slid into her car.

Chapter 22

The door on the battered Honda groaned under the weight of the resounding slam that punctuated Fran's final threat. As Fran started the car and revved the engine, she shifted gears, bunny-hopping away from the curb. Luke didn't know whether to laugh or swear. He folded his arms across his chest and watched her drive away.

"Damn," he muttered, feeling more turned on than mad. The sound of an approaching car reminded him he was standing in the street wearing nothing but a pair of running shorts that, right now, revealed exactly how he was feeling. He willed the slowing car to keep going. His normally comfortable, loose shorts felt like a pair of skin-tight biker pants.

The car stopped and idled quietly beside him as the window silently glided down. A woman leaned out resting her arms on the door and propping her chin on top of them. Her sunglasses perched on the end of her nose as she studied him over top of the lenses.

"I'd say good afternoon, but it looks like for you it already is," she said and smiled knowingly.

The smile affected her whole face, lifting her cheeks, making her eyes glimmer with mischief. He couldn't help but grin back at her. Casually, he draped the t-shirt over the waistband of his shorts.

The motion amused the woman in the car. She was likely in her fifties but had a timeless beauty that would never fade. Meryl Streep*ish*, he decided. Aging well and likely to be hot into her sixties or seventies.

"Can I help you?" Luke asked.

She straightened and pushed the glasses back into place. "Yes, sadly with directions only. I'm looking for 4587 Pinewood."

Luke pointed down the hill. "Take a left at the bottom of the hill. Drive about six more blocks, right on Oak, then left on Pine Drive. Pinewood is on the right. You'll know you're in the right area when you see the white house at the end of the block, the one with all the stone work and Roman-style statues. And the four-foot tall tomatoes bushes," he added as an afterthought.

"My, my, all that wood. No wonder it's so hard to find. Thank you for the directions, young man." She paused and gave him another long look, her eyes raking over his body. "Remember, never be embarrassed to align your sacral chakra. Blocked energy can lead to poor health in all areas of your life."

She flashed him another mesmerizing smile and drove slowly down the hill, the BMW Hybrid convertible as silent and sleek as its driver.

Luke shook his head, bemused. At least he wouldn't have to have a cold shower. Chakras? Why did he feel like he'd just received sexual advice from a perverted yogi?

He walked up the stairs and let himself into the house. The air inside was cold on his skin after standing in the hot sun. The layers of sweat left from his run raised a ripple of goose bumps. Stripping off the telltale shorts, he headed into the bathroom for a shower. He set the water to the perfect temperature and stepped under the rain shower head. Standing in the warm spray, he let the water sluice over his body.

The bathroom was the first room he'd renovated when he bought this house. He'd ripped out the tub and replaced it with a giant open-concept walk-in shower. The tiles lining the stall looked like old wood baked gray by the sun. The white-washed walls and the faded gray vinyl-planked floor reinforced the vintage feel.

His thoughts returned to Fran and her threats. No way would she carry them out. She was too sweet to go out of her way to make his life hell. He frowned. At least he thought she was. She had said something about her Italian Nonna being Sicilian. Fran said her

Nonna thought that the movie *The Godfather* had given people the wrong impression. It made Sicilians look soft. At the time Luke had laughed.

No, he shook his head and rinsed the shampoo out. Fran was a kitten. She couldn't hurt anyone, she didn't have it in her. Look how upset she was over the death of her 'pussy.' No way was she up to the stresses of working in his lab. That thought made him feel a little better. He was saving her a lot of grief. The long hours and meticulous pacing would kill her. Yeah, he nodded. She would be happier somewhere else. He swung the lever on the tap to off, grabbed a towel and rubbed dry.

Wrapping the towel around his waist, he headed into the kitchen and grabbed a beer. He carried it out to the patio and settled into his favourite chair, looking out at the water. He took a sip and frowned. Maybe he shouldn't be too smug. He didn't really know Fran well enough to predict the probability of her actions. What if she did make good on her threats?

He took a gulp of the beer. The amber ale tasted good after his run. Slowly, still thinking about Fran and her threats, he leaned forward and put the bottle back on the table. He flopped back in the chair and stared at the retreating ferry. Damn. This could be a problem.

To be fair, it wasn't all Fran's fault. He could have been honest with her. He could have said, *"Hey, I'm Luke Tanner rock-star scientist. I do a little stripping on the side because . . ."* Nope. He never told people he met that he was a Chemistry prof at the university, and he certainly didn't advertise the darker part of his life. He would have to make Fran see for herself that they couldn't work together. Not even possible. He wouldn't be able to keep his eyes or hands on the job and off of Fran. Fran had to go.

Still, he reflected, he should prepare himself. A little research was always a good thing. Before he declared war, he needed to know what he was dealing with. Leaving the beer on the table, he went back into the house and grabbed his wallet and his phone. Somewhere in his wallet was Sunny's card. She'd given it to him at the club one night. Nothing sexual, he liked Sunny, but she was way too high maintenance for him. Look at the way she had treated J-Dawg. Yeah, the guy was a jerk but she had left him sobbing in the locker room after she broke it off.

Luke grinned. Dallas had almost kicked J-Dawg's ass when he'd caught him using his towel to wipe his snotty nose. Yup, Sunny was gorgeous and funny, and not his type in any way, but she did have something to offer—information on one Francesca Romano.

He called the number on the card. Surprisingly, Sunny picked up on the first ring.

"Hi Sunny, this is—"

"Danger." Sunny laughed. "I recognised your voice. I'm glad you called. I wanted to thank you for saving Franny the other night."

"No problem. Sunny, I was—"

Sunny carried on as if he hadn't spoken. "Yeah, I kind of abandoned her. I don't know if you know but Jason, I mean J-Dawg, and I decided we were better off apart. It's okay," she continued. "It was all very civil."

Luke rolled his eyes. Civil, right. Jason blubbering and banging his head on the row of lockers in the change room civil.

"Right, I'm sorry for . . ." What? Her loss, nah. He moved on with the conversation. "I wanted to ask you about Fran."

Sunny's voice cooled slightly. "Not subtle at all. You know I love you, but you and Fran are *defs* not compatible. You aren't going to get any information out of me. But I do want to thank you. Craig kept bringing her drinks and she kept drinking them. I heard she really cut loose. I wish I could have seen that. Fran's usually so straight and narrow she makes a ruler look crooked. She's super focussed on school."

"Is she from around here?" he asked.

"Port Fling born and raised. She's a good Italian girl with an old-school mafia Nonna. Don't even think about it," Sunny said and laughed. "If Nonna doesn't scare you, her nine older brothers will. Watch out for Sal. He's super protective. It can be a little over the top."

Yeah, well, he wasn't worried about Fran's brothers. He didn't plan on meeting any of them. Besides, he was confident that he could handle anything the brothers threw at him. He had grown up in some pretty tough foster homes and spent enough time in juvenile detention to learn how to lead with his fists. He'd also learned about petty larceny and how to read through a lie.

Funny, he hadn't thought Fran capable of covering up something this big. Why hadn't she told him she was his new grad student? Right, he answered himself, when would she have offered up that little tidbit. They were too busy getting naked in the shower.

"You still there, Danger?" Sunny asked.

"Yeah. You were saying that she's really serious about school. What's she going to do when she's done?"

"God, don't ask her. She'll start blathering on about green chemistry and catalytic chemical processes. Believe me, you don't want to know."

He did actually. What Sunny considered boring, Luke was totally absorbed in. The problem was: if Fran was as deeply immersed in greening the world as he was, it might be hard to get her out of his lab.

"Yeah. That sounds over my head," Luke muttered, deciding to wrap up the call. He hadn't gotten anything out of Sunny but warnings to steer clear.

"Fran's a sweetie, but she's too serious to spend time with you. I'm sorry honey. It would be like a kitten and a tiger." Sunny was silent for a second and then added, "I know you guys spent time together, probably had some great sex, but she's not for you. Defs not the type to have an open relationship with a stripper/actor. I have some wild girlfriends that I could hook you up with if you like but leave Franny alone."

"Uh, no. I'm good, Sunny. Thanks for the warning. Good to know." Luke rolled his eyes. Stripper/actor? What had Fran told Sunny about him?

He chatted a few minutes longer about Beaujolais and when its release date would be. For someone who swore chemistry was way over her head, Sunny knew a lot about the fermentation and clarification of wine. He guessed she didn't see science as part of the process.

When he ended the call, he had the beginning of an idea. He would treat Fran like he would any other student. He would keep shovelling on the work and she would give up in no time. No way was Fran up to the gruelling pace of working in his lab. Satisfied with his plan he headed into the bedroom to erase all traces of Fran.

Chapter 23

Fran's hands shook. She wrapped them around the steering wheel and forced herself to slow down. What had she done? Blackmail? What? Did she think she was some mobster going all *Godfather* on Luke? Blackmail? What the hell are you thinking Fran?

Her adrenaline spiked and crashed leaving a tsunami of guilt to wash over her. It started at her eyes. She brushed away the mascara-stained tears with the back of her hand. She didn't care where she was going, she just knew she had to get away and clear her head, erase the memories of her time with Luke. Unfortunately, someone else had other ideas. Her phone rang for the millionth time and she glanced at the call display. Damn, it was Nonna again. If she didn't pick up, she'd never hear the end of it.

"*Ciao*, Nonna," she answered on her speakerphone, trying to sound breezy and cheerful.

"*Ciao*, Francesca. You take care of your little problem?" Nonna asked.

"Yep, just a big misunderstanding. It's all good now."

"Misunderstanding? Really?" Nonna was skeptical.

"Yep." Fran bit her lip. She was a terrible liar, especially when it came to Nonna.

"Okay, we talk about this later. When you get here?" Nonna demanded.

Oh my god, she'd completely forgotten. Maria's shower! She sniffed and blinked away another tear. Could this day get any worse? It was a nightmare already. She had promised Cousin Mar she'd arrive early and help setup. With all the Luke drama she'd been so totally self-absorbed, she'd forgotten. *Worst. Cousin. Ever.*

"I'm so sorry, Nonna. I got caught up and couldn't get away. I'm driving there right now." Fran screeched to the side of the road and pulled an illegal U-turn.

"Okay good. Pick up more cheezies and chips. I think Antonella broke up with another boyfriend. She is eating like is end of world."

"No problem, Nonna. *Ciao*."

"*Ciao*." Nonna hung up.

Antonella, Fran's curvy cousin was always either: a) madly in love, skinny and on top of the world, or b) eating her way through the *Worst Breakup Ever*. Fran shuddered and swore to herself she would not become another Antonella, pinning her entire existence on a guy.

She pulled into the Safeway parking lot, grabbed a Kleenex and vigorously wiped the streaks of mascara off of her face with a spit wash. Dumping the contents of her purse onto her lap, she unearthed her bottle of concealer and dabbed at the dark circles under her eyes. Satisfied with the touch up job, she finished with a light coat of her trademark red lip gloss and eyed her face in the rear-view mirror. Not bad. Not perfect, but enough to ward off her nosy family. She'd tell them she was overtired and overworked. It was half true. She'd just omit the little part about her being heartsick.

***

"So, then they told me just one more push and I swear I felt my whole hoo-ha ripping from front to back. I kid you not. But then suddenly, I heard screaming and she was there on my chest. I suddenly didn't care about the pain and the 40 stiches that followed. Isn't she cute?"

Fran's cousin Maria held up her wrinkled firstborn to Fran for closer inspection.

"Mmmm. She's adorable. Congratulations, Maria." Fran gave her cousin a weak smile.

Fran had never been one to swoon at the mention of blood, or guts, but Maria's twenty-minute-long birth story had left her a little weak in the knees.

"Did I tell you about the afterbirth? Looked like a giant piece of liver *floppin'* around on the table. I thought I was gonna hurl!" Maria leaned towards Fran.

Fran felt her stomach churn. She needed to get away from Maria and her graphic stories, or *she* was going to hurl.

"I'd love to hear about your afterbirth, Maria, but first you need to eat. Can I bring you some cannoli?"

"Sure." Maria was successfully distracted at the mention of cannoli. "You know me, I'm a sucker for cannoli, plus I gotta keep my milk supply up. Nonna said her cannoli is great for that. Speaking of milk supply, my nipples are huge. They look like giant flying saucers! Not to mention the bleeding and the scabbing. Lots for you to look forward to one day, cousin." Maria shook her head and nudged Fran.

"Wow. That's great Mar. I'll be right back."

Fran turned away abruptly, almost bumping into Cousin Cristina. Perfect, she gave Cristina a quick hug, steered her into Maria's path, and made her escape. Behind her she heard Maria restart her story.

"It was ten o'clock at night and I was making a sandwich when suddenly my feet were soaking wet. I thought I'd peed myself again!" Maria's voice was drowned out by the other shower guests as Fran put more distance between them.

For a second, Fran suffered a pang of guilt. Poor Cristina. She was way too sweet to interrupt Maria. She'd be stuck there for hours. Oh well, way to take one for the team. So far, everyone had taken their turn hearing the infamously gory birth story. Besides, little Chris was a nursing student. She could share the story of blood and guts with her fellow students later.

Fran made her way to the food table and grabbed a bright pink paper plate. She eyed up the spread in front of her: Nonna's cannoli, Bev's spinach dip, Sue's pasta salad, Waverly's brownies. Everything looked amazing. Normally she'd be piling her plate sky high, but the Luke drama had left a rock in her stomach and no room for food. She grabbed a plain piece of bread and a few tortilla chips and moved away, nibbling half-heartedly at the food on the plate.

"Francesca, eat! You so skinny you going to blow away." Nonna placed another overflowing platter of cannoli on the table and wiped her hands on her apron before reaching over to squeeze Fran's arm.

"Hi Nonna. Nice apron. Who gave you that?" Fran asked giving Nonna's papery cheek a kiss. With luck, Nonna would be distracted by the question and forget how Fran looked.

Nonna ran her fingers over the apron's Italian flag and looked down at the ornate lettering boldly proclaiming *Mangia.* "Who else but that brother of yours."

Good, Nonna had taken the bait. "Which one?" Fran asked innocently.

Nonna shook her head and dashed her hopes. "My girl, you look so pale." She placed her soft hands on Fran's cheeks and stared into her eyes. "And sad."

Fran bit her lip. "I'm okay Nonna."

"No. You not." Nonna moved her hands from Fran's face and patted her shoulder. "You need cannoli."

Nonna grabbed Fran's plate and plopped the largest cannoli onto it. "Eat," she commanded.

Fran dutifully took a bite. "Delicious." She smiled, lying through her teeth. Normally it would be true, but right now everything tasted like sand-paper.

"Keep eating," Nonna commanded, watching Fran chew.

Fran complied, tasting nothing.

"Hello Francesca, Nonna." Waverly moved away from Zia Rosa and approached them. She was laughing at something Rosa had said, and a little smile curved her lips.

"Ah, Waverly, you looking very orange in that sweater, like a big pumpkin! How are you?" Nonna smiled syrupy sweet as she gave her friend a kiss on the cheek.

"I'm fabulous, Nonna. You're looking great as always. I swear I've seen that same flowered pattern of your dress somewhere else. Perhaps on a couch I once owned back in the 1970's." Waverly returned the veiled barb with her own sugary smile.

"Thank-you. Some things so classical they never go out of style, and some things never in style to begin." Nonna returned, not batting an eye.

"So true, but all of the generations have different ideas about style, don't they? Are you force-feeding the guests your cannoli again, Nonna?" Waverly retorted, pointing to Fran's huge serving.

"Mind your own business, Waverly. The girl looks pale, she needs cannoli." Nonna snapped. Waverly knew just what buttons to push with Nonna and cannoli was definitely one of them.

"You say cannoli is the cure for everything, I say chocolate. Science only agrees with one of us, and it's not you, darling. Try one of my famous Mayan chocolate brownies, Francesca, sure to cure any malady. It's a proven *scientific* fact." Waverly casually dropped a giant brownie on Fran's plate, winked and walked away.

"Oh, that woman." Nonna muttered something in Italian under her breath.

Fran didn't quite catch what she said, but she was sure it wasn't flattering. Just as well, she decided. She didn't want to get caught up in a throw down between the two grandmas. She shook her head. Waverly and Nonna had a complicated love-hate frenemy relationship comparable to two ninth grade girls. They openly insulted each other, yet if anyone else dared to insult the other, they'd defend their 'friend' to the death.

"Are you and Waverly having it out again, Nonna?" Antonella called from the end of the table. Her plate was piled high with cheezies, her fingers tips stained orange.

"Only place Waverly and I have it out is the yearly bake-off and that no competition. I always win." Nonna snorted rudely, turned around and walked away.

"Hey Franny. Who peed in her espresso?" asked Antonella, sliding up next to Fran, her mouth full of orange puffs.

"Hey, Ann." Fran greeted her cousin with an awkward one-arm hug. "Don't take it personally. Waverly just knows how to get under her skin."

"Uh-oh, was she insulting her Cannoli again?" asked Antonella.

"You got it." Fran nodded.

"When are those old bats gonna learn? If you're always worrying about what other people think and stuff, then you're never gonna be happy. You know?"

"Exactly," Fran agreed, taken aback. This didn't sound like the usual depressed, post break-up Antonella.

"You know, Franny. It's taken me thirty-two years but I finally learned I don't have to make myself different for no one. I'm happy with me. Cheezie eating, big butt and all."

"Good for you Ann. I'm really happy for you. Hopefully I'll get there one day."

"You will Franny. And you know what? Now that I'm happy with me, I've actually met a really nice guy, who accepts me for who I am. Hot Italian temper and all."

Fran smiled as Antonella shoved another couple of cheezies into her mouth. Antonella was right. Hopefully one day soon, Luke would be a distant memory and she'd meet someone great. Someone who didn't lead a double life—simple, sweet stripper by night—brilliant but evil chemist asshole by day. Fran's mood momentarily darkened but lifted a minute later when she heard Sunny's voice in her ear.

"Why are you hiding out here, friend? Dodging the graphic birth story?"

"That and the rising storm between your Grandma and my Nonna. It's getting closer to the annual bake-off and the claws are out." Fran turned and gave Sunny a wink.

"Oh man. Is Waverly insulting Nonna's cannoli again?" Sunny asked.

"You know it."

"I swear that woman should come with a warning on her forehead. She's a shit disturber, disturbing people's shit wherever she goes."

Fran and Sunny giggled.

"What's so funny, ladies?" Waverly sidled up from out of nowhere.

"Nothing." Fran instantly stopped giggling. Waverly always made her feel like she was ten-years-old again.

"We were making fun of your ability to get under everyone's skin." Sunny answered matter-of-factly. It seemed Waverly didn't have the same chastising effect on Sunny that she had on Fran.

"It's really not my problem if some people take offense to my purely innocent observations." Waverly smiled serenely.

"Uh-huh, sure." Sunny sarcastically matched the serene smile.

Waverly ignored Sunny's barb. "So, what were you ladies up to last night?"

"Nothing." Both Sunny and Fran answered at the same time.

"Nothing, really?" Waverly could detect a lie like a champion bloodhound. "Then why, my darling Granddaughter, did I hear you were out with Jason again? The very same Jason you supposedly broke up with only three nights ago?"

No, not Jason! Fran's eyes silently pleaded with Sunny to deny Waverly's words, but she bit her tongue.

Sunny took a deep breath, a kettle about to boil over.

"It's none of your damn business, Grandma, but if you must know I was talking Jason down from suicidal thoughts. Even though he can be an ass, he's still a person and he's still my friend."

Sunny and Waverly glared silently at each other. They'd always had a complicated relationship, and right now Fran was smack in the middle of all that awkwardness.

"Well, if that's true, I'm sorry for him." Waverly's voice was low.

"Its fine. You didn't know." Sunny relented.

"No, I didn't but I'm not surprised. That young man has a dark energy surrounding him."

"Maybe his chakras are just blocked." Sunny rolled her eyes at Fran behind Waverly's back.

"No, its more than that." Waverly continued, ignoring Sunny's sarcasm. "He just seems off to me."

"Okay Waverly, sure." Sunny frowned.

"I'm serious Sunny. I don't want you around him, he's not good for you."

"Good thing I'm old enough to make my own decisions and base them on more than voodoo and spirit mumbo jumbo," Sunny challenged.

Fran froze and waited for the bomb to explode.

Waverly didn't answer. She stared at Sunny for a long moment, and then silently turned and sauntered away. Despite being a sex therapist/baker, an expert yogi and a meditation guru, Waverly had a temper that could scare the quills off a porcupine. It didn't come out often, but when it did you'd better run for cover. Sunny's temper was no better, although she'd never admit she was anything like her colourful Grandma. Fran had witnessed some pretty intense dish-throwing episodes between the two of them over the years.

"Sorry, that was awkward," Sunny joked.

"Was it true? About Jason?" Fran asked, meeting Sunny's gaze. She usually stayed out of her friend's love life but she was worried for Sunny. Voodoo or not, Waverly was right, Jason was bad for her.

"Yes, unfortunately it is true. Although, I think it was more of a plot to get me over to his house. When I arrived he conveniently had a candlelit dinner set out for us."

"Jason cooked?"

"He put a frozen pizza in the oven and burnt it." Sunny rolled her eyes. "But I have to give him props for trying. It was kind of sweet."

"Sunny," Fran warned.

"Its fine, Franny. We're just friends." Sunny waved her off.

"Pinky swear?"

"Oh sorry, are we twelve again?" Sunny joked but complied, hooking her pinky around Fran's. "Pinky swear. And how about you Fran? Did you make up your mind? Are you going to see Mister Muscles again?" Sunny wiggled her eyebrows suggestively.

"No, we're done. Fun while it lasted."

"Hmmm, he'll be disappointed about that. I think he's really into you. He actually called me earlier, trying to get the deets on you."

"What?" Fran screeched.

A silence fell over the room. Fran looked up to see curious eyes watching her and Sunny. She grabbed Sunny's arm and dragged her into the corner. Leaning in closer, she demanded, "Sunny, this is very important. What exactly did he ask you?"

"Whoa, down there horsey. I thought you weren't even into the guy." Sunny smirked at Fran. She was wearing her, *I've got a secret* face.

"Sunny, I'm serious." Fran hissed. "Tell me."

"Okay. Um, he asked about where you grew up and about your family. Don't worry I didn't tell him much."

"That's it." Fran confirmed.

"Yes."

Fran breathed a sigh of relief. "Okay, that's good."

"Wait, there's one more thing. He also wanted to know what you were studying in school and if you were serious about it."

Fran felt the blood rushing to her face. What an asshole. He was using her best friend to try and gain the upper hand!

"Is everything okay, Fran? Is this guy stalking you or something?"

"No, its fine. I'm just over it and don't want things to get messy."

"So, you're gonna call it off? Party's over?" Sunny checked.

"Party's definitely over." Fran confirmed. That was the understatement of the year.

Chapter 24

Luke pounded another nail into the fence panel and used the back of his arm to swipe the sweat away from his eyes. He glanced over at the stack of lumber piled high at his feet and asked himself why he was banging nails in the heat of the day after a grueling 10k run.

No, he knew why. It was because he would rather be banging Fran. Working outside prevented him from going inside and facing the traces of Fran that lingered there. How could she have left such a deep imprint after only one weekend? Everywhere he looked, he found memories of her—his bed, his shower, his kitchen counters—hell, even his laundry room. Maybe that was because they'd gotten busy in every room, on every surface of his house. Right, it was all about the sex. That was all it was. Freaking, get over it already.

He swung at another nail, cursing as the head of the hammer slipped and whacked his thumb. Shit. He clenched his hand and dropped the hammer to the ground. This wasn't working. He looked at the line of boards he'd put up and picked the hammer up again, this time pulling out the nails he'd banged in. The boards were crooked. If he left them as is, he'd have another visible reminder of Fran.

His phone rang. He didn't recognize the number and almost ignored it. No, he shrugged and swiped the answer button. Conversation would give him a diversion.

"Hello," he growled into the phone.

"Is this Danger Dark?" the male voice on the other end of the call asked hesitantly.

What the hell? No one from the club had his number. They left messages on his land line.

"Who's calling?"

"It's Jason."

Luke frowned. "Who?"

"J-Dawg, man. You know, from the club."

Luke hesitated. "How exactly did you get my number?"

It was a good thing he hadn't identified himself when he answered. Who the hell gave J-Dawg his cell number?

"I got the number from Sunny. That's what I wanted to talk to you about. She had it in her phone memory. Why would she have your number in her phone, dude? That's not cool." J-Dawg—Jason's—voice cooled.

"Look, *Jay*-son, maybe you should ask Sunny that." Luke wasn't in the mood for this high school bullshit.

"Dude, Sunny and I have a thing. I know you may have heard we broke up but that was just a fight. It's not cool to move in on another guy's woman, you're violating the stripper code man."

Luke held the phone away from his ear. Stripper code? Was this guy for real?

"Look, J-Dawg, clearly you need to talk to Sunny."

"She's hot, I know that. That's why I'm banging her." J-Daw continued, ignoring Luke. Dude, either you back off on your own or I'll make you." J-Dawg/Jason's voice turned threatening.

Luke was silent for a second. ". . . Are you threatening me?"

"No, man, I'm just telling you how it is. She's my property, she's sold." the other man laughed.

The sound made Luke want to reach through the phone and punch him. Property? Seriously, what did Sunny see in this loser?"

"I'm just telling you, she's off the market. Stay tuned for the wedding announcement. She's one of the girls you put a ring on. She's hot and she makes good coin, so I'm not letting her get away, you know what I mean?"

"Yeah well, good luck with that."

"What do you mean by that?" The voice on the other end turned threatening again.

"Look *Dawg*, I'm busy. What do you want?" Luke impatiently grabbed the hammer again and eyed up another crooked board.

"*Nothin'*. I'm just giving you a friendly warning. Stay off my turf."

"Right. Sunny's not a person, she's your property. Later." Luke ended the call, shaking his head. Jeez, Sunny could do better than J-Dawg/Jason. What the hell was she thinking?

His phone rang again. He glanced at the screen and saw it was the same number as before.

"Look J-Dawg, don't call me again. You're pissing me off."

Silence. The phone call ended.

Luke pulled off another board and his phone rang again.

What the hell? Same number. This time he didn't bother answering. He didn't have time for Jason's little dramas, between work and Fran he had enough drama.

Chapter 25

Fran was exhausted. She'd felt guilty about showing up late to Maria's shower so she'd stayed behind to help clean up and then stopped for groceries on the way home. She couldn't wait to unload her stuff and soak this terrible day away in a bubble bath with a glass of wine.

She lifted the bag of groceries onto the counter and bent to give Muffin a pat. He swished his tail and walked away.

"Snob," Fran said, amused by the cat's haughtiness.

Muffin was the most stand-offish of the cats. Luke had said that calling a male cat Muffin was like calling a male stripper Tiny. Fran pursed her lips. She was doing it again, thinking about Luke. She should be thinking about how she was going to deal with tomorrow, now that she'd blackmailed him into keeping her in the lab.

She'd done the right thing. It was the only thing she could do. If that was true than why did she feel so bad? She should feel good about this. Nonna would be proud to see her Sicilian blood win out. It's not as if Luke was playing fair, he'd already called Sunny looking for some dirt on Fran.

Fran's phone rang. She glanced down to see who was calling. Shit. It was Sal.

"Nonna, no . . ." she moaned. "Why would you do that?"

Fran would bet her left arm that Nonna had broken her promise not to tell anyone and gone directly to Sal about the whole 'Luke situation'. Her finger floated over the ignore button. Could she ignore his call? Sal was doggedly persistent when he set his mind to something. Better to diffuse the situation now.

"Hello Salvatore," she answered, trying to keep her voice extra light and breezy.

"Hello favourite sister."

That was the running joke in the family, out of ten kids, Fran was the only girl.

"How's it going Sal?"

"Fine, busy with work but I'm good. I know I just saw you yesterday but I'm working up in your neck of the woods at the university. Maybe we could catch lunch one day this week, I'll even buy. How about you? How was Maria's shower?"

"It was good. Nice to see everyone and catch up. Are you building the new physics lab? How's that going?"

"Meh, It's okay. Dad's still riding me, you know how it is. How about you? How was the big first day in the lab?"

"It was great. Just fabulous. Like really, really wonderful. Great!" Fran silently kicked herself. She was trying to sound natural, like she was over-the-moon happy, but it sounded all wrong.

"Francesca." Sal's voice was stern.

"Salvatore." Fran mocked his tone.

"Don't lie to your big brother. I know when something's wrong."

"Really, Sal? And how do you know that?"

"Uh, I just know. I'm psychically connected to you or something. It must be a twin thing."

"We're not twins Sal."

"We're less than a year apart, close enough!"

"Still not twins." Fran rolled her eyes. "Say, have you talked to Nonna by any chance?"

"Uh, Nonna? No, not at all. Why?"

"You're as bad a liar as I am Sal."

"I don't know what you're talking about."

"Sal," she warned.

"Ah, you got me. Nonna just called and told me everything."

Fran sighed.

"Don't be all pissy at her Fransie Underpantsie, she was worried about you. She said you looked as pale as a ghost at the shower. What's going on?"

Fran ignored the hated nickname. "It's fine Sal, forget about it. I took care of it."

"So, you ordered a hit on Professor *minchia*?" Sal swore. "I'm assuming this is the jerk you were all doe-eyed over yesterday? I could go pay him a visit and kick his ass for you. He's probably a soft loser who never sees sunlight outside of the lab."

"No Sal, stay out of it. I took care of it." Fran nervously paced the kitchen. The last thing she needed was Sal getting involved.

"How? How did you take care of it, Fran? What did you do?"

"Just resorted to some low-level blackmail."

"Nice. I didn't think you had it in you."

Fran rolled her eyes. Sal sounded genuinely proud that she would stoop to criminal behaviour to get her way.

"I'm not proud of it but I learned from the best," she said.

"Ha, you got that right. I'm still squeezing you for that time you spilled red wine on mom's favorite chair in the living room."

"You managed to convince her that Nonna got tipsy and did it!" Fran started to laugh remembering the look on her mother's face when the eleven-year-old Sal offered to make Nonna clean up the mess.

"It was the perfect lie. Mom and dad would never confront Nonna. Too terrifying."

"You've got that right," Fran agreed.

"In fact, if the blackmail against the professor backfires you could just send Nonna over to his house. She'd talk some sense into him in a second."

"I know she would and I know you would too. But I'm serious Sal. Please leave it alone. I need to take care of this by myself. I'm not Fransie Underpantsie anymore. Ok? I'm big girl Francesca. And I need to learn to stand on my own two feet."

"Okay, I'll leave it alone." Sal grudgingly agreed.

"Thank-you."

"But you'll always be Fransie Underpantsie to me, little sis."

Chapter 26

"Have you turned down the Bunsen burner on that hydrochloric acid yet, Ms. Romano?"

Fran stiffened and muttered an Italian curse bad enough to send Nonna looking for her bar of soap. She kept her back to Luke as she answered.

"Yes. Dr. Tanner. I have turned down the temperature." She silently rolled her eyes. *Same as when you asked me five minutes ago*. So far, Luke had been nothing but civil. Yes, today marked day four of working with a civil pain in the ass.

Fran wasn't buying any of it. She knew exactly what he was trying to do. He was trying to drown her in work. He was trying to break her, but what he didn't understand was that being a woman in the man's world of chemistry, she'd always had to work twice as hard and put in longer hours. She'd had to prove that she was up to the task, that she wasn't soft.

It was completely unfair and she hated the double standard, but she was used to it. So, while he thought he was breaking her under the pressure, it was just another ordinary day in the lab for Fran. He wanted to hand her extra work, give her extra hours? Fine with her.

"I'll need you to stay late and work on this experiment, Ms. Romano. Sarah needed to take some time off and Monica has had to step out for a while to run an errand for me."

Fran smirked but said nothing. Sarah had gotten Dr. Tanner into a beaker-full of crap with the higher ups. She'd been overly emotional the last two days and Luke had rebuked her for it in a very public manner. Word had it that Dr. Tanner was now enrolled in some very intensive 'sensitivity training.'

Sexist pig. Serves him right, thought Fran. Although if she was playing devil's advocate she would agree with Luke that Sarah was being entirely inappropriate, crying to everyone that her married lover refused to leave his wife and kids for her. The experiment they were performing was incredibly dangerous and time sensitive. Sarah was putting everyone's safety at risk with her lack of attention—but still, Luke didn't have to embarrass her in front of the entire lab.

So here they were, Friday evening and, where was she? —stuck in the lab with Dr. Luke Tanner. Everyone else had a life. They had all gone home and were probably half-way through their first glass of Chianti after a hard day's work. But her—oh, no, she was here in the lab listening to rock star Tanner ask her for the fiftieth time if she'd turned down the heat. She snuck a glance at him. He was working next to her at the table, completely focused on pouring the sulfuric acid. His lower lip was pushed out in concentration, a lock of his dark hair falling into his eyes. She practically had to sit on her hands to stop herself from brushing it away.

His arm grazed hers as he leaned over to double check the burner temperature and her skin tingled, both with desire and annoyance.

"I thought you said you turned the temperature down on the HCL." He accused, gesturing to the burner.

"I did," Fran answered. She folded her arms over her chest. Count to ten Fran. He's playing with your emotions, trying to get you to flip out so he can tell Etherridge you can't handle the pressure.

"Not low enough." Luke shook his head. "It should have hardened by now and it's still soft. Now we need to restart the whole process."

Fran let out a loud whoosh of breath. They both knew the temperature on that burner was perfect. He was testing her.

"Oh, I apologize Ms. Romano. Am I keeping you from something?"

"No. It's okay." She shrugged, giving a little smile, and then testing the waters, she added, "I'll just call Felipe and let him know I'm going to be late." Ha, take that! She didn't really have a date but Luke didn't need to know that.

Luke's mouth flattened into a hard, thin line. "Okay Ms. Romano, you do that. In the meantime, I'll keep an eye on this burner as you don't seem to grasp the dangers of exceeding the auto-ignition temperature." He turned his back on Fran and began fiddling with the equipment.

Fran clenched her jaw shut. No, she would not give in to her desire to have her own personal episode of auto-ignition. She counted to ten and then twenty. Slowly she took in a deep breath. She was good, calm, Zen. She grabbed her phone off the table and sauntered casually towards the door as if looking for a measure of privacy to make her call. She pretend-dialed a number and held the phone to her ear, listening to pretend rings, contemplating how fast her pretend lover would answer.

Three seconds was good enough, she decided. If she was going to conjure up a pretend lover he was going to be waiting for her call. "Hi Felipe? It's Fran." She giggled. "Aww, the other night was great for me too. Oh, stop! Listen, I'm stuck at work for a while, so I'll be late tonight." She paused as if listening and then continued, "That's so sweet Felipe! I'll be counting down the seconds too. I know. Okay, see you soon." And then she ended it with a sexy, "Bye."

Luke had kept his back to her the entire time but she could tell by the rigid line of his shoulders that he had been listening.

Stuffing her phone into her back pocket, she sauntered back, playing it cool as a cucumber.

"Okay then, Dr. Tanner. What do you need me to do to get it hard again?" She placed her elbows on the table and leaned forward just a touch, giving Luke a glimpse of her cleavage. Leaning in closer, she looked down at the contents of the burner, letting the table surface lift her breasts practically up to her chin.

"Oh look! You got it hard all on your own."

She saw his Adam's apple bob as he swallowed. His eyes zeroed in on her exposed skin.

Ha. That was a low-blow and entirely unlike Fran, but Luke deserved it with the way he'd been treating her. They locked eyes and she held her position, enjoying the heat radiating off his body, the raw desire in his eyes.

Her own desire bubbled through her like a chemical compound, ready to ignite. Right now, she wanted to tear off her safety glasses and devour Luke. He was like the tub of Hagen Daz chocolate ice-cream sitting in her freezer—she was fine as long as she didn't see it but as soon as she opened the freezer door, she couldn't resist just a 'taste' of all that chocolate goodness, only a 'taste' always turned into a giant bowl. She took her elbows off the table and turned away, abruptly breaking the spell.

Shit, what are you doing Fran? She silently cursed herself. This was killing her. Why did she have to fall for Professor Lucas Tanner of all people?

Life was so much easier when he was just a simple stripper.

She couldn't stand this much longer. The heat of his body next to hers as they worked was torture. She needed to distract herself before she did something stupid. She reached across the table to grab the beaker of left-over acid. Her hand shook slightly as it closed around the glass. She lifted the beaker and a single drop of acid spilled over the side, burning the back of her hand.

"Argh!" Fran gasped. The caustic acid seared a line of agony across her skin. Hand trembling with the effort, she carefully set the beaker back on the table before clasping her hands tightly together, fighting the urge to burst into tears.

"Fran!" Luke was at her side. He scooped her up in his arms and carried her to the sink. Setting her down, he activated the taps and frantically began scrubbing Fran's hand with soap and water.

"It looks fine, a bit red but it will heal," he said, examining the area kissed by the acid. "Here." He used his foot to pull over a stool. "Fran, you're white as a sheet. Are you okay?" Luke's own alarm was evident in his face.

"No. I mean—yes. No." The pain from the chemical burn was sizzling through her hand, up her arm. She couldn't think straight with Luke standing this close to her.

"Fran. Look at me." Luke urged, ducking to meet her eyes.

She lifted her eyes and met his. A white-hot shock ran though her spine.

She didn't care about the pain in her arm. She didn't care that he was Professor Tanner and she was just his lowly grad student. Screw this, she thought. She grabbed his shirt and recklessly pulled his body against hers.

"Fran, we shouldn't." Luke groaned.

His words said no, but the bulge in his pants, pressing up against her leg, said otherwise. He slid his arms around her waist and pulled her in closer.

"Luke," she breathed, nestling her head against his warm, firm chest.

"Fran, I've missed you. I can't get you out of my mind," Luke whispered against her neck.

"I know, me too. We need to figure this out Luke."

He leaned down and Fran's lips met his. Fireworks, explosions and heat surrounded them.

"Oh shit! The acid!" Luke exclaimed, breaking away from Fran. He grabbed the extinguisher and squashed the small fire burning on the table.

Fran looked from the powder-covered counter to Luke. Her laugh started from deep inside. She couldn't stop it. Her body shook with unsuppressed laughter—the relief of four days of pent up stress, lust and longing. She slapped her hands to her mouth trying to still it, but it didn't work. The experiment was fried, but wow, that kiss!

"It's not funny!" Luke scolded. "All that work!"

Fran sobered at his stern face but then he cracked a smile and joined in the hilarity of the moment. They giggled together like a pair of drunken teens.

"Damn," Luke said again, sobering. "We can't do this here, Fran. First your arm, now this? We'll blow the whole place up."

Silently, she watched as he ran a hand through his hair. He was staring at her, his blue eyes warm and intent, full of promises.

"I can't focus tonight. Can you come in tomorrow to help me finish?" he said.

"If you come over to my place tonight," challenged Fran, with a slow sexy smile.

"I'd love that," Luke said, smiling back. "Except . . . shit, I promised Zack—you met him on Seal Island, remember? The drum circle guy—anyways, he's an advisor. I promised I'd meet him in half-an-hour. How about I finish cleaning up here and let Monica know we're calling it quits and then meet with Zack. I'll head over to your house after?"

"Yes," said Fran. *Yes, yes, yes.* "Sounds great." She grabbed her phone from her back pocket. "I'll just have to tell Felipe we're off."

"Ha, Felipe." Luke snorted. "Fran? There's no Felipe is there?"

"No," Fran admitted, hanging her head in mock shame.

"That's cute. You were trying to make me jealous?" Luke asked, ducking to meet her eyes as he slid his arms around her waist.

"Maybe or maybe not." Fran smiled, coyly, leaning in to give him a peck on the lips.

His lips softened and she yielded, kissing him deeply. He lifted her up, so that she was sitting on the edge of the counter top with Luke standing between her legs. She couldn't stop herself. She pulled him in, wrapping her legs around his waist so that there was no longer any space between them. Her breath came faster. She could feel their need for each other as they kissed, long hungry kisses. She tugged at his shirt, pulling it free of his jeans. Her fingers touched his skin. Its heat made her forget everything. She wanted him right now, here in the lab.

"Fran, whoa, whoa, whoa." Luke returned to reality first, backing away, hands up in surrender. "You've got to go now, or I'm going to tear your clothes off," he threatened.

"Is that such a bad thing?" she teased, leaning back on the table.

"It is if Monica returns, or if Dr. Etherridge decides to pay me a surprise visit, which he has been known to do."

"Good point. Okay, you win." Fran surrendered, sliding to the edge of the table and jumping down.

She leaned towards him and took hold of his tie, leading him in for one last breath-stealing kiss. It was an old tie, plain blue and not nearly as nice as the ones Fran had picked out for him. Another kiss and she forgot all about ties.

"Fran," Luke muttered against her lips. "If you don't go, we're both going to lose our jobs. He set his hands on her hips and gently pushed her away. He was breathing hard.

"Right," Fran muttered feeling bemused. "Right." She gave her head a little shake to clear her thoughts and then gathered up her things. "I'll see you in a couple hours?"

"I wouldn't miss it for the world," Luke answered.

Chapter 27

Luke watched Fran walk away. He wanted to run after her and finish what they had started. He couldn't get enough of her, couldn't stop touching her, wanting her. Every move she made pulled him in and tugged at his heart. Who would ever think he could be so mesmerized by the swing of a woman's hips—his woman, he thought. This morning if someone had said he and Fran would be together again, he would have laughed. Now, well . . . well he was looking toward the future with a new perspective. The problems with having Fran working in the lab no longer mattered. He and Fran could do this. Lots of couples worked together and never had any trouble. He smiled.

"Dr. Tanner?"

The voice at his shoulder was so close that Luke jumped and took a step back. He swung around to find Monica standing sentinel-still watching him. Her eyes were sharp with concern, her lips pursed in a disapproving moue. Slowly, she shook her head, opened her mouth to say something and the closed it again. Oh, shit, was the first thought that popped into Luke's head, the second was damage control. What had Monica seen?

"What do you want me to do with these transfer documents?" Monica asked abruptly, shaking the sheaf of papers she held.

"Transfer doc—. Right." Luke held out his hand for the papers that would officially sever Fran from his lab. "Yeah, there's been a change there."

Monica furrowed her generous brows and shook her head harder. "You're cruising for danger there, Luke. That girl is not a brainless ninny trying to impress you. She has the smarts to go far. I've never seen anyone so orgasmic over the centrifuge 5000 before, unless it was you," she added.

Luke scowled. He'd known Monica a long time.

"It's not like that," he defended.

"Oh, it's totally like that. You got it bad boss, and you're too dumb to see what's right in front of your nose." Monica's head wagged in pity.

"Don't you have some beakers to wash?"

Monica laughed. "Just mark my words. Be careful, or your dancing days will be over."

"What the—!"

"Oh, don't worry about it. Your secret's safe with me." Monica smirked, her fuzzy brows lifted. "Danger Dark." She snorted and picked up a tray of beakers. The door swung shut behind her.

Luke stared at the closed door to the lab. Damn, damn, damn. He and Fran were back together three minutes and there were already problems. It's going to be okay Luke, he consoled himself; it's Monica. She's a friend. She would never rat him out to Etherridge. He scrubbed his hand through his dark hair making the short curls stand on end.

How the hell had Monica found out about his dancing? He closed his eyes and grimaced. He never thought about who was on the other side of the lights once he stepped onto the stage. He'd been guilty of his own brand of snobbery, believing that no one he knew from work would go anywhere near Spanky's. If he ever did, he figured that the camo paint and Deltas were a good disguise, making his moves covert.

His face twisted into a grimace. Monica watching him strip—well, that was just wrong. It was time to hang up the G-string. He had way too much to look forward to in the future to risk losing it over a strip club. He'd take up something socially acceptable like running marathons and save his dances for Fran. The smile returned to his face. He had acquired plenty of moves in his career. The idea of trying them out on Fran made him hard. Yeah, he'd do a whole new interactive routine just for her.

He glanced up at the wall clock. His appointment with Zack was for six but he'd cancel it and head over to Fran's place. He'd rather talk to her than listen to Zack drone on about the tweaks he had made to the gin recipe.

He looked towards the back corner of the lab where Zack's sill was neatly tucked away. Zack was obsessed with the recipe that he'd found in the back of an old diary his great grandfather had kept. Great Grandpa Miles had been a botanist. He had explored much of the west coast's rainforests and coastlines and had left behind notebooks filled with sketches of what he had seen and done. He'd also been known as somewhat of a genius when it came to making gin. Miles' gin was said to be the nectar of the gods, if you listened to what Zack said.

Discovering the recipe had Zack going crazy trying to recreate it exactly. He'd even tried retracing Great Grandpa Mile's route, trying to find the very spot he's picked the berries used to flavour the gin. So far, Zack had succeeded in making hooch. Luke shuddered—really bad hooch. Last year Luke had let him use a spot in the lab for his still. Old Winston had gotten wind of the fact (literally) and had gone ballistic. Actually, everyone had gotten wind of the fact. One of Zack's ingredients created a smell like a pile of abandoned jock straps.

This year, Luke had given in and let Zack use the back corner again. Winston didn't have the right to dictate how Luke ran his lab. This time, Zack had promised to make the set up look scientific. He'd gotten rid of the moonshine jug and was using standard lab equipment. He was also keeping his testing under a laminar flow hood to keep Etherridge's delicate nose from catching a whiff.

Luke pulled off his lab coat and threw it into a hamper by the door to his office. He shoved his computer into its bag, grabbed a handful of papers and slid them in beside it. The separation papers transferring Fran from his lab were next to his bag on the desk. He grabbed them and ripped them into tiny pieces, dropping them into the waste basket on the way out the door.

His phone rang. Zack, he thought, right on time.

"Hey, change in plans. I— No, wait, Shan, I can hardly understand you. Slow down."

Luke pressed the phone harder against his ear and tried to figure out the meaning of the broken words buried in the muffled sobbing. "Listen, I'll meet you in fifteen minutes. Yeah, the Bull Market Café works for me. See you there."

He checked the time. It's okay, he told himself. Fran knew he had a meeting with one of the other profs. She wouldn't expect him to be free for a couple of hours. He would go to the coffee shop, meet Shannia, find out what was going on and then catch up with Fran. No problem.

He dug his car keys out of his pocket. What the hell *was* going on with Shan? She was tough as stone. She wouldn't lose it like this unless it was something really bad. Shannia, the Ice Queen always kept it together. She was the fixer, the rock in the storm. The only way that she would ever call Luke for help was if she was into something that was way over her head.

He grabbed his bag and slung it over his shoulder. Change of plans, he'd drive to the Bull Market, not walk. That way he'd be able to go straight to meet Fran after he found out what had made the tightly wound Shannia finally snap.

***

Luke found a parking spot in front of the coffee shop, proof positive that only good things were coming his way. It didn't feel right to be this happy. It was like tempting fate. No. Focus, Luke. Stop thinking about yourself and think about Shan. She wouldn't be having an epic meltdown unless there was something really wrong.

The Bull Market Café was down on Main Street, close to the water. The early fall sunshine meant that the tables clustered at the front of the café were full. That suited Luke fine. He'd rather be tucked away in the back. He shook his head in disgust. Why did he feel like he was cheating? He and Shan were never an item. It was always Shan and Evan. Luke's faint smile slid from his face. Yeah, Evan. His sense of well-being drained away. The last time Shan had been this way was all about Evan.

He stepped through the door and joined the back of the line. The café was full to capacity. Both baristas, plus Elliot, were working the front.

"You want what? Speak up. I can't hear you," Elliot ordered the soccer-mom-type woman standing in front of him.

One of the other baristas looked up from the design she was creating on a Grande cappuccino. She handed the cup off to the woman in front of the pick-up counter and took a tentative step towards Elliot with her hands up, as if something was about to fall and she could catch it.

"I want an extra-large decaf coffee with skim milk. An extra-large? Skim milk?" the soccer-mom repeated. She looked annoyed. Her foot tapped impatiently.

Luke winced. Elliot, aka, the coffee Nazi was about to go off the deep end.

"What do you think this is? McDonalds? If you don't know how to order a coffee in a specialty beanery, get out of my shop and don't come back. We—"

"Here's your coffee," the other barista slid a Vente coffee across the counter and waved aside the customer's money.

"No, it's on the house today. Happy Friday," she said smiling brightly and taking the next order in line.

Elliot was still muttering about coffee etiquette. He looked up, caught Luke's eye and pursed his lips in challenge, daring him to make just one order faux pas.

"I'll have a Grande Americano, please," Luke said. He had planned on ordering a small coffee, but after witnessing Elliot's mood he decided to play it safe.

Elliot made Luke's drink. His beady eyes studied Luke over the bejewelled glasses perched on his long nose. There was the vaguest hint of a smile on his face but he didn't give in to it.

Luke moved to the pick-up counter and paid. He had spotted Shannia right away. She was in the corner furthest from the door. The over-sized sunglasses perched on her nose made her look like a Hollywood star hiding from the paparazzi.

Luke picked up his coffee and crossed to the table.

"Shan?" he said

The blonde looked up from the table. Seeing Luke, she jumped to her feet and flung herself into his arms. Reflexively, Luke hugged her back, giving her a shoulder to cry on. They stood that way for a minute.

"What happened?"

Shan drew in a slow deep breath.

"Jax's working at the club."

"Okay," Luke said waiting for her to go on.

"I found out about it on Saturday and I stopped him from going."

Luke didn't say anything. That explained why the club had called him to fill in. He started to relax. This wasn't so bad. Of course, Shan would be mad that her younger brother was stripping at Spanky's but it wasn't a reason to go off the deep end. Shan had put herself through nursing school working at Spanky's. Luke had done the same thing.

He muttered, "Hello pot. I'm kettle."

"What?" Shan demanded.

"Just saying, you can't freak on the kid for doing something that you did yourself."

Shan gulped in a big breath. She pulled her glasses off, revealing swollen, bright blue eyes.

"I also found a baggy of ecstasy in the pocket of his jeans." Shan glared at him accusingly.

"Did you ask him about it?" Luke asked gently.

"No. I couldn't."

Of course, she couldn't. Back in the day when Luke and Shan worked at Spanky's, her boyfriend Evan had been the star attraction. Evan—the life of the party—he made them all laugh and forget their problems. Unfortunately, Evan's happy-go-lucky personality was fueled by whatever drug he could get his hands on. Shan had called Evan out on his drug use and look what happened.

"I can't do this. Last night he didn't come home. I was working nights. I know he wasn't there this morning when I got home," Shan whispered. Her eyes welled with tears.

"You don't know, Shan. When did you find the drugs?"

"This morning."

"There's more to the story than this. Don't be so quick to jump to conclusions," Luke said.

Shannia glared at him. "Look, this isn't my first rodeo. I—" she stopped. Her face froze into what Luke privately called her bitch face expression. It was a cold guarded look that said *Go away*. It was protection when she was feeling vulnerable.

"What?" Luke said.

He started to turn around but Shannia broke out in another round of sobbing. Luke sighed and stood up, moving around the table to wrap her in a hug. She was soaking the front of his button up shirt and snotting all over his tie. Now he'd have to go home and change his shirt after Shan was done with her meltdown. Awkwardly, he patted Shan's back and wished he was with Fran.

Chapter 28

The imaginary elephant that had been sitting on Fran's chest had finally gotten up and left. She hadn't realized how much the distance between her and Luke had affected her. How much she really missed him. Now, with the sun casting a soft glow over Port Fling and a new sense of peace in her heart, she strolled Main Street, revelling in how truly beautiful her town was.

The warmth of the Friday evening acted like bait in a trap luring the people of Port Fling out of their homes in droves. Everyone wanted to grab one last chance to get out and enjoy the last of the sun before the rains came. The usually friendly town was practically vibrating with good will.

Fran stepped around a double stroller and avoided a runny-nosed toddler. A pair of new moms and dads had stopped on the sidewalk to 'ooh' and "*ahh*' over each-others' bundles of joy. Two senior couples were facing off on the life-sized chess board in the town square. Their good-natured calls of '*gotcha*!' and '*darn, I never saw that move coming!*' echoed behind Fran as she made her way down the street. She was over the moon happy—and sappy. She felt as if she was in a musical, that any second, the whole town would break into song and dance. She laughed out loud. What was it about Luke that made her so corny?

Her elation ebbed, microscopically draining away as she stepped closer to the Bull Market Café. *Don't order a small, it's a tall. Do not screw this up,* she told herself. *Say tall, not 'small'.*

Elliott the town 'coffee Nazi', or 'bean purist' as he liked to refer to himself, believed coffee grammar was more important than breathing. Fran thought Elliot was not only a bit of a jerk, but mildly terrifying as well. He'd held a high-pressure job as a Wall Street stock-broker before leaving New York to come to Port Fling to supposedly take it easy and enjoy the slower pace of life. The problem was, Elliott didn't know the meaning of easy or slow. Everything in his world was intensely intense and efficient, like a male Martha Stewart on steroids.

There was a right way to order coffee and a wrong way, no in-between. God forbid some poor unsuspecting tourist enter the shop and order a 'small' instead of a 'tall.' Fran had made that mistake. She shuddered remembering the dressing down Elliot had handed her. She'd been banned from the café for weeks!

She took a deep breath as her hand closed around the metal door-knob, and silently prayed Elliot wasn't there. Ah, she was in luck! It was Lucy at the counter, the sweeter-than-pie barista who was the *yang* who brought some much-needed goodness to Elliott's *yin*.

"Hey Fran, great to see you! How are you?" asked Lucy, her entire face lighting up as though Fran was her favourite person in the world.

"I'm wonderful, Lucy. How are you?" returned Fran, matching the beam on Lucy's face.

"Good, good." Lucy's smile wattage amplified. "The usual?"

"You've got it," confirmed Fran with a nod.

The 'usual' was Elliott's famous Macchiato, which he swore he was the first to invent, a supposed fact which he was currently in the process of suing a large coffee chain over. Elliott was also mildly delusional.

"Here you go, Fran," said Lucy, passing Fran's drink across the counter.

'No! No! There's no way the Paradise blend is a proper dark roast!" Elliott's voice carried from the back. "Listen to me! Did your mother drop you on your fucking head when you were an infant? Because I think you have some fucking brain damage! There's NO fucking way that's a fucking dark roast!"

The conversation ended with the sound of a phone slamming down.

"Well, I think that's my cue to leave," said Fran, her eyebrows raised.

Lucy smiled and shrugged. "Just like any other day, full of *f-bombs*."

Fran laughed and turned away from the counter. She scurried to the back of the coffee house. She wanted to get as far away from Elliott and his *'f-bombs'* as possible.

There was a couple locked in an embrace standing by her usual table in the back corner. Only a trace of the man's profile was visible, but she'd recognize him anywhere. Her stomach lurched like a sinking boat. Luke! No, it couldn't be. Someone nudged her to move, to step aside and let them pass, but Fran's feet were rooted to the floor, her eyes locked on Luke and the trashy bottle-blonde he was hugging. Fran swallowed the taste of bile. Luke's hand was rubbing up and down the blonde's back, his arms holding her close.

Sure, he was going to meet one of the advisors. He had played her. She was such a gullible idiot. Of course, Dr. Lucas Tanner wouldn't be a one-woman kind of man. He could have any woman he wanted and apparently what he wanted was a blonde who looked like a super-model.

"Hey, don't just stand there. You're holding people up."

Elliot's booming voice caught the blonde's attention. Her gaze met Fran's with a look that said, "He's mine."

You can have him, Fran thought.

She gasped feeling physical pain. *No, no, no.* She had to get out of here before she made a fool of herself, before she suffered an epic meltdown in the middle of the Bull Cafe. Blindly, she stumbled towards the door. She dropped Elliot's famous Macchiato in a garbage can on the way out. *Damn you Luke Tanner. How could you do this?*

Chapter 29

"I'll call him," Luke said squatting down to meet Shan's eyes through the lowered window of the Mustang convertible. He couldn't help glancing at his watch.

Shan looked back at him, reached up and lowered her sunglasses so that he could see her eyes. Her bloodshot, swollen eyes. He winced.

"He respects you. He'll listen to you, Luke."

"I'll go home and do it right now," Luke soothed. Shan looked better but she was still on edge, still scared and sad. Damn Evan. The guy had had a great future, an awesome girl and a brilliant mind. He'd been a good friend too. He'd blown it all in a minute, partying with a bunch of guys he figured were living the life—women, blow, booze.

"He's not Evan."

"I know. It's just . . . I don't know, call it PTSD. It brings it all back, and . . . I don't want it to be Jax."

"It won't be. Jax and I have talked about Evan and what happened. Evan was a 22-year-old idiot, we all were. You can't guard Jax every minute. He's growing up."

Shan grimaced and shoved the glasses up her nose. She started the engine, let it idle and looked back at Luke.

"Please just call him," she said.

Luke nodded. Shan put the muscle car in drive. Engine growling, the car pulled away from the curb. Luke watched her turn the corner and disappear from sight. Damn. Now he had to go home, change his snotty shirt and talk to Jax, when all he wanted to do was go see Fran. He crossed the road, climbed into his car, and settled his Bluetooth device onto his ear. He found Jax's number in his phone list and dialed. Jax picked up on the first ring.

"Luke! I'm not using drugs! I don't even smoke weed! You have to tell Shan to back off or I'm moving out!"

Luke slid into a space behind a dump truck and turned his jeep towards his house. He started laughing.

"How the hell did you do that—figured out why I was calling before I said anything?"

"Because Shan always calls you when she's freaking out about something. Why doesn't she just ask me? Why doesn't she trust me?"

"Come on Jax. You know why."

"Evan." Jax was silent for a second, and then, "The guy was a loser. She should just write him off as a mistake."

"Hard to forget a boyfriend you did CPR on in the locker-room at a strip joint," Luke said mildly.

"Yeah, I guess so. Look, J-Dawg gave me the E. I was going to flush it but I forgot about it."

"I figure it was something like that. So, what's with you and Spanky's?"

Luke could almost hear Jax's shrug through the phone.

"*Meh,* it's nothing. I don't know if it's for me. Good money, but probably not worth the hassle factor. Crystal freaked when she heard I did it."

"Crystal?"

"My girlfriend."

"That new?" Luke asked. He turned into his driveway and parked.

Jax talked for a few minutes about college and Crystal and they ended the call. Luke was smiling as he walked into his house. Jax was fine. He had his head on straight. He'd call Shan later and tell her to back off.

***

Luke changed into jeans and a white t-shirt, grabbed his wallet and phone and headed over to Fran's. He passed a convenience store selling flowers and wine on the way and stopped and went inside. One full wall of the store showcased flowers, enormous bouquets of them. He didn't know what types of flowers they were, but he figured Fran would like the bright oranges, reds and yellows. The wine was red. She'd probably like that touch of colour as well. He paid for his purchases and got back into his car.

He parked in front of the tiny rancher Fran rented, picked up his purchases and walked to the front door. He didn't see Fran's beater car anywhere, but he'd said he'd be a while, so he figured she must have stopped somewhere on the way home. No matter. It was nice sitting on the porch. The sun was shining, the birds chirping. Across the road a couple of kids were playing basketball. Luke put the flowers in the shade and leaned back on his elbows. He'd wait. His stomach rumbled. Maybe she'd stopped for groceries. He smiled picturing Fran bustling around the kitchen wearing nothing but a frilly apron. Down boy. He shook his head. He had it bad.

***

Fran cradled her phone in one hand and one of Sunny's *Knock-you-on-your-ass margaritas* in the other.

"Oh look, another text from Professor Asshole," Fran held up her phone to show Sunny. "I can't even look at these anymore. He's texting me as if everything is fine. As if he wasn't just in the arms of some other woman.

Where are you Fran? she mocked, reading the texts out to Sunny.

What's wrong baby? I'm at your house with flowers and wine. I miss you.

Two hours ago, I would have drunk up these lies. Pathetic!" She threw her phone across the room. "Now all I want to drink is this margarita." She held up her glass for more and Sunny complied.

"So, let me get this straight: Danger Dark is actually Professor Tanner, *the* Professor Tanner who your placement is with?" Sunny checked, gulping her drink.

"The very one."

"And you're sure it's just not another stripper alias of his? Like, he's really a world-renowned chemist?" Sunny couldn't seem to wrap her mind around the fact that Danger was Professor Luke Tanner.

"Yep. He's a gorgeous, world-renowned chemist-slash-stripper who could have any woman he wanted, so why would he stick with just me?" Fran choked out. The numbness was fading and the alcohol was kicking in, making her even more emotional.

"What? Why would he stick with you Fran? Are you joking? He'd stick with you because you're freaking gorgeous and super-smart and funny and kind. Do you want me to go on, because I will?" Sunny gestured, sloshing some of her margarita over the side of her glass.

"Thanks, Sun." Fran smiled weakly.

Sunny stood and grabbed the pitcher of margaritas, topping up both their glasses. "We need a plan," she declared.

"A plan?"

"Yes, a plan. You need to punish him, to make him suffer." Sunny paced the room, drink in hand.

"Yes!" Fran stood and stumbled slightly. "But how?"

"Hmmm, let's see." Sunny tapped her glass. "You should look super-hot, show some cleavage. Not enough to seem obvious but enough to make him sweat. And be cool, act like you guys were never an item. Treat him like he's just your nerdy Professor, like he means nothing."

"Yes!" Fran agreed. "He has a weird thing about red lipstick!"

"Then pile it on." Sunny grinned wickedly. "And most importantly, whatever you do, don't admit you saw him with that blonde bimbo. Don't give him the satisfaction of knowing that he hurt you. Make him believe you just changed your mind, you were bored of him."

"Ugh, how am I going to pull this off Sunny? I'm a terrible liar."

"No problem, honey. I'll set the stage for you. Give me your phone." Sunny held out her hand, "I think it's time we sent Professor Tanner some texts."

Chapter 30

Hi Beautiful. We seemed to have our wires crossed. I'm at your place thinking about you and waiting to see you again. Luke texted.

He had called Fran's cell but it had gone straight to voice mail. Maybe the battery had died. He took a sip of the wine he'd poured into the empty Starbucks cup from his car. Thank God for screw lid wine bottles, he thought silently toasting the air. But where the hell was Fran?

His phone pinged. He grabbed it and eagerly read the message.

I'm running a little late. Wait for me. [heart, kissy face, winky face] I'm so hot for you.

That one made his eyebrows raise. He smiled. "Oh baby, you have no idea," he muttered. He wouldn't have expected Fran to write that. She was usually more careful, a little more uptight. He sighed and took another sip. At least she had finally gotten back to him.

Baby, I can't wait to see you. Let's skip dinner and go straight to dessert. He grinned and added, **I have a special treat for you.**

The phone pinged again as he was reaching for the wine bottle.

Sweet cheeks, I'm thinking about dessert. I'm looking for some special toppings just for you. [cat face with heart eyes, lips, tongue] **Don't worry. I'm coming.** [heart, heart, tongue, lips]

Luke frowned. He wouldn't have pegged Fran as an icon-happy kind of girl. He shrugged and leaned back on his elbows. I'm coming. Yeah, you will be baby. He smiled and drained his cup.

"Excuse me." An elderly couple stood at the edge of the grass. They wore matching windbreakers and corresponding frowns. "Are you looking for Francesca?"

Luke sat up. "She's on her way. She says she'll be here in a minute." Luke held up his phone.

The couple looked doubtful. The woman's mouth pinched into a tight frown of disapproval. "You aren't planning on drinking and driving, are you? You've finished that bottle and I have to tell you, I will be calling the police if I see you get behind the wheel."

"Yes, ma'am, I mean, no I won't be driving. I'm not going anywhere."

He grinned. Nope. He was going to be right here, waiting for his dessert. Screw supper. He wasn't hungry for food anyway.

"Well, see that you don't." The woman straightened and latched onto her husband's arm, towing him away from Luke and the drunken debauchery taking place on the porch.

Luke looked down at the wine bottle. He reached down and tipped it up, pouring the last few dribbles into his cup. Good thing Fran was on her way home. He was feeling a bit of a buzz. Sitting in the sun drinking a bottle of wine by yourself wasn't the best idea. He looked at his phone again. He'd missed another text.

Oh baby, are you ready for me? I'm ready for you. Hottt, wetttt, aching . . . [tongue, tongue, red lips]

What was with the Fran the porn star texts? He screwed the lid back onto the bottle and set it neatly beside the bouquet of summer flowers he'd bought for her. They were starting to wilt in the heat. Come to think of it, he was starting to wilt in the heat.

Sweetie are you going to be much longer? he sent.

This time it probably took her fifteen minutes to get back to him.

Sorry, they have a sale on at Victoria's Secret. I'll be there soon. I promise. [kissy face, kissy winky face, heart]

Luke looked down at the time on his phone—eight-thirty. There wasn't even a Victoria's Secret store in Port Fling. What the hell was she doing? He sat on the porch for another half an hour but Fran didn't appear. The older couple did, walking slowly past the house, looking pointedly from the bottle to the car.

Hey Fran, you must have gotten hung up somewhere. I'm going to head out. I'll see you tomorrow. His finger hovered over the heart icon. What the hell, he added it and pressed send. That was a first for him. Icons weren't his thing, but if that's what Fran wanted, he'd add sappy emojis to everything he wrote.

It was a nice evening. He'd walk home. It would help him walk off the buzz from the wine, maybe cure some of his sexual frustration.

As he was walking his phone pinged with another text from Fran:

This isn't going to work babes. You're being waaaay too clingy for me. I'm bored. No hard feelings? [thumbs up, margarita, balloon]

What the hell? Luke felt like he'd been hit by a bus. Was she serious? She had to be joking. This didn't sound like Fran at all. He dialed her number but it went straight to voicemail. He walked faster, calling the number again, this time leaving a message.

"Hey Fran, it's Luke. I just got your text. Are you serious? Did I do something? We need to talk. Call me. Please."

He hung up and jogged the last few blocks to his house. Opening the door, he stepped inside and caught a glimpse of his reddened face in the mirror. This couldn't be happening. For the first time in his life, he'd actually opened up and let someone in, and now, she was going to stomp on his heart and throw him away?

He jumped as his phone pinged again:

Leave me alone Luke. I don't want to talk to you. Get a hint. You're annoying AF.

No emojis this time. She was definitely serious. He felt like he was going to be sick. She'd played him and he had fallen for it like some stupid lovesick kid.

Chapter 31

Fran blew a chunk of hair out of her eyes and reached for another beaker. The long rubber gloves were too big for her and they were making her fingers prune up. Luke thought he was going to make her quit by putting her on dish duty, hah! He had no idea what after dinner clean up looked like in the Romano household. Washing fifty beakers was child's play compared to a full dinner service for twelve, or eighteen for that matter. There were always a few strays kicking around.

"Hey Fran." Monica called from behind her. "We're going for drinks, want to join us?"

"No, thanks though. I still need to wash down all this equipment. Boss's orders." Fran gave a weak smile. With Sunny's help, she had sent Luke some drunken texts after she'd seen him at the coffee shop with blondie. Needless to say, things had been 'awkward AF between them' (as Sunny would say). At first, Fran had almost felt a bit guilty. Luke had appeared genuinely sad—like a little puppy— probably hoping to lure her back in. But Fran's guilt quickly faded. When his sad act didn't work, he'd decided to change tactics and push her out by piling on the menial tasks.

"Wow, you really must have *rubbed* Professor Tanner the wrong way," Lyndsey tittered joining Monica. The suggestive smirk on her face made Fran itch to wipe it off.

"Lyndsey, be nice!" warned Monica. "Just leave it, Fran. I'll come in early tomorrow and help you. So will Lyndsey." Monica gave Lyndsey a pointed look.

"Sure, whatever." Lyndsey waved Monica off. "Let's just get out of here. I need a drink."

So did Fran. She hadn't been sleeping well and had barely been able to force any food down. She felt as worn as an old shoe. She looked down at the sudsy water and tray of beakers remaining and started to shake her head no. A spark of lost backbone broke through her pity party. Nope, she was done, she was pulling the plug on kitchen duty for the day.

"Okay, twist my rubber arm. I'm in." Shrugging off her lab coat, Fran balled it up and threw it in the hamper.

"Where to?" she asked grabbing her sweater.

"Bookends," Lyndsey smiled and licked her lips. "It's delicious. There's a bunch of navy guys here taking some courses in engineering. Can you say *freee* drink night?"

Fran laughed. From what she'd seen of Lyndsey so far, drinks and parties were what she was all about . . . and stories. Lyndsey was more connected than Google. She had the dirt on everyone and spread it lavishly, layering it on, twisting it into clever little rhymes and innuendos. Right now, she was having a field day with Sarah's sordid love affair with her married man, and Luke's need for sensitivity training. She'd even speculated that Professor Tanner had his own secret life, a married woman or two on the side. Fran rolled her eyes—if only she knew.

Bookends was on the other side of the campus from the lab, near the offices and library. The late afternoon sun was warm on Fran's face and the scent of the flowers blooming in the gardens bordering the sidewalk heavy in the air. It felt good to get outside and breathe something other than chemicals. The laminar flow hoods and exhaust fans were always going but sometimes the air still felt a little stale.

The bar was the worst kept secret on campus. The place was a dive; full of dark, cobweb-filled corners and sticky tables but the drinks were cheap and it was always crowded with students looking to blow off some steam.

"What are you having, ladies? I'll buy," Lyndsey offered as they pulled up some mismatched chairs to a round table.

"Bloody Mary." Monica answered.

"I'll have the same please," Fran echoed.

"Coming right up." Lyndsey grinned and headed off to the bar.

She muscled her way in front of a short blonde wearing a soccer team sweatshirt and sidled up to a tall clean-shaven man who looked like a weed in a hipster garden. The guy probably didn't even own a plaid shirt, Fran mused.

"Hey!" Monica elbowed, pulling her back to reality.

"Hey yourself." Fran playfully returned the elbow.

"What's going on between you and Tanner?" Monica asked abruptly.

"You don't waste any time, do you?" Fran hedged, chuckling nervously. She had known that at some point she would have to answer this question. The tension between her and Luke must be palpable to everyone working in the lab. Hell, if you turned out the lights, you would probably see the sparks flying between them.

"Nothing's up." Fran shrugged, trying to appear nonchalant. "Tanner just took an instant dislike to me and tried to get me transferred out. Instead of rolling over and admitting defeat like he wanted, I fought back. And now he's pissed and making my life hell." Fran crossed her fingers under the table at the lie.

"He can be such a jerk." Monica shook her head. "I had a feeling he wasn't going to like you. Like I said, you're too pretty and our last couple of pretty students didn't have a lot going on upstairs."

Fran opened her mouth to protest but Monica held up her hand.

"I'm not saying you're that way, Fran. You clearly know your way around the lab. I just think Tanner took one look at you and made up his mind. The weird thing is, I thought you guys had smoothed things over. When I talked to him the other week it seemed like you two had reached an understanding? But I guess not. You'll just have to keep working on changing his mind."

"I'll try, but I don't know. I'm thinking it might just be easier to transfer." Fran sighed. Two weeks ago, she would have never uttered those words. If she had, she would have voluntarily taken a dose of Nonna's special secret Sicilian cure-all. She had worked so hard to get this specific placement . . . Right. That was before she had unknowingly started a sexual relationship with her Prof. Now the thought of going through a full year with Luke, without the forbidden sexual relationship, seemed impossible.

"Hang in there." Monica gave Fran's shoulder a squeeze.

"Thanks." Fran quickly blinked away the moisture pooling in her eyes, wishing she could tell Monica the whole story.

"Drinks, ladies." Lyndsey interrupted, appearing with the round of Bloody Marys.

"Cheers." They clanked glasses and took a sip.

"Alright, ladies, let's talk some work gossip." Lyndsey grinned.

Fran tensed. She did not want to talk to Lyndsey about Luke. She didn't trust her like she did Monica.

"Did you guys see that perv Etherridge drooling at the cheerleaders practice the other day? *Gaw*, the guy is so *skeevy*," Lyndsey shuddered.

"I don't know. I don't think he's that bad." Monica shrugged and looked down at her stubby nails.

"Not that bad? Are you kidding me? You know how they say people resemble their pets? I heard Etherridge has a ferret. Fits perfectly!" Lyndsey did an impression of a ferret with her hands up and lower lip tucked in.

"That's so true!" Fran laughed. "He does look like a ferret!"

"Guys, come on. Have some respect." Monica scolded. "This is one of the most brilliant minds of our time you're talking about here, and I think he's kinda . . . cute."

"What?" Lyndsey howled, slamming her hands on the table, making the glasses jump. "Cute? You're joking! You're a total freak if you actually think Etherridge is cute."

Even in the dark bar, Fran could see Monica's face coloring. Her green eyes looked hurt.

"He is very smart and he's not totally hideous looking." Fran tried to be diplomatic and came to Monica's rescue. Privately, she had to agree with Lyndsey. The guy gave her the creeps.

"See Lyndsey, Fran thinks he's cute too, I'm not a freak." Monica stuck out her tongue like a first grader.

"Fran did not say he was cute Monica. She said he wasn't totally hideous, which is just another way of saying he's a total *skeev*. Right Fran?" Lyndsey questioned, pulling Fran smack into the middle of their debate.

Fran hated being the one to decide an argument, especially when she just couldn't agree with her friend. Growing up, her brothers had used the same trick—divide and conquer— use her support to win what ever argument they were having. No, this time, she wasn't going to get sucked in. It was better to be a fence sitter when it came to subjects like this, where someone's feelings were at stake.

"I think he's not totally hideous. You both make valid points," answered Fran diplomatically.

"Thank you, Fran," said Monica, winking.

"Oh whatever, Fran. That's was a politician's answer if I ever did hear one." Lyndsey waved Fran off and started gossiping about Sarah, the emotional lab tech whose life sounded as drama-filled as an episode of *General Hospital.*

Fran sipped her drink and watched Monica regain her composure. Was there something going on between Monica and Etherridge? Etherridge and Monica? Fran's nose wrinkled. No way. She discarded the thought. Etherridge was way too uptight to risk a clandestine relationship.

"Right, Fran?"

Fran looked back at Lyndsey. She looked annoyed and impatient.

"Uh, right," Fran answered tentatively.

"Ooh, do tell," Lyndsey said sitting back in her chair.

"Do tell what?" Fran said suddenly nervous.

Monica shook her head in disgust and gulped down the rest of her Bloody Mary.

"Lyndsey thinks you and Dr. Tanner are getting it on," she said.

"Oh my god. No!" Fran said in horror. "No Lyndsey, we are not!" They weren't, Fran told herself. Not anymore. That made it true, right?

Lyndsey looked disappointed. She huffed out an impatient breath. "What*ever.* You guys are lame. I'm going to find some action." She stood and headed back towards the bar. A Navy officer was standing near it with a few of his friends. Lyndsey headed in that direction.

Fran turned back to Monica and found two more Bloody Marys had arrived. Monica shrugged apologetically.

"I needed a drink," she said and took a big gulp.

Fran agreed wholeheartedly. Why did she have the feeling that she'd just dodged a bullet. She didn't trust Lyndsey. Too bad the girl had come out for drinks with them. She had a bad feeling that the Luke discussion wasn't over. When it came to compromising information, Lyndsey was a super computer, spitting out the dirt when she needed to spin some truly malicious gossip. Fran should have stayed in the lab cleaning beakers.

"You know Winston isn't a bad person," Monica said quietly.

Fran looked at her.

"He's lonely. He had his PhD by the time he was twenty-one. He didn't learn how to interact with people so he comes off over-bearing. On top of that, he grew up with a mother who was snobbish and clingy."

"Uh huh," Fran said non-committedly. She did not want to be having this conversation.

Monica took another gulp, drained the glass and signalled the waitress for another.

Fran looked down at her half-empty glass and debated whether to join her in one more. What the hell, she'd catch the bus home.

Monica talked on about Winston, his loneliness, his passion for time management strategies. Fran stared at Monica in disbelief.

"Um, Monica . . . are you and Professor Etherridge . . ." Fran's voice trailed off and she gave her head a little shake.

Monica stared her down. "No." She paused and straightened in her chair. "No more than you and Professor Tanner are doing it," she added defensively.

"You and Professor Tanner are doing it?" Lyndsey dropped into her chair at the table. "Oh man, that's a juicy little morsel."

"Lyndsey you can't tell anyone," Monica said, adding fuel to the other girl's gossip fire.

"No, Lyndsey, we're not, it's not!" Fran protested.

The smirk on Lyndsey's face made Fran sick.

"Oh whatever, Fran, relax! I won't tell anyone. You girls are boring me, I'm heading out with my new friends," she said, leaning over to grab her sweater. "See you Monday." She winked and left to join the group of navy officers leaving the bar.

"Oh my god. What the hell, Monica?"

"Oh Fran, I'm so, so sorry. I didn't mean for her to hear that." Monica looked worried. "Umm, Fran?"

"What?"

"You might want to think about some damage control. Lyndsey kinda has a big, okay huge, mouth." Monica added under breath, "At least she didn't hear me say Winston and I are a thing."

"Great. Thanks for the warning Monica, unfortunately it's a little late." Fran drained her drink, grabbed her purse and sweater, and stood.

She had the same terrible feeling she got when a chemical equation went horribly wrong, like something was about to go boom.

Chapter 32

Monica was standing beside the centrifuge 5000 as Luke entered the lab. She lifted the clip board she'd been recording data on, glanced at Luke and turned back to her work.

Good, Luke thought, walking past her to reach his office. He didn't need to listen to Monica's relationship advice. He closed the door firmly, but not hard enough for it to be considered a slam.

He'd seen the back of Fran's pony-tailed head as he'd passed through the room. She was wearing her hair sky high—high enough to swing back and forth like an angry cat's tail. He'd bet money that she was wearing a sexy pout with her power lipstick again too. Do Me Baby red, he thought sourly. There should be a law against hot, red lipstick. He'd never thought about that before, but now it was all he could think about.

Fran was making him crazy. His desk was covered in papers. He'd forgotten about Winston's weekly special taskforce meeting yesterday, and he'd actually agreed to let Zack have even more space for his 'chemistry experiment.' He was screwed.

He sank into his chair and rubbed his hands through his hair. It had been one week since Fran had stopped talking to him—stopped talking, stopped smiling, stopped touching. One week since he'd sat on her porch for two hours waiting for her to show up. One week since he'd finally given up and gone home, since she'd dropped the bomb on him—the Dear Luke, I'm dumping you by text bomb. Like a dumbass, he'd never even seen it coming. He snorted. Right, he was clingy, she was bored. She didn't have the guts to tell him in person. She could barely make eye contact with him.

Why? He thought they were on the same page. What had he done?

He shoved a stack of papers to one side and picked up a pen. He hadn't done anything. A week ago, he thought they were on the mend and then suddenly, for some unknown reason, they weren't. She was treating him exactly like she was supposed to treat a prof who was responsible for grading her in a set-in stone A, B, or C scale—although with Fran, he wanted to use a modified bell curve.

No . . . stop. He shook his head. He had to quit thinking about Fran that way. She didn't want him. She had made that abundantly clear. No more unprofessional thoughts. No more trying to pick the best spot to check out the hint of black lace that her V-necked shirt revealed. No more acting like a sulky high schooler in lust with a cheerleader, hoping her pompoms slipped. What she wore didn't matter. He had to focus on her credentials and try to act more like Winston. Maybe he should send out an email with a list of expectations for deportment during laboratory operating hours.

Luke stood and grabbed his lab coat. Pulling it on, he resolved that from this second onward he was going to start behaving like the highly-trained professional he was. He opened the door and stepped into the lab. Two lab techs standing beside Fran broke off their animated discussion and scattered when they saw him.

Luke growled under his breath.

"Did you say something, Dr. Tanner?" Fran asked coolly. She crossed her arms at her chest. The movement lifted her breasts and the black lace was no longer just a hint.

Luke gulped. "No . . . I forgot something in my office." He bolted.

Alone in his office, he sagged against his desk. What the hell was the matter with him? One glimpse of black lace and he was done. Damn, but what a glimpse. That's it. He straightened. He was sending a memo on proper dress code for the lab. Fran knew exactly what she was doing to him. The little smirk on her face made that abundantly clear. Why though? That was the question that he needed to answer. Why wouldn't she talk to him?

Damn. He was so desperate for advice that he'd even called Sunny to see if she knew what was going on. Sunny, hah, that was a misnomer if he had ever heard one. Sunny had been colder than the most wintery day—the most wintery day in Nome, Alaska that is. Sunny had greeted him with a frosty hello and then told him that she wasn't interested in pursuing their friendship. Pursuing their friendship? What the hell was that supposed to mean. Sunny ended the conversation with, "Why don't you and J-Dawg go find a couple of icy blonde bimbos? Neither one of you have a clue how to treat real women, especially hot-blooded Italian women." She had hung up before he could say anything.

He hadn't even known that Sunny was Italian, he brooded. And why did that matter anyway? Luke rested his chin on his fist and looked down at his desk. The hand-delivered letter that he'd received from the ethics board made things even worse:

Dear Professor Tanner,

> *It's come to our attention that Francesca Romano, the PhD student placed in your lab at the beginning of the semester is requesting transfer to another position. We are concerned that her request marks the failure of yet another grad student to complete their mentorship schedule. Ms. Romano is the fourth grad student in the past two years who has been unable or unwilling to remain in a working environment overseen by you.*

The university frowns on any form of harassment, mental or physical and will be conducting a thorough review of your file. In the meantime, please let us know if there are any courses we can offer you in the way of further sensitivity training that will facilitate a smoother working relationship with the students.

Sincerely,

Harriet Flett

Ethics Board Chair

He crumped the paper and tossed it overhand at the overflowing can in the corner of the room. Yup. His golden record sure tarnished fast. What was he supposed to do with that letter—write back and pinkie swear he'd be all nice and give every grad student a gold star? What were they, a bunch of toddlers? If PhD students couldn't cut it in a real lab, it wasn't his problem.

One thing for sure, he wasn't going to beg Fran to stay. He would make up a reason for her wanting to leave and spin it in such a way that Winston would buy it. God, he covered his face and groaned. He had to fix this. *Fix this*, he sighed. If he knew a way to do that he wouldn't be sitting on his ass doodling Fran's name on a lab report.

Someone cleared their throat. Luke glanced up at the door.

"I knocked," Fran said defensively. She glanced down at the report and her mouth twitched into an almost smile. She supressed it. "You look like you need a moment. Would you like me to come back later?"

"No," Luke said. The word came out shorter and snappier than he meant it to. He couldn't help it. He was tired and unhappy and Fran was . . . Fran was gorgeous, untouchable and as hot as fire. Damn. He slouched lower in his chair.

"I have the stats you wanted."

She stayed by the door, making him stand and come to her. It put him at a disadvantage and he didn't like it. In fact, he didn't like any of this, but two could play this game. He could be just as professional and detached as she was. He stood. Fran took a tiny step back. Was she checking him out?

Interesting. He stretched. Alright, it was a patented stripper move but it got Fran's attention. She shoved the sheath of papers towards him and her fingers touched his. A jolt of energy shot through his hand.

Fran huffed out a tiny sound of shock and jerked her hand back. The papers fluttered from her open fingers and blanketed the floor.

"Shit," Fran muttered, dropping to her knees to pick them up.

"Leave it. I'll get them," Luke said stepping towards her.

"No, it's okay, I have them."

Luke half-bent towards her meaning to take the papers from her. She looked up at the same time. Her mouth dropped open in an expression of surprise. The Do Me red lipstick was killing him. All he could think of was—

"*Doctor* Tanner!" Winston Etherridge the III blocked the doorway, his stocky body forming a wall graffitied in brown tweed and dun corduroy, topped with a nattily tied green and yellow spotted cravat. "I had *no* idea that this type of behaviour was taking place here. Ms. Romano, this is dreadful. No wonder you have asked for a transfer from this lab. Forgive me for doubting your reasoning."

Fran got up off her knees and climbed awkwardly to her feet. Her face was as red as the bow she tied around her cat, Princess Fiona's neck. A sheet of paper rested near the door, behind Winston's left foot. Fran bent, scooped it up, tucked it into the pile and placed the stack on Luke's desk. She gave Luke a look he couldn't interpret and bolted from the room.

Winston closed the door. "Well? What do you have to say for yourself? The university takes a very dim view on sexual harassment. We have strict guidelines dictating the standards of behavior we expect our professors to adhere to. This is highly inappropriate." He flopped into the chair beside the desk and overcome by Luke's lapse from grace, fanned his face with his hand.

"This is not what it looks like," Luke cut in. There was another sheet of paper beside Winston's shoe. Luke nodded towards it. "Ms. Romano tripped and dropped a stack of papers. She was picking them up—papers. She dropped papers." He bent down and picked the paper off the floor. "She tripped." Luke could feel his cheeks reddening. "She was picking them up," he repeated.

Winston shook his head. "I will speak with her and see what she has to say about the situation, although . . ." Winston thought for a moment. "I don't understand how you are able to work when you allow your lab people to wear red lipstick and such low-cut shirts. I had hoped you would have learned your lesson after the debacle with Ms. Mathers. It's not acceptable deportment for a university lab environment. Your staff should dress more like Monica. Perhaps she can speak with Ms. Romano regarding acceptable work wear. Yes, I'll speak with Monica." Winston nodded decisively and lurched to his feet. "I shall deal with you later." He patted the thin comb-over of hair flat against his head and sailed out of the room. Luke could hear him calling to Monica.

Luke closed his eyes. This wasn't happening. It was bad enough Winston was going after him, but he had a career. He could weather Winston's remarks, Monica would back him up.

What about Fran? She only had her academic background to protect her. If Winston went after her, her future could be tarnished before she even got started. He closed his eyes. This couldn't be happening.

Chapter 33

Fran splashed ice cold water over her face and looked up at her reflection in the mirror. Her eyes were ringed with deep, dark circles. Her usual rosy complexion looked dry and dull with permanent frown lines developing around her mouth. It had not been a good week. No, that was an understatement, it had been an awful, terrible, hellish week all rolled into one.

She had thought it couldn't get any worse, but now thanks to accidently dumping papers all over the floor, Dr. Etherridge thought she was doling out sexual favours to her mentor. She could lose all her credibility. It would undermine her years of hard work and make her a cheap joke.

Chemistry was a boys' club, and Dr. Etherridge was the leader of that club. He would love the chance to neatly rid his department of his supposed top-ranking female student by writing off her good grades as the result of years of giving all her professors blow-jobs. Her brother Sal would say it gave a whole new meaning to the term 'head of the class.' No, for Etherridge, nothing was better than adding proof to his belief that women weren't meant for the chemistry world.

Damn. Fran needed to talk to Luke and fast. They had to sort this out and get their story straight or both of their careers were going to end in shame and scandal. So far, it had proved impossible to talk to him at the university. The rumours were already spreading like sunburns on a nude beach. Everyone was watching them, waiting for a lingering glance or an inappropriate touch. Yesterday, Fran had overheard someone refer to her as "the swing of Fling, everyone gets a pump." She wanted to throw up. How could things have gone so wrong, so quickly? She had to talk to Luke tonight.

She picked up her phone and looked up the number for Spanky's.

A man answered on the third ring. "Hello Spanky's. Craig speaking."

"Hi there, Craig, I was hoping to come in with some of my girlfriends tonight. Girls' Night yeah!" she tried to instil some peppiness into her voice but it just came out weird. She hurried on, "Anyway we're looking for a good time and we were wondering if our favourite dancer Danger Dark will be working?"

"Hold on, let me check our schedule."

We're looking for a good time? Fran winced, she could feel her cheeks turning red. The guy probably thought she was a whack job, that the ladies were looking for sex. She could hear the sound of papers being shuffled on the other end of the line.

"You're in luck. Danger wasn't supposed to work but another dancer cancelled so he should be filling in."

"Okay, great, thanks," said Fran.

"No problem, see you later."

Fran ended the call and dropped her phone onto the counter. This was good. Luke was working. She'd go to the club and talk to him. They would figure out what to do about this mess. Spanky's was a good place to confront Luke, there would be lots of people around and she could fix this once and for all. It's where everything started and where it should end. A logical conclusion to an experiment gone woefully wrong.

Her phone rang and she glanced down at the call display. Great. Sal. Again. Please, not now, Sal, she silently begged. He'd been texting and calling her more than usual, claiming his twin psychic connection was going crazy.

"What, Sal?" Fran answered abruptly. She wasn't in the mood for Sal's brand of small talk. She didn't want to hear how Manchester United's, Sal's favourite soccer team, season was going.

"What's going on with you and your professor?"

Silence. Fran stared blankly at the phone.

"Fran? I know you're there. What the hell is going on?"

Fran sat down on the edge of the bathtub. Her legs were too rubbery to hold her weight. Could this week get any worse? Yes. The answer was a big fat yes. Sal getting involved amped up the chances of an epic disaster by one hundred percent. Fran closed her eyes in pain.

"I don't know what you're talking about," she hedged, hoping Sal would just go away.

"Yeah, you do, Fran, you bloody well do. Don't try and lie to me."

"Why are you asking me this?" How the hell had Sal gotten a hold of this little tidbit?

"I went for beers at that book place, the campus pub. A couple of guys were talking about the chemistry lab and Professor Puff Ball Tanner, your Professor Puff Ball. They said he was doing his PhD student in exchange for a bump in her grades. They said that she was a hot little Italian who they wouldn't mind taking for a swing."

Fran could hear Sal's rage through the phone.

"Sal, what did you do?" Fran asked unsteadily.

"Nothing," Sal said sullenly. "Mario held me back."

"Mario?" Fran said faintly, stifling a moan. Oh God, if Mario had been there she was really going to hear about it.

"Yeah, Mario shoved the guy and knocked the table over. Beer all over the place. We got tossed out of the bar and banned from going back."

"Sal, that's assault. You can be charged."

"Nah," Sal said. "The guy hit Mario and broke his nose. If there's any assault it's on him."

Another long silence.

"Is it true?" Sal asked softly.

Fran gulped back a sob. "Sal, just leave it alone, okay? I'll fix this. It isn't what you think. Please?"

"I dunno Fran. You told me you were going to handle it before and look what happened. Just let me talk to him. I can straighten this out for you. I know I can."

Fran felt like she was in an elevator, plummeting to the ground. If Sal got involved, it would be catastrophic. She had to choose her next words very carefully.

"Sal, listen to me. I've been a good sister. I've kept my head down and put up with a lot of teasing. I've never asked you for much but I'm literally begging you to leave this alone. If you get involved I will lose this placement and everything I've worked for and I will completely blame you."

It was harsh and not true but she was desperate. Sal was silent for a second and she held her breath, praying it had worked.

"Wow. Okay little sis, I'll back off. But promise me, you'll call if you need anything."

"I will." Fran agreed. "Thanks Sal. Love you."

"Love you too, Franny. Be safe." Sal hung up.

Fran buried her face in her hands for a minute, and then swiped away the tears and turned the water back onto cold. She was going to fix this.

Chapter 34

Luke flicked off the lights in the lab and headed out the door. It was the end to a lousy day, a day that could screw up his career and ruin Fran's before it even started. What the hell was he going to do? Etherridge was going after Fran. Luke knew that. Monica had already warned him Etherridge was scouting around for a new placement for the lab. In fact, he'd found one—male of course. Monica said Winston was doing his happy dance—luckily, she hadn't elaborated on what that meant.

Luke shook his head in distaste. He'd walked into the lab to find old Elliot deep in conversation with Monica. If the guy had a tail, it would have been wagging. Worse—Monica looked like she was enjoying the attention. She'd even been smiling. She'd stopped doing that when she saw Luke's face.

Etherridge had left and Monica had cornered Luke by the Centrifuge 5000.

"Look, Luke, you have to tell Winston, no. He can't replace Fran with Kevin. There is no way that's going to work. It would be like swapping a Ferrari for a 1978 Toyota. Do not let it happen."

"Monica, Fran hates me. She doesn't even talk to me unless it's something to do with statistics."

Monica shook her head violently, pursing her lips in disgust.

"That kiss I saw didn't say that." She looked at him in pity. "For such a brilliant scientist you really are dumb."

"And you're so smart—why? Did you even notice that Winston has the hots for you big time?"

Monica sighed and shook her head again, more gently this time.

"Luke, Luke, Luke, you're so busy being a Rockstar scientist that you've forgotten to be Danger Dark. Sweep that girl off her feet. I'll take care of Winston."

Monica reached into the pocket of her lab coat, pulled out a tube of bright red lipstick and smoothed it over her lips. She made a kissy face at Luke and continued, "If you let Fran go and Kevin replaces her in the lab, you are going to have to look for a new lab manager because I will quit. I've told Winston the same thing. He thinks I'm joking. Don't you make the same mistake." She was out the door before he could answer her.

Luke drove home, mulling over Monica's words. He entered the house to silence and for the first time in his life felt lonely, like he was missing something. The answering machine light was flashing. Only two people called him on the house phone.

He pressed the play button.

"Hey, Danger. Feel like working tonight? The new kid bailed on us again and we're short in the line up. We could really use your help. Call me back. It's Craig." *Beep*.

Luke sighed. He didn't feel like dancing. The last thing he wanted to do was get naked in front of a group of screaming women.

The next message started with, "Lucas Robert Tanner, what on Earth do you think you're doing?"

Only one person in the world called him that. He took a deep breath and waited.

"Call me back now. I'll be at the lab, call my cell." *Beep*.

Great. Could it get any worse? He tossed his keys onto the table and grabbing his cell headed out onto the deck. He may as well get comfortable. Professor Anna Foster only used that tone of voice when she planned on schooling someone. He hadn't heard it since he was an angry thirteen-year-old who'd blown up the apple tree with a home-made explosive. Back then, he'd been a foster kid fresh out of juvie, not the adopted son of Detective and Professor Foster.

He speed-dialed the number. Anna answered on the first ring.

"What's up, Mom?"

"Why do you think something is up? Can't I just call my son for a chat?" Anna asked.

"You could, but I just talked to you on Wednesday so you probably wouldn't."

The woman on the other end of the line laughed. "You know me too well." She paused as though getting her thoughts in order. "I was up in Port Fling today . . ."

"You should have called me, we could have met for lunch."

"No, it was a quick jaunt. I needed to meet with one of my colleagues in the physics lab. The thing is, we got to talking about ethics and managing labs peopled by PhD students, anyways . . . your name came up."

Luke breathed out a sharp breath. He had never shared the fact that his mother was an astrophysicist working with NASA in Seattle. Likewise, Anna kept the information her son was heading the chem lab at the university private. They'd started doing it when Luke was working on his master's degree. They had both agreed that Luke's work should be judged on its own merits, not who his mother was. Anna said there was way too much of that happening in the world of academia. Besides, Luke's dad Brent Foster was a detective with the Seattle police. He'd already taken more than his share of ribbing over being married to a rocket scientist. If word got out that his son was following in Anna's footsteps, he'd never hear the end of being a dumb bunny in a house of *Brainiacs*.

"And?"

"The scuttlebutt is that Dr. Luke Tanner has been getting it on with one of his students."

"Mom," Luke tried to cut in.

"No, no, let me finish because there's more and you've got to hear this."

Was Anna laughing or crying? Luke tightened his grip on his phone and waited.

"I had a phone call this morning. Unknown number, unknown name. It was a voicemail left on my phone. A threatening voicemail."

"What the hell?"

"No, let me finish. The caller was a woman with a heavy Italian accent. She said something like, 'You tell your son to leave my Francesca alone. I call cousin Dario. He fly here and deal with Professor Luke Tanner. *Accura!* You tell your son stay away from my Francesca. She work too hard for your son to kick her from her lab. Family! You warn him. *Ciao*.'"

Luke was silent.

"Oh, and she made sure to tell me that she has links to the Mafia too, so to beware."

"*O-kay*," Luke drew the word out. Anna was laughing openly. "It's not funny."

"But it is. Your dad ran the number and I called it back. Nonna Romano isn't the only one capable of using a little research to find someone."

"Nonna? Fran's grandma?"

"We had a nice chat. Nonna is a lovely woman who's concerned that you have plans to ruin Francesca's career. She told me all about her granddaughter. She sounds like a very sweet girl. Not your usual one-night stand bimbo." Anna's voice hardened.

"What the hell, Mom? Bimbo?"

"At least you didn't meet this one at a strip club." His mom joked.

Luke didn't answer.

"Oh no, no, no. Please tell me that you aren't still working at one."

Luke remained silent. Anna had never liked the fact he'd paid for school by stripping. She and Brent had wanted to pay for everything, but Luke refused their help. He wasn't going to dig into their retirement fund when he had a perfectly legal way of making his own money.

"Honestly, grow up Lucas! You're too old to be working at some low brow strip joint. Do you know what this could do to your career?"

"I know how old I am, and I know how to run my own life, Mom. Anyway, I've got to go. Bye." He hung up without waiting for a reply. Maybe he was a bit harsh but he was a grown man, no one told him what to do. Going back inside, he called the number of the previous message.

"Yeah, Craig, It's Dark, I'll work tonight." He hung up. Screw it. His career would have to handle one last dance.

Chapter 35

Fran dressed with care, wanting to look nice but not too sexy. She wore one of the few power suits that she owned and minimal makeup. Tonight, she needed to draw a very professional line between the two of them. While she wanted to look good, she had to make it clear that she meant business as well. That meant that she had to meet Luke's eyes without letting him see the desire burning in their depths. She couldn't risk giving him the chance to see into her soul, plus, the last thing she needed was to look like a kid confronted by a particularly delicious candy that was impossibly out of reach.

She fed her fur babies and headed out to Priscilla, her beat-up but reliable old Honda. She was going sober and solo tonight, no Sunny. Sunny would just talk her out of ever seeing Luke again, tell her to take a new placement and move on. But Sunny didn't understand how the academic world worked.

If she left Dr. Tanner's lab amidst all these rumours, anything she accomplished from this point on would be tainted.

Fran took her time driving across town. It gave her a chance to rehearse what she planned to say to Luke. No matter what he said or did, she had to keep it together. She had to make him see that if they were going to get through this, they had to present a united front. They were going to have to go to Etherridge and convince him that it was all a misunderstanding. Maybe they could say it was a joke, an early Halloween costume Fran was trying out. Right, she was planning on dressing up like the kind of girl who slept with her prof for marks. She swallowed against the lump in her throat. A broken giggle escaped her. She'd pay to see Etherridge's face if she said that.

The lot at Spanky's was full and she had to park on the road. Damn, she had wanted to park as close to the door as possible. *Get in and out as quick as you can. That way there will be less distance to travel when you're running away from your last meeting with Luke. Less people to see your tears.*

***

The show at Spanky's was in full-swing. Her plan had been to get there early and catch Luke before it started. Now she was going to have to suffer through his dance and then go backstage to see him, all sexy and sweaty and half-naked. It would be so much easier to draw the professional line between them if he was dressed in a puffy jacket and Capri pants, or overalls, something equally unsexy.

Maybe she'd hide in the bathroom during his dance. At least then, she wouldn't have the image of his gorgeous naked body burned in her brain. Although, if she was totally honest with herself, the image of his hot naked body was already burned into her brain. She shook her head trying to shake the desire for Luke out of it. If only if were that easy.

The air in Spanky's was as stifling as a tropical, humid jungle. Fran smirked—if it was a jungle, the ladies were wild cougars. The crowd two weeks ago, were mewling kittens compared to this group. A leather-clad woman next to Fran jumped onto a table in an attempt to launch herself onto the stage.

"You! Get down from there now!" yelled a brawny bouncer in a ripped t-shirt. He grabbed the woman's leather tassels and yanked her off the table. "You're outta here!" he growled, as the clearly drunk patron staggered and tried to wriggle out of his grasp.

"Boo," a bachelorette party of biker chicks hissed as they lost one of their gang. They didn't let their loss affect them for long. A few seconds later a brunette in a bedazzled white leather bandeau top yelled, "I'm getting hitched bitches! Woo hoo! Smash these babies!" The group roughly *cheers'd* and downed creamy-looking shots before slamming their glasses down on the table.

"Ladies! Have I got a treat for you! A real cowboy from the Wild, Wild West! Put your hands together, and your legs apart, for J-Dawg!" yelled the DJ.

Sunny's ex-fling Jason sauntered on-stage to Kid-Rock's *Cowboy* song. The crowd went nuts. Jason's chest was oiled and bare. His leather vest hung open, letting his abs play peek-a-boo with the lights. The giant fake gold cross around his neck, rested on his hairless skin. J-Dawg was wearing his chaps with nothing underneath.

This was one dance Fran didn't want to see. She tuned Jason and the noise of the crowd out. She looked around, searching the club for a glimpse of Luke. He could be anywhere and she wanted to be sure that she didn't miss him in the press of people. She didn't see Luke, but someone else caught her eye. A blonde woman was standing a few feet away on the other side of the crazy bachelorette party. Her white shirt glowed under the touch of the club's black-light. She looked more stunningly beautiful than the day Fran had seen her locked in an embrace with Luke at the Bull Market Café.

Fran swallowed the bitter bile rising in her throat. A pathetic part of her had still hoped somehow, she and Luke would patch things up tonight. *Stupid!* She was hopeless. There was no way he could explain away the blonde's presence here tonight. It was too much of a coincidence. Fran studied the blonde's profile thinking she wasn't happy to be there. And she clearly wasn't impressed with the group of drunk biker chicks bumping her table and spilling their drinks on her white shirt.

"Hey!" The blonde protested, standing up and shoving her chair back. She grabbed a napkin and started scrubbing what looked to be strawberry daiquiri off her shirt. "What the hell is wrong with you?"

A short dark-haired girl with hair gelled back into a mullet shoved the blonde. The blonde pushed back and the dark-haired girl landed in the lap of the bride. The bride had chosen that second to down a Bob Marley shot. The green, yellow and orange layers dripped down her chin spattering her white bandeau.

The bride-to-be shrieked and jumped to her feet. "You bitch!" she screamed.

Fran winced as the bride stumbled backward impaling one of her entourage with the heel of one zebra-striped stiletto.

Nonplussed, the blonde grabbed another napkin and returned to mopping strawberry off her shirt. Three of the biker bachelorette party-goers swarmed towards her, burying her in a barrage of insults and colourful drinks.

Hey that's not fair. Sure, the other woman was with Luke but she didn't deserve to be jumped by an out of control bridal party. Maybe she didn't even know about Fran. Even if she did, 3-on-1 wasn't a fair fight.

Growing up with nine brothers, Fran had learned how to elbow her way into a crowd at a young age. She used those skills to break through the tight circle forming around the blossoming fight.

"Is there a problem here?" she asked, sliding up next to the blonde and putting on her tough-girl Italian accent.

"Who the fuck wants to know?" asked a biker chick with a half-inch-wide gap between her front teeth.

The biker chick stepped towards Fran, flipping up her beer bottle so that she was holding it by the neck. Beer poured from the mouth of the bottle soaking the floor. The woman squinted at Fran. She swayed side to side, clutching the bottle, swinging it like a baton.

"You guys are so weak that it takes three of you to take down one tiny blonde?" Fran challenged, glaring back.

"Step-off, bitch!" one of the chicks yelled.

Something sailed past Fran's head. It smashed into Jason who'd been prancing around at the front of the stage using a broomstick horse as his prop.

Jason screamed like a baby. Fran lifted her eyes from the women in front of her and half-turned to see what had happened. Blinding pain ripped through the right side of her face. Her head snapped back from the force of the punch thrown by one of the biker chicks she hadn't been watching. Reeling, she dropped to one knee, her hands shooting to her face. *What the hell! She punched me!* Fran hadn't even seen it coming.

Arms came from behind her, roughly pulled her to her feet and dragged her backwards, away from the rapidly developing scrum in front of the stage.

"I didn't need your help, you know," hissed a voice in her ear. Fran turned to find the blonde she'd tried to rescue.

"Seriously? There were three of them and one of you."

"Whatever. I can take care of myself," the other woman returned. "What the hell is wrong with you? If you can't handle yourself, stay out of the way." The blonde, turned on her heels, flipped her hair out of her eyes and walked away.

"Wow. You're welcome!" yelled Fran, at her retreating back.

Gingerly, Fran touched the right side of her face. Already, her cheek was blowing up like a balloon.

"Here," a voice said from behind her.

One of the bouncers handed her a bag of ice. Carefully she placed it against her face and nodded her thanks. The thought of hashing things out with Luke no longer sounded like a good idea. Clutching the ice, she turned and pushed her way out of the club. Tomorrow, when she faced Dr. Tanner, she would have a broken face to go along with her broken heart.

Chapter 36

The stage lights came on when the brawl started. Luke had been standing next to the curtain, half-amused as he watched J-Dawg rip off Dallas's routine and half-wishing he'd said no to coming in tonight. He tugged the curtain further to the side to catch a better perspective of the fun. The white lights painted everything and everyone with a stark, unflattering reality. The truth wasn't kind, Luke decided, getting an eyeful as J-Dawg staggered naked off the stage.

"Help me. Call an ambulance. My nose, not my perfect nose," Jason wailed holding his face.

Someone had thrown a beer bottle that glanced off J-Dawg's right temple. A goose egg that rivalled the horn on Dallas's fake unicorn was already sprouting on his temple.

Hearing a sound at his left shoulder, Luke turned around. Dallas had managed to sneak up on him once again. He was wagging his head thoughtfully, wearing his habitual cowboy hat, chewing a stick of pepperoni.

"That's gotta hurt," he said, watching Jason howl as someone pressed a bag of ice to his face.

Luke shrugged. He thought it was fitting that J-Dawg was the one on stage when the fight started. When Luke walked into the locker room, old J-Dawg had greeted him like they were best friends, as if he hadn't been spamming Luke with threatening texts and phone calls warning him to steer clear of Sunny.

"What's up, man. We're cool right? Sunny's hot, man. I get why you'd want to poach her. She's a lotta woman, if you get my meaning." What the hell was Sunny thinking?

Dallas watched Jason carry on, moaning and calling for his mother. Finally, he muttered, "There is something seriously off about that guy." He yawned, rolled his shoulders and cracked his neck. "Hey, special forces man, you're up next."

Luke snorted. "Maybe not. You see the war out there?"

"That's not war. It ain't even a battle." Dallas took another bite of the dried meat.

Luke was about to answer but caught a glimpse of himself in a mirror at the edge of the stage. The bright lights illuminated his face, making the gray of the camo paint glow and the dark green stand out in bars of shadow. The special-forces gear looked all wrong, like he was a kid dressing up to be something or someone he wasn't. He frowned and dropped the curtain.

This was who he was, the persona he had built to get through life. It was his fall back when the Rockstar scientist role didn't fit. Tonight though, it wasn't doing it for him. It wasn't working. Tonight, he didn't want to be here. He didn't want to get naked and dance.

"What?" Dallas was watching him. "You afraid to go out there?" Dallas pulled the curtain aside and looked out. "Party's over, dude. What? You bailing?"

Luke shook his head and looked through the opening in the curtains. The bouncers were mopping up after the fun, rounding up the biker chicks, herding them towards the door. The bride-to-be looked like she had gotten the worst of it. Her fake leather bandeau had slid up and one breast popped out. Luke watched as she tucked it in and leaned over to grab her purse.

The studded black-leather purse with its metal initials and long tassels would make a formidable weapon if the fight moved outside. The B-T-B flung the strap over her shoulder, grabbed a glass and chugged one last parasol-topped drink. She said something to the bouncer and made a rude gesture. The bouncer grabbed her arm. She shook him off and staggered towards the door, her entourage falling in behind her.

"This place is lame. Let's get out of here bitches!" She belched loudly earning a chorus of *woo hoo's* and *fuck this!* The other women fell in behind her like rumpled ducklings staggering after their not so classy mother.

"*She's* cute," Dallas observed.

Luke jumped. He'd forgotten about Dallas. He thought he'd headed back to the locker room.

"You're pretty quiet for a guy your size," he said testily, returning to his view through the curtain.

"Sometimes, that matters," Dallas replied.

Luke didn't answer. He had spotted a woman standing at the edge of the stage, close to where the action had started. She looked like Fran. Was it? He shook his head in disgust. He was starting to see Fran everywhere. He had to get over it. The whole Fran thing was impacting his life and not in a good way.

Luke dropped the curtain and crossed to the edge of the stage where the DJ sat. Harley was leaning back in his chair, feet resting on the edge of the stage, watching the free show as the biker chicks departed. He jumped when Luke tapped him on the shoulder.

"What?" Harley demanded, pulling off his headphones.

"Change of plans," Luke said. He leaned over so Harley could hear him. "Play this instead." He told

Harley his new pick and returned to where Dallas was still standing at the edge of the stage.

Dallas looked down at him. His eyes were shadowed by the brim of his cowboy hat. Luke had the uncomfortable feeling that the other man could see straight through him.

"Hey, things change, man. Life turns. You know you can't control everything. Sometimes you have to know when to walk away," Dallas said. He turned and left Luke alone on the stage.

The lights dimmed. Luke waited for the opening bars of the music. *Candy Shop*—50 Cent—*Uh huh, so seductive* . . . He rolled into the routine he'd perfected at the start of his career. It was cheesy, but a good swan song to end with. He'd planned something slower but this was better. This time he didn't worry about pleasing his audience; he just danced, changing things, doing whatever felt right.

The song ended and he realized he hadn't got naked. Oops. The boss wasn't going to like that. He turned around to leave the stage and found himself nose to nose with Hector Bartlett, the owner and CEO of Spanky's.

"What the hell was that?" Hector demanded. His beefy face was bright red, almost as red as his blood shot eyes. "I can fire your ass for that," he threatened. "You pull this shit again and—"

Luke shrugged. "Yeah well, too late. I quit." He brushed past Hector and headed towards the locker room.

Behind him, he heard a mixed course of boos and cheers from the front of the club. Whatever. A smile lifted the edge of his mouth. It had been fun. Sweat rolled down his forehead and into his eyes. He blinked it away and pushed his hair back. He felt better than he had in days.

He had a long hot shower in the dressing room and changed back into his jeans and '90's vintage Seahawks t-shirt. Bundling the special-forces outfit, face paint and G-string into his gym bag he took one last look at the battered locker and combination lock. Lifting the lock from the door, he tossed it into the bag and jammed it all into the overflowing garbage can. Picking up his Delta glasses, he considered them for a minute. They were the one memento from his dancing days that he was going to keep. He tucked them into the front pocket of his jacket. Tonight, he wasn't hiding.

He shouldered open the door to the locker room and made his way to the bar at the back of the club. Now that the special event Ladies' Night was over, the doors had opened to the public. The ratio of men to women had changed. Craig was manning the taps at the back bar. He raised his eyes at Luke's sun glass-free face, reached up and lifted a dusty bottle of scotch from the shelf above the bar. Picking up a clean towel, he polished two highball glasses, holding each up to the light and inspecting it before placing it back on the counter. He cracked the seal on the Bruichladdich Black Art 24-year-old spirit and poured two fingers into each glass

Behind Luke a line up was forming. Craig ignored it and nudged a glass towards Luke.

"That's it then," he said solemnly. "It's the end of an era."

Luke nodded slowly. "It feels like it's time."

"Cheers," Craig toasted, lifted his glass in salute. "*Fad saol agat*. Long life to you."

Luke looked at him curiously.

"Gaelic," Craig said before draining his glass.

Luke nodded and downed his own drink.

"Yeah, yeah," Craig waved off the complaints of the disgruntled customer beside Luke and returned to taking drink orders.

"Luke?"

Oh god, now what? Luke closed his eyes for a second and then turned around.

"Shan," he said flatly.

"I need to talk to you."

"Twice in a week? That's got to be a record, lucky me," Luke said and then felt a stab of guilt.

Coming here would be tough for Shannia. The last time she'd been to the club was when she'd found Evan overdosed in the locker room. That night was one for the books. Everyone had known that Evan liked his coke. What Evan and the rest of them didn't know was that Evan had a little heart problem that meant that the coke made his heart blow up like a balloon. By the time Shan found him, he was pulseless, breathless and dead. That hadn't stopped Shan from doing her all to bring him back. That was probably why she had chosen emergency room nursing. She was always trying to bring Evan back.

"You know I wouldn't come here unless it was important," she said. "I'll have one of those," she said gesturing at Luke's glass.

Craig shook his head. "If you want scotch, you get the usual stuff."

Shan looked irked, and then relented. "Just water." She waited until Craig filled a glass, passed it to her and moved away.

"I saw your dance," she said leaning back against the bar.

"Yeah," Luke observed, "and . . ."

"I take it you're done?"

"Yup, the time has come."

Shan nodded silently.

"Look Shan, you can't control everything. Sometimes you just have to walk away." What had the world come to? He was quoting Dallas.

"Like you did?"

"I didn't walk away. She dumped me."

"Wait, what are you talking about?" Shannia looked confused

"Nothing," Luke muttered. "Look, sorry I forgot to call you but I talked to Jax like you asked. He's not using, so leave him alone. It's his choice to strip. You made the same one in order to get where you wanted to be. So did I. He deserves the right to choose just like we did. Jax isn't Evan, so give him his space. Okay?"

"I know you're right. He's old enough to make his own mistakes. I'm just worried." Shan sighed.

"I know I'm right. Don't worry so much, he's a good kid. He'll figure it out." Luke straightened and put his glass back on the bar. "I need to get home. Thanks for the drink, Craig," he said, giving Craig and Shan a quick wave. He left the club without a backwards glance. He wouldn't be back.

Chapter 37

Fran slammed her car door. The hinges groaned and for a second, she was afraid that the door was going to finally fall off the rusted body. What a night. She'd barely slept. Every time she rolled over, the shooting pain in her face woke her. Her right eye was swollen and rimmed by a nasty purple-black bruise that even the thickest layer of concealer couldn't quite hide. She had finally given up on the makeup and settled instead on wearing her sunglasses. She'd come up with a lame lie about going to the optometrist.

The walk from her car to the lab only reinforced just how awful the night had been. Every step jarred her head and launched a resounding throb through her cheek and into her eye. Her face was ballooning larger by the second. What she wanted to do was crawl back into bed, pull the blankets over her head and hide, but calling in sick at this point would make her look even guiltier to the judgemental, holier-than-thou Dr. Etherridge. She had to ride out the days until her transfer went through.

Fran slid through the door and quietly pulled on her lab coat. She looked around the empty lab, committing the uncluttered counters, the unadorned walls to memory. Taking a deep breath, she inhaled the familiar scent of chemicals and briefly closed her eyes. No, she could do this. Slowly, she flexed her shoulders trying to work out the tension and find the moment of Zen-ness that Waverly was always harping about. It evaded her.

Fran sighed. It was hard to be at harmony with yourself when your emotions were simmering like a pot about to boil over. She straightened and moved over to the counter. At least here in the lab she could forget everything. Working on her latest project would force her to concentrate. *Your last project*, a little voice mocked. She blinked away tears.

The test she was running was painstaking, the experiment requiring precise, methodical care. It needed all of her attention and a lot of prep work. She entered the stock room, gathered the chemicals and carefully measured them out, pouring each into a separate beaker. As she worked, she revelled in the silence. She was early today. No one else had arrived.

The silence didn't last long. The sound of the lab door slamming behind her back made her flinch. She didn't turn around. She knew exactly who had just entered the lab. There was only one person inconsiderate enough to let the door slam behind him—Luke.

"Morning," he called gruffly as he trudged through the lab to his office.

"Morning," she returned coolly, carefully eying the chemicals in front of her, not the cute butt sailing by.

The butt stopped and reversed.

"It's just you and me again today. Sarah and Ran both called in sick and Monica and Bob are in Hever's lab." He paused. "What's with the sunglasses? Are you hungover or something?"

"Nope. Not hungover," answered Fran, shortly. "Just an appointment with my optometrist this morning."

"That's a pretty early appointment," he observed, his eyes boring into her, trying to see past the dark lenses.

"She starts early, or at least on time, unlike some other people I know," returned Fran coolly. There that should shut him up. Luke was always late.

Ignoring him, she bent down to check the level of her pour.

"What the hell, Fran? Is that a black eye?" He stepped closer and reached for her glasses.

"Don't," she threatened, brandishing a long-handled set of crucible tongs and stepping away from his touch.

Relentless, Luke moved towards her, his fists were clenched at his sides.

"Who punched you, Fran? I'll kick his ass!"

"No one. It's fine," Fran mumbled, avoiding his eyes. She added lamely, "I tripped."

"You tripped? Really Fran?"

"Really." She rubbed at a non-existent scratch on the counter.

"Fran, tell me who did this to you? Please."

She looked up. His face was earnest, lined with genuine concern.

"Okay, I didn't trip," she admitted. "I was hanging out at Spanky's with some friends last night and I kind of got in a fight."

"A fight? You?" He grinned, relaxing his posture. "Wait, with the biker chicks? That was you?"

"Yes." She rolled her eyes, embarrassed now. "It was stupid."

"I've had a few black eyes in my day. Let me take a look," he commanded, moving in and gently removing her sunglasses.

She stared down at the ground. She felt his breath on her face, smelled his familiar scent. He leaned closer, examining her eye.

"It looks like it will heal but what about you? Are you okay?" he asked softly.

His hands were resting gently on her shoulders and she looked up into his eyes. Her fingers itched to reach up, take his face in her hands and kiss him. Then she remembered the blonde.

"I'm totally fine," she snapped, pulling away from his touch. She grabbed the sunglasses from off the table and rammed them back onto her nose before turning back to her work.

"Okay, sorry." Luke was frozen in place, his hands hanging at his sides. His face had a tight, hurt expression.

"It's just too bad I'm not a leggy blonde," she mumbled under her breath.

She snuck a sideways glance at Luke. He looked as if he had no idea what she was talking about. For a few seconds, he stayed still, watching her, then he shook his head and stalked towards his office.

Fran's hands trembled as she rearranged the equipment one more time. She couldn't concentrate. Seeing Luke's confusion had gotten the wheels in her brain turning again. Maybe it was totally innocent between Luke and the blonde? He seemed to genuinely care about Fran, was hurt by her coldness. *Argh, are you 12-years-old? Get over it!* When had she gotten so pathetic that she was moping over a guy instead of enjoying the challenge of an experiment? But . . . what if? What if there was still a chance? Maybe if she just talked to him—

"No!" she yelled, slamming her hands down on the table.

"Fran? What's wrong?" Luke turned back, alarmed.

"I'm done, Luke," she exploded. "I'm done with it all. Your lab. Us. I can't stand another second!"

Luke's mouth dropped open.

"But Fran—"

"No. Don't try and talk me out of it. My mind is made up. This environment is toxic. You're toxic. I can't work like this and I never want to see you or this lab again."

She threw her lab coat on the floor and ran out, slamming the door behind her.

Chapter 38

What the hell just happened? Luke stared at the closed door to the lab. He'd thought that things were going well. Hell, he was congratulating himself that he had managed not to grab Fran and kiss her silly when he'd lifted her glasses to reveal the puffy black eye discolouring one side of her face. He shoved a glass beaker to the side and yanked off his protective goggles.

"What the hell?" he repeated out loud.

Fran had admitted to being at the club last night. She'd confessed to being part of the biker chick bar fight. That meant she had come to Spanky's to see him. Why couldn't she just say that? Cut to the chase and say, "Luke, I want you. Let's go back to your place, lock the doors and get naked?"

Nope. He growled. Not Fran. Since he had met her, she had turned his world upside down and sideways. He reached over and twisted the gas up on one of the Bunsen burners. Now what? What was Fran doing?

He planted his hands on the counter and stared blindly at the softly boiling chemical in the beaker. He was so screwed. If Fran left the lab he didn't know what he would do. He had gotten used to her— her illegal pony-tails and red lips—red lips that made him spend his days thinking of the possibilities.

This had to be his fault. He straightened. His relationships till now were pretty close to all one-night stands. Any woman who tried to get closer gave him a reason to move on, Yeah, he had an attachment issue. He'd spent the years hopping from foster home to foster home. The fact that his alcoholic mother wouldn't give him up for adoption meant his longest time in one place was from two-years-old to the year he turned five. He'd cultured a hard shell to get through life. Blah, blah, blah. He knew all the psycho-babble bull shit, but he could only use his past as a fallback excuse for so long. He'd ended up getting adopted by Anna and Brent Foster in his teens and he was pretty sure the odds of a kid getting adopted after the age of 9 or 10 were akin to winning the lottery.

The truth was that he was terrified of commitment, terrified of losing his independence, and most of all he was terrified of falling too hard and getting his heart broken. To be honest, maybe he had been holding back. Fran must have sensed that and pulled away. The texts about him being 'too clingy' were probably a test to see if he'd stick it out. He'd failed horribly.

Anna Foster would laugh if she saw him right now. She'd warned him that the women he dated were 'bimbos,' in it for the short haul. She always said that sooner or later love 'em and leave 'em would end and he'd be in real trouble. And now, here he was.

"Hey? What's with the death stare?"

Luke looked up and found Zack standing beside him.

He forced his facial muscles to relax and nodded hello. Great. The last thing he needed right now was Zack and his "I'm an unencumbered free spirit" crap.

"What's up?" he asked, hoping Zack would take the hint and go away.

Instead Zack pulled up a bar stool and planted himself beside the counter.

"You know," Zack mused. "You should try some yoga or meditation. You're starting to remind me of Winston. You've got that same scowl and some seriously negative karma radiating from your outflow." He said the words lightly, studying Luke with shrewd eyes.

"Seriously, Zack, why don't you go away? I'm busy right now."

"Busy?" Zack nodded slowly. "Yup busy. That's why you're standing in the same place muttering to yourself. Really busy."

Luke snorted and turned away. He moved a beaker and lifted a set of tongs.

"Yeah, you might want to put something in there before you put it on the burner," Zack observed.

Luke dropped the tongs and swung around to glare at Zack.

"Are you here for a reason? Or did you just come in to annoy me?" he asked.

Zack grinned. "Nope, I came to tell you that I think I've got the perfect blend of botanicals for the gin. I spent the last few days gathering Juniper berries and I'm ready to craft the perfect spirit."

"Right . . . gin. We have to talk about this right now?"

"Nope. We can talk about your problems with Fran if you want because it doesn't take a rocket scientist to know she's the cause of your negative energy."

Luke frowned. "Do you always talk like that? It sounds weird, you know. It makes people think you're a little off."

"Quit trying to change the subject. What's going on with you and Fran? It's taking over the gossip circle in the staff room. I hear that the ethics board is at loggerheads on how to deal with your questionable actions. In fact, there's a whole memo coming out telling us how to act according to university protocol." Zack raised an eyebrow and waited.

"Shit," Luke said and sank down onto the stool next to him.

"So, maybe you want to tell me how first Fran is your fabled girlfriend, but then she turns up in your lab as a picked placement?"

Luke was silent. He had underestimated Zack. He'd thought he was just a hipster, beach bum, hippy dude. He should have remembered the other man wouldn't be teaching at the university if he was an airhead. How much of Zack's persona was a cover—like his own stripper personality—covert moves, smoke and mirrors?

"I met Fran the weekend before the semester started. We hit it off. We didn't spend a lot of time discussing what we did in real life. I had absolutely no idea that I would walk into the lab and find her here."

"You threw her under the bus to get rid of her."

Luke frowned. "I couldn't work with her."

"Did you even try?"

"No. Can you imagine what would have happened if the ethics board got hold of that?"

Zack snorted. "You mean what's happening right now? Exactly this would have happened but dude, you've made it ten times worse."

Silence, and then Zack said, "Look, I'm not telling you how to run your life, but you better get your head straight. Fran seems like a nice girl and doesn't deserve to have her reputation and career trashed just because she met you."

Luke didn't answer. There was nothing to say. Zack had just reinforced what he already knew.

Zack stood up. "Look, I gotta go. Later, man."

The door swung shut behind him.

Luke groaned and buried his face in his hands. This was getting out of control. He had to do something.

Chapter 39

The timer pinged. Luke frowned at the beaker of chemicals, watching the slow roll of the glue-like fluid in the beaker. With Fran gone he had to finish the experiment alone. *Well, buddy, you did it to yourself. Get used to it.*

"Dr. Tanner?"

Luke looked up, nodding blankly.

"Fran asked me to fill in for her. She said you needed an extra pair of hands."

Luke stared at the eager face of the student in front of him. He'd seen him around but had never spoken with him. The guy was hard to read, broadcasting an air of confidence, acting as though he knew what he was doing, but the brief times Luke had watched him, he'd noticed some of his technique looked questionable.

Fran was right though, he did need help. Still . . .Luke hesitated and started to shake his head. He stopped. The fact that Fran cared enough about him to not bail on him completely meant something, didn't it? The process he was working on was in its final stages. At this point, if anything went wrong, it could be catastrophic.

"How's your chemical processing technique?" Luke asked, still studying the young undergrad. The kid looked like he belonged in high school but he wouldn't be here if he wasn't capable of working in a lab.

"It's great, sir. Top notch," Kevin assured him.

Kevin, huh. The kid hadn't introduced himself. Luke only knew that was his name because his badge was dangling from his neck on a long-woven cord. Luke frowned. He hated that practice. Things that dangled from strings were never a good idea in a lab environment. He opened his mouth to tell Kevin to take it off but the timer on the burner dinged again. Luke turned away to check the results.

Kevin was either incredibly self-assured or he really did know what he was doing. He went straight to work, carefully titrating and mixing chemicals. Luke watched until he was satisfied it was safe to turn him loose.

His thoughts returned to Fran. Why had she been at Spanky's last night? Had she had a change of heart? Clearly, she was there to see him. She'd told him that the only reason she was at the club on the night they met was Sunny had dragged her there kicking and screaming. And the comment about his tastes running more towards leggy bleached-blonde bimbos—what the hell was that supposed to mean? Luke frowned trying to puzzle it out.

The evening had been quiet aside from the biker chick bar brawl. He'd done his last dance, showered, had a good-bye drink with Craig and headed for home. Shan . . . he'd talked to Shannia for a bit, but by then, Fran would have been long gone. He knew that, because after he'd left the stage, he'd looked for her.

He glanced over at Kevin. He was eagerly timing the temperature on a covered beaker, leaning forward as he watched the numbers on the display. That stupid badge was dangling into the space between him and the beaker.

As Luke watched, Kevin reached for a clipboard lying beside the burner. The badge dropped lower, hanging between Kevin and the beaker of nitric acid. Kevin tossed the badge over his back so it was out of the way and returned to his preparations for pouring the leftover nitric acid into an empty chemical waste storage container.

Luke looked away, thinking about Fran again. Why would she think Luke was interested in blondes? The only woman he was into was a fiery Sicilian brunette. Considering the time he and Fran had spent together, she had to have seen that she was the only one he was interested in.

He sighed and shook his head in disgust. He couldn't figure it out. The only blonde he even knew was Shannia, and the two of them were strictly friends. He grimaced imagining Shan and him as anything else. They'd kill each other. Nope, the only blonde he'd been close to recently was Shan when he'd met her at the Bull Market Cafe.

He stopped, his hand hovering between the control on the Centrifuge 5000 and the table. That was it. He had the sudden clear image of Shan's angry gaze staring past his shoulder at the Bull Market Café, warning something or *someone* away. He hadn't turned around because Shan had succumbed to another round of tears. It made perfect sense. Since Evan's death Shan had developed the philosophy that if she couldn't be happy, then no one could.

Fran thought he had something going on with Shan. Luke felt a surge of anger towards Shannia and then almost laughed. He might have if he hadn't looked up to see that Kevin had switched off the air flow on the hood. The next thing he saw was the organic solvent label on the container Kevin was holding.

His heart stopped. He took two steps towards Kevin.

"Stop! You're—!"

Too late! The nitric acid reacted with the trace of organic solvent remaining in the jug. The violent explosion picked Luke up spinning him like a rag doll. The force of the blast flung him over the counter. He slammed into the wall on the other side and bounced off of it. He flung his arms out, trying to stop the momentum of the fall. His head struck the edge of the centrifuge with a sickening *thunk*. A blinding green light lit the room and darkness closed Luke's eyes as the world vanished.

Chapter 40

"Dammit, Sunny, where are you?" Fran cursed Sunny's answering machine again. She'd already left five messages. She'd considered going to Sunny's apartment. Where was she when Fran needed her?

Fran had pulled over to the side of the road. She couldn't focus on driving. Her mind was in turmoil. She needed some serious girl time. She needed to get drunk. No, that was what had started all this in the first place. She let out a strangled cry at the memory of her first night meeting "Danger" or "Luke" or "Dr. Tanner" or whoever the hell he was. He wasn't hers, that was for sure. She had just pretty much guaranteed that they were over for good—yelling and slamming her hands down on the table— storming out of his lab like a freaking psycho.

Rihanna's song *Umbrella* blared on the phone, making Fran jump. She grabbed the phone.

"Sunny?" she answered frantically.

"Fran?"

Thank god. It was Sunny!

"Fran? Is everything okay? I saw that I missed a million calls from you and stepped away from my conference for a minute to call you back."

Shit, her conference! Sunny was at a wine conference in Napa; Fran had completely forgotten. She cleared her throat and tried to steady her voice before answering. "Oh shoot, sorry. I totally forgot you were away. I'm fine. Everything's fine."

"Really? You don't sound fine. Do you want me to come home?"

"No, I'm fine. I'm fine!" Fran said, trying to sound as if she meant it.

"No, you're not. It's Luke isn't it." It was a statement not a question. Sunny's nose for guy troubles was sharper than a bloodhound's.

"Yes," Fran started to cry. "It's just, I ended it and I know I've done the right thing, but if it was the 'right thing' why does it feel so wrong? Why do I feel like complete and utter crap? Shouldn't I be relieved? Maybe I should have let him explain?"

"No sweetie, it's totally normal to feel like crap after a breakup and you definitely did the right thing."

"I guess so. But I didn't feel like this after Ricky."

"Ha, Ricky! Ricky was beige. He was nothing. He was boring. Easy come, easy go. Luke is red. He's hot. He's dangerous, like, his stripper name is actually Danger! He's just all wrong for you. When someone captures your heart, and your passion, even for just a short time, well it's hard to let go but you definitely should let go Fran. He cheated on you! Don't give him a chance to explain. He'll just suck you back in like Jason did with me, over and over and over again. You need to make a clean break. Learn from my mistakes and forget about that loser."

That wasn't what Fran had wanted to hear but when Sunny put it like that it made complete sense. "That was actually really good advice."

"Don't sound so surprised!" Sunny laughed. "I've been around the block a few times and learned a couple of things here and there."

"Thanks, Sun."

"No problem, sweetie. I'm just sorry I'm not there for you in person. What you need to do is have a junk-fest pig out tonight. Watch chick flicks, cry and get it all out of your system. Then start fresh tomorrow. But whatever you do, don't call Luke. You can always call me if you need some reinforcements. Sound good?"

"Sounds good," agreed Fran, feeling a bit better as she hung up the phone.

***

No junk fest would be complete without some of Waverly's famous 'boobie brownies', chocolate goodness in a round shape, topped with pink Hershey's kisses for 'nipples.'

Waverly was bent over polishing the case when Fran came in.

"Hello, Francesca," she greeted Fran as she stretched her arms overhead. "Oh, but my back is sore, I've been polishing knobs all day." She gave Fran a suggestive smile.

"Hi, Waverly," returned Fran, ignoring the perverted comment. It was best not to encourage Waverly. "Any of your famous brownies left?"

"Have a craving, do you?" Waverly asked, making no move to head around to the other side of the counter and serve Fran.

"Yep." Fran smiled tightly. She wasn't in the mood for conversation.

"Are you going to tell me what happened?" Waverly went back to cleaning the glass.

Darn. So much for getting in and out. "What do you mean?"

"I mean last time I saw you, you were oozing with the sex glow and now you're all dried up, or should I say cried up?" Waverly turned and gestured to Fran's sunglasses.

"Ha, ha, very funny. It just didn't work out and I don't want to talk about it." Fran shrugged, blinking back tears. Would they never dry up?

"Why?" Waverly probed, putting on her therapist voice.

"Why?" Fran bit her lip and decided to spit it out. "Because I saw him on a date with a gorgeous blonde."

"How do you know it was a date? Did you ask him?" challenged Waverly, scrubbing at a stubborn spot on the counter.

"Well . . . no. But they were hugging and they looked very cozy."

"Hugging?" She turned around to face Fran, hands on hips. "Do you not hug your grandma, your brother, your mom? Does a hug instantly signify wrongdoing, Francesca?"

"No but lying about where you were going to be and who you were going to be with does."

"True. What did he say when you asked him about it?"

"I didn't exactly ask him."

"Ha! Your generation with your fancy phones and *twatbook*! Always sharing all the details of your personal life and thoughts and dreams online: what you had for breakfast, what it looked like and then what time you pooped it out. Honestly! But when it comes to a real conversation? Phew! Sit down face-to-face and talk to him. None of this he said, she said garbage!" Waverly gave Fran a light swat on the leg with her cloth.

"It's not that simple, Waverly." Fran shook her head. It wasn't, was it?

"No Francesca, it is that simple. Putting aside this misunderstanding: Do you like him?"

"Yes."

"Do you like to spend time with him?" Waverly ticked off on her fingers.

"Yes."

"Do you have a common interest, something that gets you both wet?"

"Um, gross but yes."

"Do you find him attractive?"

"Yes."

"Okay, and most importantly do you have fabulous sex?"

"Waverly," Fran protested. She did not want to discuss this with her friend's grandmother.

"Come on Francesca, we're adults here, just answer my question!" Waverly urged.

"Yes." Fran sighed. *Yes. Oh, yes.*

"Five out of five. See it is that simple. You passed the compatibility test." Waverly held up her five fingers to Fran as proof.

"But Sunny said—"

"Stop right there," Waverly interrupted, wagging a finger in front of Fran's face. "I love Sunny but my granddaughter has no business giving anyone love advice. She's your best friend, you should know better than to take Sunny's advice! Career? Sure. How to dress? Not my taste, but some people might call her stylish. But love advice from Sunny, Francesca? Really? I always thought you were smarter than that!" she chided.

"Oh God." She was totally right. Fran loved Sunny to death but taking love advice from her was like asking a three-year-old if your outfit looked good. They might give you an answer but it probably wasn't going to be accurate.

"Forget the brownies. You need to go find him and sort this out now." Waverly ordered pointing at the door.

"You're right. I've been an idiot." Fran agreed.

"I know. I'm usually right. I'll bill you later." Waverly laughed. "Go," she said pointing at the door again. "What you really need to do is both get completely naked and practice some yoga positions together to unblock your chakras; I find downward dog particularly stimulating for my sexual energy."

"Um, yes, we'll try that for sure," Fran returned. "Thanks for the advice, Waverly!"

"Good-luck Francesca."

Chapter 41

Fran climbed back into Pricilla praying the old car would start right away. She bounced away from the curb and merged into the long line of traffic. Taking the exit to University Circle Drive, she tried calling Luke's cell phone. It went straight to voicemail. He usually turned it to silent mode when working in the lab. The clinical trial he was working on was volatile. He couldn't afford to take the risk of the phone going off at a critical moment. Fran felt a stab of guilt. She shouldn't have left him in a lurch with Kevin. She knew Kevin wasn't the strongest student, but, she consoled herself, he was better than having no one.

Luke would still be at the lab. She'd find him and they would talk this out. She nodded feeling more confident with every passing second. Yes. They would work this out like adults. Waverly was right, no more high-school drama and mixed messages; no more jumping to conclusions. She merged onto the branch road leading to the lab.

Traffic clogged the street leading from the parking lot. It was bumper to bumper. Fran frowned. She rounded the corner. Earlier, the lot was half-full, now it was clogged with firetrucks and police cars. *Looks like someone burnt toast again or wanted to get out of an exam.* Every time a big exam was scheduled, someone pulled the fire alarm. She grinned. Some students would do anything to buy more time to study.

She parked one lot over and climbed out. Now she was here, she wasn't in so much of a hurry to go inside. She was scared and hopeful at the same time. This talk would make or break the relationship between herself and Luke. She was done with all the back and forth, done with never knowing where she stood.

Frowning, Fran sniffed and looked towards the lab. The heavy odor of chemicals hung in the air. Another firetruck roared up the road and turned into the lot. Engine quieting, it idled, lights slowly revolving in a red strobe. For once, there was none of the usual milling about as the firefighters waited for the all clear to be given. Fran moved slowly, climbing out of the car, her eyes locked on the flashing red lights. A deep sense of foreboding engulfed her. So many firetrucks—was something actually on fire?

She jogged towards the lab, weaving between the trucks, trying to get a better look at the building.

Yellow tape stretched from tree to tree, preventing the crowd of curious students from getting closer. Yellow tape? What was going on? The smell was stronger now. She took another delicate sniff of cloying smoke. It was heavy with a pungent chemical that caught in her throat. Oh my god. She knew that smell. She touched her face with shaking hands. The experiment—Luke!

Fighting off rising panic, Fran pushed through the crowd and ducked under the tape. She ran towards the building. Screw the tape. What was happening inside? Where was Luke? He should be here, protecting his turf, bossing the firefighters around, directing traffic.

"Miss!" A firefighter jogged towards her holding out his hand, waving her back.

Fran ignored him and kept moving.

"Miss! Stop right there!" He stepped in front of her. "Does the yellow 'caution' tape mean anything to you?"

"Yes. Sorry," Fran answered, dazed. This couldn't be happening. "I work in the lab. It's not a real fire, is it?" She couldn't take her eyes off the thick black smoke billowing from the air vents.

"There was an explosion in the lab. We managed to contain the fire before it spread. Well, they did," he added grumpily. "I drew the short straw and got stuck with crowd control. Get back behind the yellow tape." He pointed.

"But Professor—my boyfriend . . . Was anyone hurt?" Fran stood her ground, not giving way.

"I can't answer that but I'm sure Professor Boyfriend is just fine," he answered flippantly, trying to herd her back behind the tape.

"Please, just tell me?" Fran begged, digging in her heels. "Was anyone hurt?"

His grim face was all the answer Fran needed. Her bottom lip quivered. Tear welled up in her eyes, rolling down her cheeks, dropping off her chin.

"Oh God, Luke," she whispered. "This is all my fault." Her teeth began to chatter as a violent involuntary shudder took over her muscles.

"Oh shit, don't cry. Here." The firefighter looked alarmed. He draped his coat over her shoulders and led her to a nearby bench.

"Sit," he commanded. "And don't move. I'll go find out who was injured and let you know. Your boyfriend's name is Luke?"

"Yes. Professor Luke Tanner." Fran nodded, pulling the coat tighter around her shoulders. She was such a fool, leaving Luke alone with Kevin, today of all days. She knew how dangerous that experiment was. If Luke was hurt, she'd never forgive herself.

A few minutes passed before the firefighter returned. He sat down next to Fran, his body positioned to face her.

"What's your name?" he asked.

"Fran," she answered flatly, terrified. He was stalling. "Please just tell me."

"Fran, I'm Josh." He spoke with a deliberate calm, the type of low-key passivity used to deliver bad news.

It had the opposite effect. "Just tell me!" Fran yelled.

"Okay," he said, his voice still calm and measured. "There were two people in the room. They were both badly hurt. One of them is Professor Luke Tanner."

"Oh God!" Fran jumped to her feet. The coat dropped to the ground. "Where is he? I need to be with him." She turned towards the parking lot and then back towards the lab. Where was her purse? She needed her car keys.

"I can't . . . Where's my purse?" She gulped in a long sobbing breath. "I can't . . ." Nothing was making any sense. She had to see Luke.

"Fran."

Josh the firefighter's voice sounded a long way off. "Take a big breath," he ordered. "Good, now another one." He watched until satisfied she wasn't going to faint. "You're in no state to drive, Fran. My Captain's given me clearance to take you to Port Fling Hospital." Gently, Josh took hold of Fran's arm and guided her towards one of the fire/rescue vehicles parked in the lot.

***

The drive to the hospital took an agonizing fifteen minutes. Fran fidgeted, bouncing her legs up and down, trying to control the anxiety buzzing like ravenous African bees beneath her skin. Faster, faster. Why didn't he turn on the siren and clear traffic? Didn't he understand this was an emergency? Her toes pressed down on an imaginary gas pedal. *Come on. Come on.* If strength of will could propel the car through traffic, she would already be there, parked, and racing to Luke's side.

"Can you go any faster? Maybe turn the sirens on?" she asked. Her foot was pressing so hard on the imaginary pedal that her toes were going numb.

"No, sorry. Rules are that we can only turn on the lights when we're heading to an emergency. You're Mario Romano's sister, aren't you?" Josh asked, changing the subject, as he steered the truck around a corner.

"Yep." Fran nodded briefly. She clenched her fists. Would they ever get there? She was in no mood for chit-chat. Thankfully Josh seemed to recognize that and lapsed back into silence. Fran closed her eyes and tried to still her mind, shutting away the thoughts swirling through her head. Please let Luke be okay. Please don't let anything happen to him. What if he was badly hurt? Worse, what if he was dead? Her stomach jumped up into her throat and choked her. Finally, they reached the road leading to the Emergency Department parking lot.

"Do you want me to come in with you?" Josh asked kindly.

"No. Thank you. I . . . I need to get in there. I have to know." Fran unbuckled her seat belt and steeled herself to face the truth.

Josh slowed the truck.

"Thanks." Fran jumped out before they were at a full stop.

"Good luck," Josh called to the slammed door.

She gave a quick wave and jogged through the ER doors. Stepping inside, she had to stop and search for the reception desk.

She ran towards it, forcing herself to slow down, and not run past it.

"Luke Tanner," she gasped. She couldn't catch her breath. Leaning forward, she planted her hands on top of the counter and tried again, saying, "I'm here to see Luke Tanner. My husband." The lie slid off her tongue like butter. She knew hospitals never gave information to a non-family member.

"Luke Tanner?" The clerk repeated, "Let me see what bed he's in."

Fran's fingers drummed impatiently as the clerk click-clacked away on the computer.

"I'm sorry, ma'am, but I can't give out any information. You'll need to talk to the physician. If you'll just wait, I can see if he's available." He pointed to a seat.

"I'm okay," Fran waved off the seat. "Please, just hurry," she begged.

The clerk nodded, stepped away from the desk and approached a man dressed in green scrubs. The man—doctor—turned and looked at Fran. He said something to the clerk and approached her. The doctor looked tired. His eyes were deeply shadowed. His mouth set in a straight line. The lump in Fran's throat doubled in size. She wanted to throw up. Oh God, he was going to tell her Luke was dead. She hadn't made it in time. The defeat on the doctor's face told the story and it wasn't good news.

The adrenaline she'd been running on abruptly drained from her body. Wordlessly, Fran stared at the doctor, her eyes pleading with him to tell her everything was fine. Her body was numb. She couldn't move her limbs. This wasn't happening. Luke couldn't be dead.

"There must be a mistake," she choked out, before the doctor could speak. "He can't be dead. I just saw him."

The doctor frowned. He shook his head and placed a hand on Fran's shoulder.

"I'm so sorry, Mrs. Reiner, he's in critical condition. We've done everything we can. We've air evacuated him to Seattle. He'll get good care there. You should sit down."

"What did you say?" Fran shook the doctor's hand off.

"I said, I'm sorry, ma'am."

"No, what did you call me?"

"Mrs. Reiner."

Fran let out a strangled, maniacal laugh. "I'm Mrs. Tanner."

"Oh, Mrs. Tanner!" The doctor's demeanor changed. He straightened, looking taller, more confident. "I'm incredibly sorry, Mrs. Tanner. It has been a hell of a long day and the clerk gave me the wrong name. Mr. Tanner is in serious but stable condition. He hit his head quite hard, so we're watching him closely. He's also suffered some smoke inhalation."

"He's alive?" Fran checked. The switch from sorrow to happiness threatened to launch her through the ceiling.

"Yes, but he's not out of the woods yet," the doctor cautioned. He gave her a weary smile and rubbed his face. "I apologize again for the mix-up, Mrs. Tanner. You can see him now if you like, he's in the trauma room." He gestured to the room behind him.

"Oh, thank you!" Fran gushed. She wanted to wrap the doctor in a bone breaking hug or smother him with kisses. She settled for a quick handshake.

Okay, Fran. You've got this. Big breath. Be calm. She inhaled and exhaled, afraid of what she would find on the other side of the door, preparing herself for the worst.

Luke was motionless, his body lined up in a straight unnatural line. The narrow bed looked too small for him, the crisp white blankets draining what was left of the colour from his face. His eyes were closed, his lashes dark smudges surrounded by sooty shadows. An oxygen mask covered his mouth and nose and he was connected to machines that monitored his heartrate and blood pressure. *Beep, beep, beep.* The electronic eye on one machine blinked owlishly at her. *Blink, blink, blink.* Beside Luke, a woman in scrubs straightened from taping the intravenous attached to his arm. She turned at the sound of the door opening.

It was the gorgeous blonde from the coffee shop. The woman from Spanky's.

"Oh, sorry," Fran uttered faintly, backing out of the room.

"Fran, wait!" the blonde called. "Come in, he was calling for you earlier."

Fran swallowed her tears. Slowly she turned back to face the blonde. She stared into the other woman's eyes and saw only sympathy and concern. Unsteadily, Fran took a step, moving past the other woman to reach the far side of the bed.

Standing over Luke, she looked down at him, afraid to reach over and touch his hand. His hair was singed, his face blackened and bruised but the rise and fall of his chest was steady and regular.

"I'm Shannia." The blonde's face held the hint of a smile. "Luke's nurse and his *friend.*" She emphasized the word. "You may have seen Luke and I together and assumed the worst but we've been through a lot. He's like a brother to me. That's it. So, if you have a problem with us, then that's your deal, not mine." The blonde abruptly turned away and began fiddling with some equipment at Luke's bedside.

Fran opened her mouth and then closed it again. Shannia definitely wasn't emanating warm fuzzy feelings, but she appeared to be telling the truth.

"Okay," Fran said, believing Shannia's story. *Enough drama already*. A weight lifted off her chest. "Shannia? Is he going to be alright?"

"He has a head injury. It's minor but it's definitely time to wake sleeping beauty. Now that you're here he might be a little more willing."

Chapter 42

Something was beeping. *Beep, beep, beep.* It went on and on, each beep setting off an accompanying throb in his head. The sound was messing with his dreams. As if sensing his restlessness, a cool hand stroked his hair back from his eyes. He smiled, enjoying the touch. The smile hurt. He frowned. That made it worse. He tried to open his eyes and groaned.

"Luke?"

It was Fran's voice. Fran was in his dream? Of course, she was. She was always in his dreams.

"Talk to him again," another voice ordered.

Luke frowned again. That was Shan's voice, the last voice he wanted to hear in his dreams, especially when Fran sounded so close.

"Luke?" Fran repeated.

Her soft hand trailed down his cheek. He tried to turn his head into her touch. It hurt too much. He groaned again.

"For god's sake. Luke!" Hands landed on his collar bone, pinching his trapezius muscles. Shan's voice bellowed in his ear. "Luke! Open your eyes!"

"Go way," Luke mumbled, squeezing his eyes closed more tightly.

"You're hurting him," Fran's voice protested.

"I need him to open his eyes and respond. He has a head injury."

Shan pressed harder. Luke winced and moved his arms.

"G'way . . ." he mumbled.

"Luke, open your eyes. It's Shan. You're in the hospital."

"You're hurting him. Get the hell away from him."

Good, Luke thought. His little mafia sweetie would make Shan go away. He heard the sounds of a scuffle and tried to open his eyes. Neither Shan nor Fran were looking at him. They were standing nose to nose like two cats growling over a mouse.

"Hey, a little quiet here." Why did his voice sound so far away?

"Luke!" Fran moved away from Shan. She dropped down into a chair beside the bed and grabbed a hold of his hand. The strength of the grip hurt his fingers. He hoped she never let go.

"Luke, open your eyes," Shan commanded moving to the other side of the bed.

"If I do will you go away?" he mumbled, his eyes still closed.

Shan laughed. "Squeeze Fran's hand."

That one was easy. He wasn't planning on letting go of it. He opened his eyes and stared into the whiskey-coloured depths of Fran's beautiful eyes.

"Good. Move your feet."

"What happened," Luke demanded. He tried to sit up but an avalanche of pain dropped over him. He flopped back against the pillows, too stunned to move.

"There was an explosion at the lab. Oh my god, Luke. I thought you were dead. I never should have left. I'm so sorry." Fran dashed away her tears with her upper arm. She didn't let go of his hand.

"It's okay, Fran. How could you have known?" Luke consoled. He closed his eyes again, scrunching them shut against the memory. "I remember. Kevin poured nitric acid into a jug with organic solvent . . . He'd shut off the flow hood. Wait. Is he—?"

"They air-lifted him to Seattle. Try and rest." Shan raised the head of the bed.

"You yell at me to wake up and then tell me to sleep?"

"You'll be back to your regular charming self in no time I see," Shan said. "Why she likes you, I'll never know." Shan left the room, gently closing the door behind her.

Fran rested her forehead on Luke's arm. He couldn't see her eyes anymore.

"Are you crying?" he said, pleased and alarmed that she cared enough about him to shed tears.

"I thought you were dead. They wouldn't tell me what happened. One of the firemen at the lab recognized me. He knows my brother. He gave me a ride to the hospital. When I got here all I knew was that one man was in critical condition and they were sending him to Seattle."

Fran let go of his hand and used both hands to wipe the tears from her face.

"I thought you were going to die, Luke. The doctor had the wrong person and actually told me you were in critical condition." Fran's shoulders shook as her tears started back up.

"Shit."

"I know. Then when he realized his mistake and told me you were stable, I was so relieved. He said I could come in to see you. I walked in and saw Shannia, I just assumed she was here with you, that you guys were together."

"Fran, there's nothing between Shannia and me. Honestly. We're—"

"I know Luke. It's okay."

Luke grabbed for her hand and missed. He moaned. He hurt everywhere.

"Shh." Alarmed Fran took hold of his hand and held on tight. "The blast threw you around. Nothing broken, but you're pretty banged up. They said you have a closed head injury."

Luke tried again. "Shan and I—"

"Would kill each other in ten minutes. I know," soothed Fran. "I figured that out pretty quickly. Man is she ever ice cold."

Luke smiled weakly in relief. Whatever painkiller Shan had shot into his intravenous was starting to work. He felt dreamy and happy.

"She called your parents," Fran said. "They're here waiting. Shan's gone to get them from the waiting area." Fran stood up. "I'm going to go so you can see them."

"No," Luke said. His voice was croaky. He cleared his throat and said more strongly, "You aren't leaving me again. Every time you go something bad happens. Sit your little mafia butt back down."

Fran smiled. "Alright, Dr. Tanner. I'm on it."

Luke's parents entered the room hesitantly. Their faces were lined with fear and worry. Anna had been crying. Luke had never seen her look so lost, so fragile.

"Luke! Are you okay? What happened? What went wrong?" Anna Foster bent down and kissed his forehead. Her cool hand stroked his face.

Brent Foster moved towards the bed slowly, approaching cautiously. His face was harder to read. Thirty-five years of detective work in downtown Seattle meant he played his cards close to his chest.

Luke felt Fran try to pull her hand away. He wrapped his fingers around it tighter and hung on.

"I'm okay. Mom, Dad, this is Fran. I love her and when I get out of here, I'm going to marry her."

Fran gasped. Luke didn't let go of her hand. The drugs made him feel sleepy and honest. They let him say the words he had to get out. He no longer cared about hiding his feelings from the world.

Brent Foster leaned forward and shook Fran's free hand. "Welcome to the family, Fran. Good luck with this one."

Anna smiled and moved around the bed to hug Fran.

Luke met Fran's eyes. He squeezed her hand, and whispered, "I love you."

Epilogue

Three months later . . .

"Relax, honey, you look fine," Fran said.

She was watching Luke fiddle with his tie for what had to be the hundredth time. She hid a smile. She'd been doing that a lot recently—smiling, being happy, just being. Maybe she had finally found that perfect state of Waverly Zen. Whatever it was, she liked it. It beat feeling stressed and worried, trying to get the best mark, be the best—the only—daughter. Her relationship with Luke had returned to what she privately referred to as the stripper phase—the relaxed, easy-going state that marked the very beginning of their time together. Except for the sex. Luke hadn't been cleared for "contact sports" yet. They did a lot of cuddling.

"It's just a bit too far to the left." Luke frowned and made another infinitesimal adjustment to the position of his tie. "There." He nodded, satisfied that it was straight.

Fran smiled again and counted to thirty in her head. Sure enough, Luke was standing at the mirror fiddling with the tie. She walked over, reached up, pulled his head towards hers and gave him a kiss, a little one. Anything more would lead to unfulfilled hunger. She undid the tie and slowly, strip-tease style, pulled it off his neck.

"Ms. Romano, not now. Your family will be here any minute." He grinned, sliding his arms around Fran's waist.

"Dr. Tanner, please. Be professional." She mock-scolded, gently removing his hands. "I was merely getting rid of the troublesome tie. You were overdressed anyways," she teased and then added, "My brothers will make fun and they can be pretty brutal when they get together, especially Sal."

"It's not your brothers I'm worried about." Luke shook his head.

"No?" said Fran, her eyebrows raised.

"No. Its Nonna!" Luke pretended to cower in the corner and Fran laughed.

"She is pretty scary. Don't worry though, I'll protect you." Fran flexed her barely visible biceps.

"Why am I still worried?" Luke joked.

The doorbell sounded. "Showtime," said Fran. "Are you sure you're up to this?"

"Yes, honey. I'm five-hundred percent sure I'm up to this. We've been putting this off for too long. I want to meet your family."

"But everyone at once? It just seems like a bit much."

"It's like ripping off a Band-Aid," Luke teased. "I'm getting it over with in one clean sweep. Besides, it isn't really your whole family. It's just your brothers, parents and Nonna."

"I know, but they're still a lot to take. I want you to tell me if you're feeling overwhelmed. Don't be a tough guy."

"Please, Fran, I'm fine! Dr. Ravvy checked me out yesterday and gave me a clean bill of health," Luke insisted. "Now will you answer the door, or should I?"

"Okay, I'll go answer," Fran said. "But I'll be watching you."

Luke held up his hands in mock surrender as Fran went to get the door. Only Nonna waited there. Despite Luke's insistence that he wanted to meet everyone at once, Fran had decided, unbeknownst to him, to invite Nonna to arrive half-an-hour early. If Nonna gave Luke the green light, everyone else would follow.

Nonna was waiting on the other side of the door. For her meeting with Luke, she had elected to wear black, one of the prim skin-concealing dresses that the family privately called her *Don't screw with me* power suits. Her soft white hair was pulled back into a tight bun. Her face wore a stern expression. For Nonna, the jury on Luke was still out.

Fran greeted her with the usual cheek kisses.

Nonna didn't wait, she asked the question Fran knew was coming, "So where this boy?"

"He's in the kitchen," Fran replied, "making the appetizer. Nonna, be nice."

Luke had been out of the lab since the accident and he'd temporarily replaced his passion for chemistry with a passion for cooking. It made perfect sense. They were both based on chemical reactions. He threatened he was going to enter the bake-off between Nonna and Waverly. Fran had warned him not to even joke about it.

"You make him to work in kitchen?" Nonna asked, elbowing Fran, clearly impressed.

"I don't make him, Nonna, he likes to cook. Now you have to promise me you'll be nice," Fran warned.

"Francesca! Nonna always nice." Nonna's face lit with an angelic smile.

"Mmmhmmm." Fran wasn't buying it.

"Okay, okay. I be nice," Nonna relented. "Now where this boy?"

Fran led Nonna to the kitchen where Luke was working. He attacked cooking the way he did a difficult experiment in the lab, studying the recipe like an equation and measuring out ingredients with the same exact precision. He didn't hear them come in. Fran smiled. His hair had fallen forward on his face and her heart skipped a beat. Every time she saw him, she was still in awe of his beauty.

"Belissimo," She heard Nonna utter under her breath.

Ha, the old girl isn't immune to his charm either!

Luke looked up at the sound and his face lit up. "Nonna?" he asked.

"Si." Nonna replied with a nod, playing it cool.

"Hello." Luke wiped his hands on a tea towel. "I'm Luke." He crossed the kitchen to Nonna and held his hand out.

Nonna looked down at the hand, unmoving.

Oh, great, thought Fran. She's going to freeze him out.

"So, you the boy who put my Francesca through so much?" Nonna asked coolly.

"Yes ma'am." Luke said, hand still waiting.

"You a smart boy? Why you no realize how wonderful my girl is right away?" Nonna demanded.

"Yes ma'am. I was stupid for a while there but I'm a quick learner. I just want to make Francesca happy." He gave Nonna a smile that would melt the North Pole.

Nonna glared silently. Tiny beads of sweat began to form on Luke's forehead. Hah, bet he was glad the tie wasn't strangling him now. Fran waited. The seconds ticked by with agonizing slowness.

Finally, Nonna replied, "Okay, come here." She bypassed the hand, reaching up to pull Luke in for a hug.

"Phew," Luke mouthed to Fran. "I'm in!"

Nonna held Luke in a long hug. Her head reached just above Luke's navel and she tugged on his arm to bring him down to eye level.

"Wait," she said," I tell you something. I have cousin in Sicily, Dario, and if you make Francesca sad ever again, I send him after you."

"Nonna!" protested Fran with a laugh.

"No, it's okay, Fran. I understand. I will never make that same mistake again, Nonna. I promise."

"Good," said Nonna. "Now bring everyone in. They waiting out front."

"They're here already?" Fran ran to the front door and peaked out through the glass. Sure enough, the Romano clan—minus the wives, girlfriends and kids—were camped out on her front porch.

"I tell them wait. I go first, but I know Francesca only pick a good one. Now where is wine. We toast new member of family." Nonna busied herself with the corkscrew.

"She's cute . . . and terrifying," whispered Luke as the rest of Fran's family filed in.

***

Dinner was a traditional Romano occasion, loud and animated. The family loved Luke's pasta *puttanesca*, declaring it only second to Nonna's. Fran's brothers behaved very well, with the exception of Mario, who kept touching his nose, and Sal who insisted on calling Luke Poindexter and inappropriately grilling him on his salary and 401K.

"I'm glad that's over." Fran sighed after ushering the last of her brothers out the door.

"It wasn't so bad," Luke said, clearing the remainder of the dishes off the table.

"Hey, what was with you and Sal?" Fran asked. Sal had acted as though he had met Luke before.

"Nothing really. I ran into him on campus and he got pissy with me for cutting through the construction zone. I didn't realize he was your brother at the time but now it makes complete sense." Luke didn't volunteer any further information.

Fran gave him a curious look but didn't ask any further questions. She led the way into the kitchen.

"Ugh, it looks like a bomb went off in here," she moaned eying the dirty dishes that covered every available surface of kitchen counter.

"Don't worry about it. I can do it. I don't mind cleaning," Luke reassured her as he filled the sink with hot water. "I'm considering opening a business. You think it pays better than stripping?"

Fran grabbed a towel to help dry.

"Do you miss it?" she asked.

"What?" Luke teased. "The whistles, the adulation, rescuing hot drunk babes? Nah."

Luke whistled as he washed. A surge of love passed through Fran. She was so lucky. Luke was amazing. After the hospital had released him, his recovery had been rocky. He'd needed some rehabilitation for the burns on his hands, plus he'd suffered headaches from the concussion injury. Fran insisted he move in with her when he was discharged. She was terrified something bad would happen if she let him out of her sight. Shan hadn't been any help, instead she'd filled Fran's head with dire warnings about signs and symptoms of increasing brain pressure and the risks of infection.

At first, Fran looked after Luke, but slowly, as he felt stronger, he had taken over the chores and cooking. The cats were a bit of a hurdle, growling, hissing and scratching the bedroom door, incensed at being shut out. Fran glanced over at the feeding corner. All six of them were patiently awaiting the treats they knew Luke would hand out before he and Fran headed into the closed-door bedroom.

Luke pulled the plug on the sink and watched the water drain down. He looked tense. Oh, oh, she had known that having everyone to dinner was too much, too soon.

"Are you okay?" she asked, stepping towards him.

"Huh?" Luke looked up. "I'm fine, Fran." He dropped the dishrag in the sink. "Stop worrying so much."

"You're sure? You seem—"

Luke stepped around the counter and reached for her, drawing her in close and resting his chin on her head. She could feel his heart thumping beneath her ear. She snuggled closer getting the response she was used to. Luke stepped away from her.

"Not so fast there. I have something I need to say."

His face was so serious, it made Fran's heart pound faster.

"Fran . . . you know I love you, but . . ."

Fran's eyes widened as Luke dropped down on one knee in front of her.

"Luke?" His name emerged in a breathy whisper.

"I can't just live with you. I need you in my life, now and forever. Will you marry me?"

He held the ring between his thumb and index finger, holding it up in silent offer. The oval cut diamond sparkled in the glow of the kitchen pot lights.

"Luke!"

Fran dropped onto her knees beside him and threw herself into his arms to be wrapped tight against his heart where she belonged. Her lips met his in a kiss of promise and passion.

"What do you say we leave the rest of this for tomorrow?" Luke's voice was husky as he slid the ring onto her finger. He pulled her in for another deep kiss.

Fran's body tingled with desire. It had been four long months since they'd had sex and his slightest touch was making her crazy.

She kissed him back and then pulled away. "I'm not going to be able to sleep if you get me all riled up," she teased.

"Not tonight." Luke shook his head and smiled. "Like I said, I've been cleared by Dr. Ravvy. For work, for everything. So, get ready for some hot, burning love." He raised his eyebrows suggestively and then rethought. "Well, maybe not burning but definitely hot."

Fran giggled as he scooped her up and carried her to bed. There wasn't going to be any sleeping tonight.

The End

Read on for an excerpt from

Carol Kinnee

&

Kim McDonald's

next novel

UNWRAPPED

Book 2

in

The Port Fling Romance
series

CAROL KINNEE & KIM MCDONALD

Chapter 1

The overpowering smell of unwashed bodies was about as subtle as a sumo wrestler dancing in a bikini. Sunny wrinkled her nose in distaste and tried to breathe through her mouth. God, didn't these people know anything about deodorant and toothbrushes? She seriously wanted to be anywhere but here.

The Seattle passport office on a Friday afternoon was packed fuller than the opening of that hot new club she'd attended the other night. Forget *Mistletoe*, this was the place to be—if you didn't care anything about personal hygiene that was. Sunny glanced around disdainfully. A mother was picking something that looked suspiciously like boogers off her child's face with her bare hands. The woman gave Sunny a smile and shrug, as if to say 'what can you do?' Sunny smiled weakly back and glanced away, trying to hide the disgust in her eyes.

She tried not to be a snob but sometimes people were just plain gross. She grabbed the hand sanitizer out of her purse for the fifth time and vigorously rubbed her hands. She'd definitely need a long hot shower once this ordeal was over.

"Can you spare a squirt of that for me? I'd like to bathe in it but I'll have to settle for just the hands for now."

Sunny laughed and turning towards the voice, met the gaze of a man with piercing bright blue eyes and tanned skin. She couldn't help herself. Lowering her gaze, she peeked through her lashes, running her eyes over his body, taking in the broad chest with perfectly sculpted arms highlighted by a tight blue t-shirt. Versace? *Good-looking and well-dressed.* She felt the familiar flutter of anticipation in her stomach that she always experienced when she met a gorgeous man for the first time.

"No problem." Sunny smiled coolly and regained her composure. She handed him the sanitizer. Their hands brushed as he accepted the bottle and she felt a pleasant jolt of energy run through her fingers. He set his magazine down on his knee before rubbing the sanitizer between his hands. Sunny caught a glimpse of the Baroque lettering on the cover—*Wine Connoisseur Monthly.* Suddenly, the Passport office didn't seem so bleak.

"Thank-you." He passed the sanitizer back and gave Sunny a smile that accentuated the deep lines in the corners of his eyes. He was older than her but not in a gross Sugar Daddy kind of way. He was probably in his forties. Sunny usually went for guys in their twenties, guys who were younger and less established than she was. So far that hadn't worked out so well. Maybe it was time to sample a new variety of man—someone older, cultured, more experienced. Someone just like the tasty dish who happened to be sitting next to her in the passport office.

"So, are you a wine enthusiast?" Sunny gestured to the man's magazine and crossed her legs in his direction, letting her skirt ride up an inch to expose maximum leggage.

"I was at one time. But I only had a couple of years to put my sommelier training to use before my restaurant branched out into different markets. Now I'm too busy overseeing. Unfortunately, I have to pay someone else to select my wine lists. But I do get my hands in the pot—or should I say decanter?—every now and then. How about you? Sorry I didn't catch your name?"

"Sunny." She made an exception and shook his proffered hand. She'd just seen him sanitize it, so she figured it must be pretty clean.

"Jerry," he returned, smiling.

"Nice to meet you, Jerry." She tossed her blonde hair over her shoulder. "I actually work for Jamieson Rogers as a wine rep, and as it happens, I just finished my sommelier training."

"Wow, at your age? Very impressive." Jerry winked.

"Thank you. It was a lot of hard work but I'm really proud of the accomplishment. Do you mind me asking what restaurant you own, Jerry?"

"Illume."

Sunny had to clench her jaw to stop from drooling. Illume was one of the hottest restaurants in the country. As for their wine list—they were always the first to discover new, cutting-edge wine blends. Sunny glanced down at Jerry's hands. No rings. This guy was a catch and a half *and* he was single! Of all the places to meet the founder of Illume!

"Wow, now who's impressive? I have to admit, I've had a crush on your wine lists for years." Sunny smiled and leaned in a bit closer. "Tell me Jerry, how do you manage to always find the most unlikely blends with that certain *something*?"

"It's simple: thirty percent nose, sixty percent dumb luck and ten percent mojo, baby." Jerry smiled rakishly.

Sunny laughed at his joke and gave a Cheshire cat grin on the inside. He was blatantly flirting with her now. She'd have him asking her to dinner in less than five minutes flat.

"You must have so much knowledge to share. I know you're probably incredibly busy but if you have any tips to give a new sommelier, I'd really appreciate it." She batted her lashes ever so slightly.

"Oh sure. I'm busy, but I always enjoy mentoring hot new talent like yourself. My friend's just finishing up in there but I'll give you my card and you can call me to set something up. We can have dinner and talk wine."

"Great! I'd love that." Sunny smiled as Jerry opened his wallet and handed her an elegant business card.

"I'm finished, Jerry." A women's voice called from across the room.

Sunny's head snapped up at the familiar sound. *Oh god. Oh no. It wasn't.*

"Waverly!" Jerry beckoned to a woman on the other side of the room. "Come meet this nice young woman I was just chatting with."

Jerry stood and Sunny saw that in the brighter light he was probably older than she originally thought but that wasn't what was grossing her out. The barf factor on this one was that his "friend" was in fact her Grandmother Waverly.

"Sunny, darling. I see you've met *my* Jerry. Fancy seeing you here." Waverly held out her arms for a double cheek air kiss. Sunny stood and numbly complied, swallowing the taste of vomit pooling in her mouth. O. M. G. She'd been flirting with her Grandma's new boyfriend? She'd hit a new low. Could this day get any worse?

"Sunshine Moonbeam Gayheart Asson Devine?" There were some snickers in the waiting room at the odd name. "Hello people? Is there a Sunshine Moonbeam Gayheart Asson Devine here?" The passport officer tapped her foot impatiently and called out Sunny's full name in all its glory for the third time. An entire roomful of bored passport clients craned their necks gawking towards Sunny as she walked up to the desk to own up to the offending name.

The answer was yes, this day could definitely get worse.

Chapter 2

Zack shivered and looked up at the morning sky. The cloud cover had thickened, reinforcing the promise that any second the skies were going to break open and rain down cats and dogs. It was typical November weather for the Pacific Northwest. On the bright side, those same clouds had warmed the ground enough for the frost to finally melt. He stared glumly at the open bog land. Good thing he hadn't hacked off his pony tail. The weight of his thick blonde hair doubled as a scarf. He tipped up the brim on his Indiana Jones-style fedora and glanced at the news helicopter circling overhead. Lifting his *Stop the Development* sign, he waved it above his head.

The motion triggered a groundswell of action in the group around him evoking roars of support that made Zack's ears ring.

The university kid beside him jumped up and down, chanting, "Trees before fleas! No heavy industry!"

"Trees before fleas?" Zack looked sideways at the kid beside him.

The kid's left wrist was chained to the bulldozer, leaving him free to use his phone with his right hand. As Zack watched he lifted his phone and snapped off a series of photos.

"Are you kidding me?" Zack said.

"Instagram, man. Gotta record the fight. Just go with it." He bellowed out another course of 'trees before fleas.' "It's our tagline. It doesn't matter what you say. It's all about stirring the pot, getting the message out there. Trees before fleas! Trees before fleas!"

Around them, others were taking up the message.

"Trees, trees, fleas, fleas." Soon the long, ragged row of protestors were all chanting the words at the top of their voices.

Zack closed his eyes and shook his head. He tried again. "This protest is to stop them from building condos on a peat bog. There aren't any trees out here."

"It's cool. We're bringing attention to our cause. The activist/college kid beside Zack grabbed his hand and punched it in the air along with his own.

Zack yanked his hand back. *Trees, trees, trees!* The call had gained enough support to overtake the *This is not a view lot. No condos on Clayton Bog* message the serious protestors were trying to get out.

Zack opened his mouth and tried to turn the call back to the point they were trying to make. No good. He smothered a yawn with the back of his hand. They'd been at the building site since five in the morning, early enough to block the first of the heavy equipment operators from firing up their machines. The tree message was stupid. There *were* no trees. They'd had to chain themselves to the actual equipment or sit across the giant swamp pads the construction workers had hauled in to keep their equipment from sinking. As for fleas—was that supposed to be some sort of deep social message?

"Stop the construction!" The shout gathered steam.

Good. Someone had managed to get the chant back on the right track.

"Trees before fleas!"

"No oil sands!"

No oil sands? What the—? Where had that one come from? Zack turned to look down the row of protestors. He met the serious brown eyes of Monica Doyle. She looked cold. Her lips looked a bit blue, but then again, that might have been from one of the new lipstick colours she'd taken to wearing. Some of her hair had broken free of its ponytail and the damp air had created a mass of frizzy curls around her face.

Monica shook her head in disgust and pulled her wrist free of the loose chain binding it to the bulldozer at her back. She stood up and crossed over to Zack.

"I'm out of here," she said. "This is just stupid. These guys have no clue why they are even here. I am not getting arrested because of them. You should come with me. It isn't worth it."

Zack shook his head stubbornly. "Stay. This is important."

"Nope. This is dumb. See you at work." Monica turned and walked away. The wind caught her long pony-tail and flipped it flag-like behind her.

"Save the bogs," Zack shouted.

The heavy rumble of big diesel engines started up. The sound worked the line of protestors into a frenzy.

"Trees, trees, trees!" the kid beside him shouted.

"Stop saying that. There aren't any trees here." Zack was starting to get seriously pissed off. These people were idiots. Three nearby girls whipped off their shirts exposing their chests.

"No shirt, no shoes, no service for women! Equal rights in everything," they shouted waving their black t-shirts over their heads.

What the hell did that even mean? The sound of sirens screamed closer. The police were done with the stand off. They were ready to move in. Zack snorted. That was fine by him. It wasn't the first time he had been arrested for supporting a cause.

Beside him he heard the jingle of chain. The *Trees not Fleas* dude was unhooking himself.

"What are you doing? Stand your ground!" Zack said.

"Sorry man, it's not that important. I've got a 4.0 standing. My old man will freak if I get arrested." He dropped his *Stop Now* sign into the mud and jogged away from the line of chanters. He reached the crowd of spectators at the edge of the bog and turned back to give Zack a thumbs up and a big grin.

Cupping his hand over his mouth, he shouted, "Stand your ground. Don't let the man bring you down."

"Pussy," Zack muttered. If things had been left to guys like that there would never have been an environmental protection act.

He tightened his hand around the chain connecting him to the machine. The cops were moving in now and the line was starting to push back. Someone threw a banana at one of the officers. The crowd cheered.

"Stay passive," Zack yelled. He didn't like the way the protestors were starting to get aggressive, pushing and shoving. This wasn't how it was supposed to go.

"This is over people. Time to go, you've made your point." One of the officers picked up a megaphone and was trying to reason with the crowd.

This was going to get ugly real quick. Zack did what dozens of protests had taught him. He sat down, tucked his head in, and waited. Rocks, sticks, lunches—whatever was close to hand started flying. It was over before it really got going. The local police had learned from past experience as well. They waded in and started making arrests.

***

"I demand a chance to make a phone call." It was the kid from earlier, Mr. Trees not Fleas. He was the one who had tossed the banana from the sidelines. The crowd had offered him up fast.

Zack leaned against the wall of the police wagon and tipped his hat over his eyes. The kid had been going off for the last ten minutes. You'd think they were leading him down death row from all the wailing he was doing.

"Shut it already," an irritated voice muttered. The upper crust British accent was at odds with the long brown pony-tail and shaggy beard of Alex Brown, a fellow veteran protestor.

"I tried that already," Zack said. "He's an architectural student and he thinks he'll get kicked out of school."

"Really? Well what do you know, I'm an architect and I mentor students in their last semester, now shut it, kid. Nothing will come of this. They'll call your folks and sent you home with no more than a spanking and a promise to keep the peace."

"Thanks, Alex," Zack said. "I was starting to get a headache."

Alex nodded. "I understand. I think this is my last protest. It's not like it used to be."

Zack nodded slowly. He was feeling the same way. Today was an exercise in futility. Monica had called it right. It just wasn't fun anymore. Too much social media presence. It was all about the selfies, not so much about the message anymore.

The van pulled to a stop and two officers started herding everyone out. The trees, not fleas chant started up again.

Zack jumped down and started to follow.

"Nope, not you. There's someone here who wants to see you." The cop pointed down the hall to where another officer was standing next to a door.

The sign on the door read—Interview Room 1. Interesting, mused Zack. Was that the interrogation room? Was water torture in his future? He smothered a grin. This had never happened before. He sauntered towards the door, paused and glanced back at the other man. The expression of smug laughter on the cop's face made him stop.

"Enjoy your meeting, Dr. Mason." The cop opened the door and gestured him in.

Zack frowned. Now what? He stepped through the door.

"No way," he said, turning around.

"Dr. Mason, have a seat."

The perfectly coiffed, elegantly dressed woman on the other side of the table checked the time on the diamond encrusted Cartier watch on her wrist. She tapped her index finger on the table surface. The red lacquered nail made a sharp clicking sound.

For a moment, she waited as though she expected Zack to say something. He kept his mouth shut. No way was he giving her any information.

"It's unfortunate," she said, "that we must meet here under these circumstances."

Zack stepped up to the table and spinning the chair around, straddled it.

Her mouth tightened in a frown.

Zack gave up on silence. "I'm not clear on what brings you here, counsellor. Perhaps you could explain. As far as I can see, I haven't been charged with anything yet."

"And you won't be." She flipped a paper around and held out a pen. "Sign here."

Zack leaned forward and pulled the paper towards him. He pushed it back at her, ignoring the pen.

"Let me put it this way." The lawyer leaned in. "I don't need you to sign this, Zachary. I have already made arrangements for you to leave."

She stood. "Make no mistake, this development site is going through." She collected her briefcase and stepped towards the door.

"Just one thing," Zack said softly.

She turned back.

"How did you know I would be there?"

She shook her head. "Zachary, I am your mother. I always know what you're doing. Besides, Facebook and social media make me aware of these events well in advance. Perhaps you should get an account, darling. There's no telling what you might learn."

She smiled and opened the door.

"Oh, and don't forget supper on Sunday. It's your Father's birthday. Perhaps you can make amends for trying to stop his development."

The door banged shut behind her leaving Zack staring at the dull grey paint. His mother had a Facebook account?

About the Authors

Carol Kinnee is a free-lance writer living on the west coast of British Columbia. She's the author of The Christmas Presence—a romantic suspense set on Vancouver Island, and the Fantasy novel—A Trail of Embers.

When she's not tied to her laptop, she's out exploring what BC has to offer.

Visit her at:

> https://www.carolkinnee.com/

> Facebook: Carol Kinnee, author

Kim McDonald doesn't have any fancy writing degrees to boast about or prestigious awards to list. She grew up devouring books (reading, not eating them—that would be weird). She lives with her darling husband and son, her overweight cat and her behaviourally challenged dog.

Visit her at:

> https://kimberlygmcdonald.wixsite.com/website

> Facebook: Kim McDonald, author

By CAROL KINNEE

The Christmas Presence

By C.A. KINNEE

A Trail of Embers